The author wishes to thank Kurt Busiek, Jon Cohen,
the Evans family, and everyone else who made suggestions
or otherwise helped in creating this novel.

MARS ATTACKS®:
MARTIAN DEATHTRAP

PROLOGUE

No one believed in the last years of the twentieth century that Earth was being watched keenly and closely by intelligences that thought themselves far greater than mere humans, and that those intelligences were not the product of some distant star system, but of Earth's own celestial neighbor, the planet Mars. After all, hadn't American and Russian probes visited the Red Planet and pronounced it devoid of life?

It wasn't until the computers crashed all over the world, half the world's nuclear arsenal threw itself uselessly away, and the Martian attack craft swept down, weapons blazing, that the people of Earth learned that they had been deceived, that the Martians had hidden themselves and their civilization from the cameras, had taken control of the computers and transmitters and fed humanity false data while they prepared their assault.

Caught off guard, totally unprepared, Earth's people fought back as best they could against the relentless assault—not just the military, but everyone, in thousands of scattered skirmishes and isolated encounters.

This is the story of a few of those ordinary people, flung into confrontation with the Martian juggernaut . . .

3

1

DEATH ON TWO WHEELS

Bud Garcia looked up at the sky ahead and frowned. He cranked the brake and brought the Harley to a skidding stop on the shoulder in front of a weathered billboard reading GELMAN MANSION 4 MILES. He kept the motor running, but put down his booted foot and stared overhead.

Lenny, Blitz, and Screwy Joe pulled up beside him. Blitz and Lenny had their chicks with them, riding post, but no one got off; they all stared at Bud. "What is it, man?" Lenny asked, his eyes hidden by his mirrored shades, his head jerking nervously from Bud to the empty highway ahead and back. "Why'd you stop? We're in the middle of nowhere!"

Bud glanced at him. "Take a look at that," he said, pointing, "and tell me what the hell kind of plane that is." Cruising far above the trees ahead of them was a green and yellow aircraft in a sort of modified flying-wing shape.

Lenny looked, then shrugged. "Crap, man, I dunno. I'm no expert."

"*I* am," Bud said. "My old man was in the Air Force until they booted him out for drinking on duty, and I know planes. I never saw anything like that."

"It's coming this way," said Blitz's girl, Nancy. She was wedged in behind Blitz; the two of them were a lot for one bike to carry. Blitz was a hulking blond brute in black leather who always said he needed a lot of woman, and Nancy filled the bill—dark hair, tight jeans, and black leather jacket wrapped around a bountiful quantity of female flesh.

Bud looked up, squinting through his own shades. Sure enough, the strange aircraft had wheeled and was heading directly toward the bikers at an altitude not far above the treetops.

"Well, you'll get a good look at it, anyway," Lenny's chick, Marcie, said. She was thin and blond and nervous, matching Lenny point for point.

"I don't think we want to," Blitz said. "Don't that look like a strafing run to you?" He didn't wait for an answer; he kicked off and rolled, ignoring Nancy's yelps of protest at the unexpected move. She had scarcely gotten a solid hold around his waist when he veered off the road and went charging across an overgrown meadow.

The other three stared, eyes flicking from the approaching craft to Blitz and back. The thing's engine made a strange, keening wail unlike anything Bud had heard before.

"I don't—" Lenny began.

Then the aircraft opened fire, and Bud pushed off.

The greenish death-rays tore bubbling black lines of molten asphalt in the highway, and when one touched the gas tank of Screwy Joe's chopper, the tank flashed into an orange fireball, flinging Joe and pieces of cycle in all directions.

Lenny was luckier; he wasn't able to dodge completely, but threw himself and his bike sideways. The beam sliced through Lenny's foot and both tires.

Marcie fell clear when Lenny threw the bike over; Blitz and Nancy were already a hundred feet away across the weeds, and Bud had rolled away just in time, mere inches out of the line of fire.

Lenny's bike had stalled out when it fell, Bud had always liked his own chopper to run quiet, and Blitz was a field away; when the sound of the explosion of Joe's Suzuki died away, there were a few seconds of near silence. Joe himself was dead or unconscious, his face and chest burned black.

Then Lenny looked down and saw the stump of his foot and started screaming. Marcie, who had been dazed by her fall, started shouting obscenities. And Bud looked up to see that weird thing in the sky wheeling around for another run.

"What *is* it?" Marcie shrieked.

"What'd it do to my *foot*?" Lenny bellowed. "Jesus, it shot my *foot* off! What the hell kind of cannon was that, some kind of laser?"

Bud didn't answer; he looked around, assessing the situation. Joe was out of it for good. Lenny was down—his foot had been sliced away, and while it wasn't bleeding the way it ought to be, Bud didn't think Lenny was going anywhere anytime soon. Blitz had split, rolling cross-country.

"Yo, Marcie," Bud called. "Need a lift?"

Marcie looked up at the flying death-machine as it dropped into line for another strafing run, looked at Lenny lying crippled and pinned under the wreckage of his bike, and looked at Bud's Harley. She didn't bother answering, just pushed herself up and ran flat-out toward the Harley.

"You son of a—" Lenny shouted.

Then the returning attack craft's death-ray cut him in half. Bud's Harley was already starting to move when Marcie vaulted on, and she barely made it, but the two of them skidded out of the line of fire.

Bud didn't hesitate; he cracked the throttle and headed over to see what Blitz was planning, if anything.

He didn't have to get close to see just what Blitz was up to. The big man had pushed Nancy off the bike to get maneuvering room, and pulled his shotgun from its special boot. Now he was driving one-handed while the gun waved wildly in the other.

Bud decided to just stay the hell out of Blitz's way; he roared across the field toward Nancy, though, to see if she was still in one piece.

The craft was swinging around for a third run, and Bud was suddenly absolutely certain that the pilot was just toying with them. One biker killed on each pass . . . that wasn't a serious attack, that was target practice.

And what the hell kind of pilot was that, anyway? Much as Bud hated the fighter jocks his father had once worked with, much as he despised all authority figures, he knew no U.S. pilot would have casually blown away U.S. civilians that way. Not even redneck cops would—the risks of an investigation and of catching hell for it were too high.

What foreign pilot would have been cruising along the American coast here? As of a couple of hours ago, when the six of them had eaten a late breakfast at the Motel 6 in Toppwood, the U.S. hadn't been at war, there hadn't been anything on the news on the TV over the bar . . .

And what kind of *plane* was that? It made snap turns like nothing Bud had ever seen. It bore no insignia he recognized, though there were yellow lines patterning the green belly. The airframe wasn't like anything he'd ever seen before—it was a lifting body, with the wings merging into the fuselage, but it wasn't the usual flying wing that showed up in the aircraft mags. What were those beams it fired? They weren't any sort of lasers Bud had encountered before, and besides, who had working laser weapons?

And it was making its third run while Blitz was charging across the weed-covered field with his shotgun raised and ready.

The death-rays, or whatever they were, flashed out again just as Blitz pulled the trigger—and the beams missed the biker by millimeters, as Blitz's cycle wavered wildly from the shotgun's recoil.

Blitz's shot missed, too—or at least did no damage.

Blitz recovered his balance, roared his bike up onto the highway and aimed it straight toward the flying craft. He braced the shotgun against one thigh and pumped, readying it for another shot.

"Come back here and take it, you murdering bastards!" he bellowed.

The flying craft didn't do the same graceful wheel this time; instead it flipped over in a screaming Immelmann, and Bud decided that the pilot was angry about missing Blitz and wasn't going to play around anymore.

"Nancy, get on," Bud barked, bringing his chopper to a mud-slinging halt directly in front of her.

She looked at him doubtfully. "Three on a bike?" she asked.

"It's a Harley," Bud said. "She can handle it. Hurry!"

The shotgun boomed again, but at that moment Bud was too busy getting Nancy squeezed in between himself and Marcie to look. Besides, he doubted that a direct hit would even scratch that thing's paint.

Because he didn't think it was a plane.

It didn't make sense that there could be a plane like that anywhere on Earth, or that if there were, it would be strafing bikers here in the middle of Nowhere, USA. So, Bud had concluded, it didn't come from Earth. And somehow he didn't think a shotgun was going to be real effective against invaders from outer space.

Then Nancy was on. He let in the clutch and rolled, and spared a second to look back over his denim-clad shoulder and see what was happening.

The alien flying machine had slowed this time as it swept down over the highway; Bud decided the pilot was taking his time. Then beams flashed out—not just the cutting green ones like laser beams, which blasted through signposts and melted asphalt, but spreading bluish ones that seemed to have no effect on the highway or surrounding terrain.

One of the blue beams swept across Blitz, though, and the big man screamed, going into sudden convulsions that sent him flying from his motorcycle. The bike skidded sideways and came to a smoking stop thirty yards up the road, while Blitz jerked and twitched wildly, head and limbs slamming against the pavement for several seconds before he lay still.

Nancy screamed, and Bud winced—she was shrieking right in his ear. Meanwhile, he was wheeling as fast as he could away from the road and the open field; he intended to get in among the trees. They wouldn't provide very much shelter from that flying monstrosity, but they were better than nothing.

By the time the thing had swung around for another run, Bud and the two women were out of sight beneath a huge old oak.

2

FLYING TERROR

Above the coastal highway, aboard the swooping MPI-AG "Death-wave" ground-attack fighter, the Martian pilot frowned. He'd been sure there were four of those odd little riding machines, but now he only saw the three he had hit.

Well, that was what scanning systems were for . . .

"Pol, what do you think you're doing?" his commander's voice said from the communicator. "Our instruments show no military units in your area."

Pol hesitated. "Well, there were four Terran vehicles moving in formation," he said. "I thought I should make sure."

"And have you?"

"Three vehicles are disabled, and their pilots appear to be dead, sir. I was about to scan for the fourth, which has taken shelter among some of those overgrown plants."

"Don't bother," the commander said. "You're supposed to be doing a sweep up the coast and rejoining us for the attack on the primary target, not picking off the enemy one by one. We have a city to destroy!"

"But the survivor—"

"One Terran can't be a threat to us."

"He could warn the others."

The commander's exasperation was now audible. "Pol," he said, "the humans already *know* we're here."

"But those plants . . . sir, almost anything could be hiding in there."

The commander sighed. "If it'll make you happy, Pol, I'll order a few biogenetic modules heaved into the area. Now, get back on course!"

"Your will." Waxtad Pol swung the MPI-AG northward, but could not resist one final sweep with the neuron disruptors as he headed away from the battle site at roughly Mach 7.

Bud Garcia spasmed as the bluish beams filtered down through the leaves and brushed over him for a fraction of a second. He lost control of the Harley as his muscles jerked and twitched, and both Marcie and Nancy were flung off as he struggled to keep the overloaded, overstressed bike upright.

He didn't manage it. He dove clear himself just before the Harley plowed into a fallen tree.

He landed hard, and by the time he cleared his head, Marcie and Nancy were both up and running.

Marcie knelt down beside Bud and asked, "Are you all right?"

Nancy stood over the Harley and said, "Oh, crap."

"What is it?" Bud asked as he pushed himself up into a sitting position.

"See for yourself," Nancy said, gesturing at the Harley's front wheel.

Bud stood and looked, and saw what Nancy meant.

The Harley had plowed itself onto the sharp stub of a snapped-off branch, and the front tire was ripped to shreds.

"Oh, hell," he said. Then he looked up. "Is that thing still flying around up there?"

Marcie looked up. Nancy shook her head. "Nope," she said. "Whatever it hit us with, that was its last pass—it headed off that way and hasn't come back." She pointed to the north.

"Well, good," Bud said. "You guys aren't hurt, are you?"

"Some bruises," Nancy said with a shrug.

"What do we do now?" Marcie asked.

"We get the hell out of here," Bud said. "Maybe we even call the cops—after all, that thing killed Lenny and Screwy Joe and Blitz. And we find out what the hell is going on, if we can."

"Lenny's really dead?" Marcie asked unsteadily.

Bud nodded.

"So how do we get out of here?" Nancy asked. "Look at your hog!"

Bud looked again, and admitted to himself that the bike wasn't going anywhere. "What about the others?" he asked.

"Joe's blew up," Nancy said. "And Lenny's . . . well, the tires got cut, and it's got Lenny all over it."

Marcie gagged and her eyes moistened.

"Blitz's should be okay," Nancy continued, "but I don't know about getting all three of us on it."

"I'm not going out on that highway," Marcie said, her voice trembling. "Lenny's all . . . I mean, what if that plane comes back?"

"So, what, you wanna *walk*?" Nancy demanded.

"Yeah, I wanna walk!" Marcie retorted.

"Hey," Bud said, "don't sweat it! I'll go out and get the bike; you two wait here." He turned and took a step back toward the road.

Just then he heard a faint, high-pitched whistling, one that was growing steadily louder. He frowned. He knew that sound from hundreds of old war movies on TV.

That was the sound of a falling bomb.

"What the . . ."

The sound multiplied—there was more than one object falling toward them.

Then the first one hit with a crunch, somewhere off to their left. Another smacked onto the highway, and a third thumped down somewhere in the distance. Bud couldn't see the first or third, but he dashed out and looked at the second one, the one that had hit asphalt.

It looked for all the world like a brass beer keg burst open on the highway, except instead of foaming brew, this thing was spewing a cloud of thick purple smoke that rolled across the road, completely covering what was left of Lenny, Joe, Blitz, and their bikes.

Bud took one look, turned, and ran back toward the women. "Gas!" he shouted. "Some kind of gas!"

"But where'd it come from?" Marcie asked.

"I don't know," Bud said. "Come on, run!" He charged on into the woods, moving well despite his size, his long black hair bouncing into his eyes and fluttering behind him—if this state had helmet laws, he'd have been breaking them.

Nancy and Marcie ran after him, Nancy pumping hard, her mouth set in a solid line, while Marcie seemed to be a collection of skinny limbs flying in all directions as she gasped and stammered.

After they had covered a few hundred yards, the three of them collapsed, panting, at the base of a huge oak.

"Are we far enough?" Marcie asked.

"I hope so," Bud said, looking back. He couldn't see any of the purple stuff—but that didn't mean he wasn't breathing it.

What was it, anyway? Nerve gas? What were the space creatures up to?

"Now what do we do?" Marcie asked.

Nancy glared at her. "We walk," she said. "I guess we can't go back for the Suzi."

"Well, *I* sure as hell won't go back there," Bud said.

"So where *do* we go?" Nancy asked.

Bud stood up and looked around, thinking. He stuck his hands in the back pockets of his jeans, pushing back his denim jacket.

"Well," he said, "Toppwood's twelve miles that way." He pointed. "Brownsburg is thirty miles *that* way." He pointed in the opposite direction. "There isn't a whole hell of a lot in between except Gelman Mansion. The Gelman family used to own most of this land, and they weren't real neighborly."

"How not-neighborly are they?" Nancy asked. "If we show up on their doorstep, are we gonna get help, or a faceful of buckshot?"

Bud snorted. "Old lady Gelman doesn't live in the mansion," he said. "Nobody lives there. It's a tourist trap. You didn't know that?"

"I'm not from around here," Nancy replied defensively. "I grew up in Texas. Picked up with Blitz at Mardi Gras and came back with him." She shivered as she looked around at the forest. "I'm gonna miss him."

"So'm I," Bud said. "Lenny, too." He didn't mention Screwy Joe; nobody was going to miss Screwy Joe, and Bud wasn't going to lie about it.

Marcie sniffled as if she were about to burst out crying, but managed to hold it in.

"So tell me about this Gelman place," Nancy said.

Bud grimaced. "I could tell you a whole hell of a lot more than you want to know," he said. "I worked two summers there as a tour guide. I probably remember the whole spiel."

"Give me the short version," Nancy said.

Bud shrugged. "Short version, this old guy, Ebenezer Gelman, was crazy as a loon. Made a fortune off half a dozen weird inventions, bought about a hundred square miles of trees and beach and swamp, and then spent most of his money building this goddamn castle of his. Managed to marry some society dame was even whackier than he was, and they had one kid, a daughter. He died in 1943. His widow lived there another twenty years before she croaked, and their daughter still owns it, but she's about ninety now and lives in Miami. She won't sell any of the land, won't let anyone build on it, so it's all still pretty wild. They run tours through the house to make enough money to keep it from falling apart. If it weren't in the middle of nowhere, they might do better at it—even at the peak of the tourist season we never needed more than two guides and a cashier at the snack bar."

"But like, it's got a phone, and there'll be people there?" Nancy asked.

"And maybe we can bum a ride somewhere?" Marcie asked.

"Yeah, sure," Bud said. "Old man Gelman had enough phones for his own goddamn switchboard, and they still worked last time I was there. This time of year there'll be a guide and a cashier, for sure."

"How far is it?" Nancy asked.

"On the coast. Three or four miles, maybe." Bud pointed. "That way."

"Three or four miles?" Marcie protested. "You wanna hike four miles?"

"I don't *want* to," Bud said, "but we don't have a whole hell of a lot of choice, do we? There isn't anything closer."

"So let's go," Nancy said.

"Yeah," Bud agreed, giving Marcie a hand up. "Let's go."

3

THE MANSION OF DOOM

"**J**esus," Nancy said as they emerged from the trees and she looked up at their destination, "that's a *house*?"

"It was originally," Bud told her. "Now it's more like a museum."

"It looks like a goddamn fortress!" Nancy said.

Bud shrugged. From this side Nancy was right—they were approaching from the south, along the beach around the end of a little bay, and this side was the part that was more or less modeled on a medieval castle. The north side was more like a French chateau, and the central courtyard imitated a Tudor village with some Gothic trimmings, while the east and west sides were . . . well, kind of a mess.

"It's *huge*," Marcie said, looking up at the turrets and crenellations.

"One hundred and eighty-eight rooms," Bud said. "They think."

"And it's on top of a goddamn *cliff*," Nancy said. "How are we supposed to get up there?"

"Stairs," Bud said, pointing around to the left.

Marcie turned to stare at him. "You mean after walking for *hours* through the woods, you expect us to climb about a zillion flights of stairs?"

"Ninety-nine steps," Bud said. "And it was maybe an hour and a half."

"It seemed like more," Marcie said.

Bud wasn't going to argue with that—fleeing in terror through a forest, with mysterious flashes going off in the distance and with several barrages of something that looked a lot like nerve gas spreading out behind him, was not his idea of a good time, and it had seemed like *forever* before they finally emerged at the foot of the cliff.

His watch said an hour and a half, though.

"Come on," he said, heading for the steps.

"Are you sure it's safe?" Marcie asked, hanging back.

"Hell, no," Bud said, not stopping. He called back over his shoulder, "I'm not sure of anything. For Chrissake, Marcie, I just saw three of my buddies blown away by what looked like some kind of Martian spaceship, and there's been all kinds of weird stuff happening ever since—those things with the gas, and those lights in the sky . . . those weren't lightning."

"What—" Marcie began, then stopped.

"Bud," Nancy said from close behind him, "what do you think is happening?"

"I don't know," he said, not wanting to tell her what he actually suspected.

He didn't want to say it because he knew it would sound crazy if he heard it spoken right out loud.

He thought that Earth had been attacked by invaders from outer space.

Hell, it sounded crazy when he *thought* it!

Invaders from space? His old man had been an Air Force mechanic in love with big machines—at least, until he started loving booze more—and little Pedro Esteban Garcia y Gonzalez had grown up hearing about the latest technology, about jets and spaceships and lasers. He'd gone through all those magazines about hot new planes and secret projects, and believed every word, but invaders from outer space *still* sounded nuts, as if he were thinking about dancing with fairies.

But what else made any sense?

He stopped about ten steps up and turned to call back to Marcie, "You coming?"

"Yes, damn you!" she shrieked as she ran after them.

Throughout the entire climb Bud debated whether or not to say anything to the girls about invaders from space. By the time they finally panted up the last step and into the kitchen garden, he had decided against it, at least for the moment.

Marcie glanced at the kitchen door with its heavy bar and padlock and asked, "How do we get in?"

"Around front," Bud explained, leading the way.

Despite their exhaustion, as they staggered out of the garden, along the flagstone path through the yew alley and out onto the front lawn, Marcie and Nancy couldn't help gazing in awe at the maze of spires, porches, turrets, and ornament that stood four stories high up on their right—four stories not counting the towers.

"Jesus," Nancy said again, "that's a *house?*"

Bud didn't answer; he was more concerned with the parking lots. The little employees' lot just outside the yew alley held one battered old Ford, while the big visitors' lot out front held a family minivan, a black Toyota, and a white Lincoln.

Someone was inside, then; the place wasn't closed. Bud hadn't been sure what the schedule was. Seeing the cars was a great relief.

At last they reached the entrance—not the never-used big front door, but the tourist entrance that had once been one of those used by tradesmen.

Bud didn't bother knocking; he just pushed inside, telling the girls, "They're all probably off somewhere on the tour, but I know where a phone is."

"You think they're still giving tours?" Marcie asked.

"Sure, why not?" Bud asked. He stepped in, into a dim world of rich textures. He had forgotten, he realized as he looked around, just what this place was like, how lush it was.

The walls were dark wood paneling with gilt detailing; the door through which they had just entered had a big panel of stained glass that spread colored light across the polished hardwood floor and faded Oriental rug. A life-sized alabaster statue of a nymph or goddess stood in one corner. The lights on the far wall were lit behind elaborate cut-glass shades. The doors in the three inside walls were carved with scenes of satyrs at play amid fruit trees and waterfalls.

And this was the *tradesmen's* vestibule!

The only concessions to modernity were printed signs beside all the inside doors—two read NO ADMITTANCE, a third said SNACK BAR & GIFT SHOP, and the fourth, which Bud remembered led to a parlor, said TOUR STARTS HERE. It was accompanied by a much larger sign listing ticket prices and tour schedules.

A maroon velvet rope was strung between two brass posts at one end of the entry hall, in front of one of the carved doors labeled NO ADMITTANCE. Bud headed straight for it.

"Wow," Marcie said, looking around.

"Yeah," Nancy said. "Bud, where're you going?"

"The guides' lounge," Bud replied as he shoved a brass post aside and pushed open the door.

At first Marcie hesitated, intimidated by luxury and the NO ADMITTANCE sign; then, as the door opened, she heard voices somewhere in the distance, beyond that portal.

She wanted to see other people. For the past few hours she hadn't seen a single human being other than Bud, Nancy, and their now-dead companions. When she heard those voices she ran, passing Nancy halfway across the room, to catch up to Bud. She had to force herself not to run on past Bud toward whoever was talking.

Of course, passing Bud in the narrow hallway might not have been all that easy. Bud was not a small man. In fact, he had a fairly traditional biker's build—which is to say, wide. Marcie followed close behind him as they walked the fifteen feet down a passageway; Nancy hung back, following only reluctantly.

At the end of the little corridor, they stepped into a large, modern, well-lit room, where they found two kids and half a dozen adults gathered around a small television.

"Hey," Bud said.

No one looked up; their eyes were all locked onto that screen.

"Hey!" Bud said, more loudly.

This time a young man looked up. "Hey," he said back. "I know you, don't I?"

"Bud Garcia," Bud said. "I used to work here."

The young man snorted. "If you've come back for your paycheck, you sure picked the wrong day!"

"No, I got that long ago," Bud said. "I wanted to use the phone— what are you all watching?"

"News," the young man said. "That's all that's on right now, anyway."

Bud frowned. "Why?" he said. "What happened?"

A young blond woman in a flashy silvery minidress looked up at him. "Where you *been*, mister?" she asked. "We've been invaded by Martians!"

"They don't know if they're really Martians," another man said.

"They're from outer space, and that makes 'em Martians as far as I'm concerned," the blonde retorted.

Bud looked at the TV.

He hadn't gone nuts, then. His theory, too wild to even tell anyone, had been right. He stepped forward and stared at the screen, at the shot of Washington in flames and dozens of those green and yellow flying death-machines, like the one that had killed Lenny and Screwy Joe and Blitz, cruising over the burning ruins.

It was all true, then. Earth had been attacked by aliens!

4

ASSIGNMENT: EARTH

Squad Leader Quisaz Hadrak sat back and wished he wasn't so cramped. Tech/Div said that the MAFB-2 Killerghost transport was ample for up to thirty Death Squad Troopers like himself; the idiots at Tech/Div had obviously never asked any Death Squad Troopers what *they* thought.

"Pilot!" the commander shouted suddenly, startling Hadrak. "Why have we slowed?"

"Vehicles on the road below us, sir," the pilot reported. "Standing orders are to check for any heavy military equipment and destroy it."

"Get on with it, then," the commander barked. "We're under orders to join the northern assault force as soon as we've cleared this area, and I don't want any more unnecessary delays!"

"Your will," the pilot said. Hadrak could almost hear the commander's uncomplimentary mental grumbling about officers. Get to the target city as fast as possible, but check out and destroy every Terran military installation along the way—who would write orders like that?

Officers, of course. Maybe some of those confounded Paeec politicians.

"Commander, one of the vehicles matches our identification profile for a light troop transport," the pilot reported. "I'm descending for a strafing run."

"Be quick about it," the commander muttered.

The transport shuddered and swayed as it swooped to the attack, spraying death-rays. Then it leveled off again.

"Target destroyed, Commander," the pilot reported. "Several of the accompanying civilian vehicles were hit, as well. However, some of them escaped—should I pursue?"

"Civilians?" The commander snarled. "Don't bother. They're no threat to us."

"One of them has turned off the main road onto a side path that doesn't show on our maps," the pilot said. "It's hidden by those big plants they have everywhere—our reconnaissance scans must have missed it."

"We don't need to know every trivial little by-road on this whole swampy planet!"

The pilot hesitated, then said, "But, sir, this one leads to an unidentified structure that doesn't fit any of our standard military or civilian profiles."

"Oh, for . . ." The commander leaned over to look at the displays. He stared.

"What *is* that?" he asked.

"I don't know, sir," the pilot replied. "That's why I mentioned it. Should I attempt to destroy it?"

"No," the commander said, frowning. He turned and looked back at the troopers, strapped into their seats. His gaze fell on Hadrak.

"Hadrak!" the commander barked. "I want you and your men ready to disembark immediately!"

"Your will!" Hadrak replied, without conscious thought. Then the order sank in. "Uh . . . disembark, sir?"

"That's right. We've spotted a structure down there that needs investigation, but I'm under orders to get this company to the front as fast as possible, and it might take a while. So I'm going to put you and your squad down to check it out, and when you've done that you're to head north on your own, by whatever transportation is available, and rejoin us."

"Your will," Hadrak said, a bit less enthusiastically.

"Show some spirit!" the commander shouted. "You're a Martian, you're a Gnard, you're a Death Squad Trooper!"

"Ready for anything," Hadrak agreed, following the training formula. "Your will."

"Should I put them down in the paved area beside the structure?" the pilot asked.

"Mmmm . . . no, let them approach under cover. Just in case. Put them down along the road."

"Your will."

Five minutes later Quisaz Hadrak stood on the pavement and watched the saucer-shaped MAFB-2 ascending. It rose steadily at an angle for a few seconds, then zipped off northward.

Hadrak watched it go, then turned to his squad—six fully armed troopers, most of them eager to engage the enemy.

"Now what, sir?" Slithree Di asked, hefting his KA-77. "Where are we? What's our assignment?"

"I thought we were going to be landing in one of the Terran cities," Tenzif Kair said. "This doesn't look like a city."

"It's not," Hadrak said. "The commander's asked us to check out a structure over that way, beyond all these big plants." He pointed.

"What if we meet Terrans?" Kair asked.

Hadrak made a noise of exasperation.

"We kill them, of course," he said.

5

CARNAGE ON
THE HIGHWAY

"**W**hat's the holdup, Mom?" Katie Winters asked, sitting up in the backseat. "Why'd you slow down?"

"Traffic," Betsy Winters replied.

Katie looked around at the unbroken lines of trees on either side of the car. "Out *here*?" she said. "We're in the middle of nowhere!"

"Look," Betsy told her.

Katie looked. Sure enough, they were behind two other cars and a semi . . . and ahead of that she couldn't tell, since the semi blocked their view.

"Can't you pass 'em?" Katie asked.

"Not all at once," her mother replied. "Not unless we hit a straight stretch."

The road, Katie had to admit, did curve a lot along here; it probably wasn't really safe to try to pass everyone at once. If someone was coming the other direction . . .

Of course, anyone who knew what was going on wouldn't be heading the other way. The Winterses, mother and daughter, were fleeing a Martian attack. Katie assumed that everyone else on this road was doing the same thing, and anyone heading the other way would be running right into the middle of the chaos and disaster that had swept over the area.

Of course, someone coming the other way might not *know* better, since the radios and stuff were only working part of the time.

Or someone coming the other way might be fleeing an even *worse* attack. Katie wished she hadn't thought of that possibility, but now that she had, she couldn't get it out of her head.

Just then the car crunched over something, and Katie looked around.

They were passing an open field and a big sign that read GELMAN MANSION 4 MILES. There was a good-sized burned area along the shoulder of the highway, and some charred wreckage that might have been a motorcycle once.

There was also some charred wreckage that might have been the motorcycle's rider once. "Ewww, gross," Katie said—though in fact she'd seen worse things back in Toppwood, when the flying saucer had skimmed overhead and blasted everything.

Had one of those flying saucers fried this biker? It didn't look all that recent, nothing was still burning, but Katie looked up out the rear window anyway.

And saw the saucer.

"Mom!" she shrieked. "It's them!"

Betsy turned and looked over her shoulder. She couldn't see what Katie was pointing at, but she didn't need to; she turned to face front again, saw the line of vehicles still creeping along at twenty miles an hour. She had hoped the delay was caused by who- ever was at the front of the line being squeamish about running over the dead bikers, but there was no sign that whoever was up there, in front of the semi, was accelerating, or planning to anytime soon. So either there were more corpses ahead, or that hadn't been the source of the slowdown.

Whatever the reasons, whatever might be going on up ahead, she reached a decision. Despite the risk of oncoming traffic, she wasn't about to sit here, last in line, as one of those infernal flying disks blasted the whole column. She jerked the wheel to the left and floored the accelerator.

The Chevy shuddered, jerked, and took off, veering wildly onto the left shoulder before she got it under control and swung it back onto the highway. Katie clung to the door handle and to the seat back in front of her, wishing she'd worn her seat belt as the Chevy charged past the two cars and alongside the semi.

By then Betsy could see what was causing the backup. The line extended another twenty or so vehicles, and at the front of the line was a National Guard Humvee with a heavy machine gun ring-mounted on the roof; a gunner sat ready at the weapon's breech, scanning the roadside for targets.

They must be looking for Martians, Betsy realized. That was why they were going so slowly—so they'd be able to spot Martians in the woods along the highway and shoot them.

Betsy wasn't interested in *shooting* Martians, only in escaping them. She pushed down even harder on the accelerator, trying to pass, then slammed on the brake as one of the other cars started to pull out of line ahead of her.

Then a shadow skimmed over, the saucer opened fire, and the Humvee exploded.

Cars immediately began veering left and right, out of line onto the shoulder, into the other lane, anywhere, as the saucer reversed direction and came swooping back toward them. Betsy already had the Chevy on the left shoulder; now she stamped on the accelerator again, trying to get past the demolished Humvee before any of the other cars blocked her way.

She didn't make it; a big blue Olds swerved in front of her, and she swung the wheel hard to the right to dodge it.

The highway was turning into a high-speed game of bumper cars when the saucer's death-rays flashed out again. Betsy saw the glow of the beam and jammed the pedal to the floor, not caring where the car was aimed.

The Chevy's right front fender slammed against a gray Honda, jarring Betsy and Katie, but it didn't stop them. Betsy kept her foot on the gas and rammed her way through, shoving past the Honda and scraping trim from the Chevy's side.

The Chevy charged across the right-hand shoulder and bumped down onto the grass; directly ahead, a big yellow shape suddenly loomed up, and Betsy swung the wheel fiercely to the left.

A car exploded somewhere behind them as Betsy recognized the yellow thing as a billboard.

Turn Here for Gelman Mansion, it said, embellished with a big red arrow and a picture of something that looked like a castle tower. Betsy had no idea what Gelman Mansion was, but "turn here" meant a side road, and that meant a way out of the growing disaster on the highway. She looked about wildly and spotted the turnoff thirty yards away.

"Hold on," she said as she sent the battered car bouncing across rough ground and foot-tall grass.

Katie held on, and a moment later they jounced up onto the mansion's access road, under the shelter of the big oaks, out of sight of the Martian attacker. Smoke or steam was beginning to come from under the Chevy's hood, but Betsy ignored it; she could worry about the car's condition later.

Behind them they could hear screams and explosions, but neither mother nor daughter paid any attention; they were both staring straight ahead. Betsy was concentrating on keeping them on the road as they blasted along at sixty-five miles per hour on a road designed for no more than thirty, and Katie was watching the skies, looking for more of the disk-shaped attack craft.

About two miles farther along Betsy realized that the steering was even more difficult than it ought to be, and that something was thumping horribly. She gritted her teeth, clamped her hands tighter on the wheel, and kept driving.

At last the car came screaming into the parking lot at the end of the drive, and Betsy slewed it to a gravel-flinging stop just short of the low stone barricade at the far end. The engine stalled out and steam billowed from under the hood.

When the dust had settled, Betsy turned to look at where they were. She took in the cliff edge, the ocean beyond, the huge imitation chateau, the three other cars in the lot.

"It's a goddamn tourist attraction!" she said.

"Does that mean the Martians won't bother with it?" Katie asked.

Betsy whirled to look at her daughter, then stopped and stared thoughtfully at the mansion.

"Maybe you're right," she said. "Maybe they'll just ignore it. I mean, nobody lives here, there's nothing they'd want . . ."

"Sure!" Katie said with forced cheeriness. "We'll be safe!"

Cautiously, the two got out of the car. Betsy turned to inspect the vehicle.

The right front fender was caved in from the impact with the Honda back on the highway, and a sharp steel corner had cut the right front tire to pieces; they had driven the last mile or so on the rim, she guessed. Steam was pouring out and boiling water was dripping steadily into a pool under the twisted bumper—the radiator was obviously done for.

"We'll have to bum a ride when things calm down," Betsy said.

"Sure, Mom," Katie agreed. "Now what?"

Betsy looked around and shrugged. She snagged her purse from the front seat and slung it over her shoulder. "Now we go inside and see—" she began. She stopped dead in mid-sentence, staring back the way they had come.

The saucer that had strafed the column of traffic, or one just like it, was cruising over the woods, low and slow—looking for them, perhaps?

"Come on," she said. "Don't run, you might trip and fall. Walk fast. Let's get inside, quick."

They were on the porch when the saucer sank out of sight, apparently landing in the woods.

"Oh, my God," Betsy said. She reached for the handle on the big front door, not looking at it—she was still staring at the treetops where the saucer had dropped out of sight.

The door was locked. The latch didn't move. She struggled to press down the lever, but it wouldn't budge and the door wouldn't open.

"Mom, read the sign," Katie said.

Betsy turned, and realized that her daughter was right—there was a neat little sign on the door, just below the fancy beveled glass. It read *Please use tour entrance* and had an arrow pointing off to the side.

"Come on," Betsy said, grabbing Katie by the hand and dragging her in the direction the sign indicated.

6

THE GATHERING STORM

"It's *real*?" Marcie squeaked. "It's really *real*?"

"You saw that thing that shot up Lenny and Blitz," Nancy said. "What do *you* think?"

"Yeah, but *Martians*?"

"That's what they say on the TV." Nancy pointed.

Just then the screen went blank.

"Oh, damn, there it goes again," said the young guy.

"Again?" Bud asked.

"Yeah," the young guy said. "It was out for most of this morning, off and on. José thought it was the Martians doing it—maybe it was."

"Who's José?"

"The kid who works the snack bar. He went down to the basement to check on something, he didn't say what. Should be back any minute. By the way, my name's Steve." He held out a hand, and Bud shook it.

"I'm the guide here," Steve said. "The rest of these folks took the tour this morning, and when we got back to the snack bar, José had the radio on, with the emergency bulletins about Martians. At first we thought it was an update of that old Orson Welles radio scare story from 1938, but I wanted to check the TV to be sure, so I came in here to see whether it was working, and it was. And when I saw what was on, I figured everybody ought to see it, so we were watching it, and then you guys showed up."

Bud nodded. "It's real," he said. "They strafed us and killed my buddies."

Just then the sound of an approaching engine reached them; Bud looked up.

"Did José go somewhere in a car?" he asked.

Steve shook his head. "No, I gave him a lift this morning, so he doesn't even *have* a car. He's downstairs."

"Whoever's coming is coming awfully fast for a tourist," Bud said.

Steve nodded agreement and clambered over stacked boxes of tickets and tourist brochures to peer out the room's one little window. Everyone in the lounge heard the squeal of brakes. Steve announced, "It's a Chevy. I don't recognize it."

"Why'd it come in so fast?" Nancy asked.

Steve shrugged.

"There were probably Martians chasing it!" the blonde suggested cheerfully.

Steve and Bud exchanged looks.

"I better go see who it is," Steve said. "I mean, I'm in charge here, and everything."

"I'll go with you," Bud said. Together the two men marched back up the little passageway to the entry hall.

No one was there. The two waited, but the door stayed closed and no one knocked.

"Maybe they're still in the car," Bud said. "Maybe they're hurt."

Steve frowned and looked around nervously.

"I'll check," Bud said. "You're not supposed to leave the building during business hours, right?"

"Right," Steve said, relieved.

Bud opened the door, leaned out, and looked both ways—and spotted a harried-looking woman in blouse and pants and a girl of twelve or thirteen in jeans and lumberjack shirt approaching rapidly along the big front porch.

"This way!" Bud called. "Come on in!"

The woman started at the sight of him, and Bud remembered that his wasn't exactly the most inviting appearance around—an inch short of six feet, 250 pounds, long curly black hair, two days' growth of beard, wearing Levi's jeans, denim jacket, black leather cap, tall black boots, and a black Coors T-shirt—not that he drank Coors, he just liked the shirt.

Or maybe she just hadn't been expecting to see anyone. She recovered quickly and pointed back up the entrance road.

"Martians!" she shouted. "A flying saucer!" Bud started to nod, started to say that they already knew, and then the woman said, "It's landing over there!"

Bud whirled. "Landing? Where?" He stared out at the trees, but saw no sign of any alien craft.

"Over *there*," she insisted, jabbing her finger in that same direction.

Bud frowned and looked back through the door at Steve, who shrugged.

"Come on, get inside," Bud said, waving to the woman and girl.

The two hurried down the porch, past Bud and into the vestibule. Bud hesitated, taking one final look around before going back inside himself.

He was glad he did because, as he peered in the direction the woman had indicated, there was a sudden whoosh. A flying saucer— not the same flying-wing kind that had attacked him and his gang out on the highway, but a traditional disk shape, like something from the movies, but clearly far more advanced—rose abruptly up out of the trees, hovered for a fraction of a second, then sped off northward at incredible speed.

"Jesus," Bud muttered. "It *did* land." He frowned. It had landed, and taken off again—but why? Had someone boarded the saucer, or gotten off?

He didn't like it.

He stepped inside and found Steve introducing himself and, out of habit, launching into a variation of the standard spiel about Ebenezer Gelman.

"Steve, that can wait," Bud said. "This lady saw one of the Martian saucers land out there along the entry road. I just saw it take off again. I don't know what's goin' on, but maybe we should all get together in the guides' lounge and talk it over, huh?"

"Sure," Steve said, catching himself.

"Thank you," the woman said. "I'm Betsy Winters, and this is my daughter Katie."

"Call me Bud," Bud said. "Come on." He led the way back to the lounge.

The little crowd gathered there looked up expectantly as Bud led the new arrivals into the room.

"This is Betsy and Katie Winters," he said. "I'm Bud Garcia. Anyone know if the phones are working?"

Steve stepped in and shook his head. "They're out," he said. "José and I tried to call a couple of times."

"Try again," Nancy suggested. "Maybe they're fixed."

Steve nodded.

"I'm Nancy," Nancy said, holding out a hand. Betsy shook it. "That's Marcie."

"I'm Tiffany," the miniskirted blonde with the gaudy makeup announced. "I'm with Tony." A big, trim, black-haired man in an expensive suit nodded acknowledgment.

"Bill Edwards," said a handsome brown-haired man, who wore a suit and tie visibly less expensive than Tony's.

"Stan Rubens," the last man, who wore a plaid sport shirt and tan pants, said. He nodded at a plump brown-haired woman and the two young boys. "That's my wife, Susan, and our boys, Bobby and Sid."

"Fine, we all know each other," Katie said. "Now, can we do something about the flying saucer that just landed out there?"

"Landed?" Bobby and Sid shrieked in unison, scrambling toward the window.

"It took off again," Bud said. "I saw it."

"We should call and tell someone," Marcie suggested, pointing at the phone on the desk in one corner.

"It doesn't work," Steve said.

Bill Edwards picked up the receiver and put it to his ear, then jiggled the cradle button a few times. "He's right," Bill said. "It's dead. No dial tone, nothing."

"Maybe we should just get out of here, then," Marcie suggested. "If someone could give us a lift . . ."

"Where would we go?" Nancy asked. "You saw the TV! The Martians are everywhere!"

"They can't be *everywhere*," Marcie protested.

"I'm not afraid of any Martians anyway," Tony said. "I'll give you a ride, doll."

Tiffany threw Tony a dirty look.

"Thanks, mister," Marcie said. She looked at Nancy and Bud. "You guys coming?"

Bud figured, from Tony's expression of distaste, that he hadn't intended his invitation to include all three of them. That wouldn't have stopped him from taking the offered ride anyway, if he'd actually wanted it, but Nancy's question had hit home for him—where would they *go*?

And what would they do when they got there? His Harley was back there in the woods somewhere with the front tire ruined, and that was about half his worldly wealth right there.

He needed time to think before he rushed off anywhere.

"Not me," he said. "Thanks anyway. You and Marcie go if you want."

Tony shrugged, and visibly tried not to look relieved. "Suit yourself," he said.

Nancy looked back and forth from Marcie to Bud, noticed Tiffany glaring at Marcie, then said, "I think I'll take my chances here."

Steve looked uneasy. "I dunno, man, I mean, this isn't a shelter or anything. Old lady Gelman might not like it if you hang around here."

"Maybe it's time for us all to be going, then," Stan Rubens said.

"Go where?" Betsy Winters asked.

"Home to Toppwood," Susan said.

Betsy shook her head. "Toppwood's not there anymore," she said. "That's where we came from."

Susan, who had been standing by the couch, sat down abruptly.

"Sounds like old lady Gelman is just gonna have to grin and bear it," Bud remarked.

"Hey, look!" Bobby shouted from the window.

"Look at what?" Nancy asked, leaning over.

"Spacemen!" Sid said, pointing.

The others stared at each other for half a second, then charged en masse for the little window.

Sure enough, two creatures had emerged from the woods and were peering cautiously at the house.

This was the first look any of them had had at the invaders themselves; up until now the humans had only seen the Martians' fighting machines. Now they could see the Martians themselves.

They were shaped roughly like human beings—two arms, two legs, a head—and were of roughly human size. The details of their bodies were hidden under sleek green metal armor, but even in armor their arms and legs seemed somewhat thinner than they should be. The shiny, smooth green surfaces and sticklike limbs gave them a vaguely insectile look.

Their heads, though, were like nothing on Earth. The green armor did not cover their heads; instead they wore clear helmets of glass or plastic that resembled bell jars, and that left their hideous faces plainly visible.

Their heads were swollen and hairless, with mottled surfaces, reminding the observers of skulls or exposed brains. Their skin was a brownish pink that was not quite the color of any human skin, but was similar enough to Caucasian to be unsettling. The small, misshapen faces were crowded down to the bottom few inches. They had no lips or noses—their dozens of long, sharp teeth were plainly visible, accentuating the skull-like appearance.

And their eyes were a baleful red that almost seemed to glow.

"Ewww," Tiffany said.

Each Martian held a gleaming golden metal thing that was obviously a weapon; they were swinging them from side to side, keeping them ready to meet any threat. Katie shuddered at the sight.

"Well, there's what that saucer landed for," Bill Edwards remarked. "Must've dropped this pair off."

"You still planning to leave?" Nancy asked Tony.

Tony peered out at the weapons the Martians were waving about. "I guess maybe not right away," he said. "Guess it won't hurt to hang around a little longer and see if those guys leave peacefully."

"Hey, Steve," Bud said. "You wouldn't happen to have any guns around here, would you?" For the first time he seriously regretted not having Blitz's shotgun.

"Nope," Steve said. "Not unless you count the antiques in the great hall and the south gallery."

"I was afraid of that."

"What should we *do*?" Tiffany asked.

"There are only two of them," Bill said.

"What, you think we should jump 'em?" Tony asked.

"No, no. But I was just thinking that two of them can't search a house this size very effectively. If we were to hide in one of the secret rooms Steve showed us on the tour, they'd probably never find us; we could just wait until they move on."

Bud considered that, and nodded. "Sounds good to me," he said.

"But how will we know when they're gone?" Susan Rubens asked.

"Didn't Steve show you the peepholes?" Bud asked.

"Sure he did, honey," Stan said to his wife. "You remember. Someone will watch through those, and they'll see when the Martians are gone and it's safe to come out."

"Right," Tony said. "I ain't much on hiding, but who knows what those things can do. Let's go."

"Come on, boys," Stan said, pulling Bobby and Sid away from the window. "Lead the way, Steve."

The entire party trooped down the hallway, through the vestibule, and on through the door marked SNACK BAR & GIFT SHOP, following Steve.

Bud was the last to pull himself away from the window. He took one last look, then checked to make sure the TV was turned off and walked out, closing the door of the guides' lounge behind him.

He had only been gone a second or two when the other five Martians emerged from the forest.

7

INTO THE LABYRINTH

"**I**'m *sure* I saw something move over that way, sir," Tenzif Kair repeated, pointing into the forest.

"And maybe you did," Hadrak agreed. "We don't know what sort of creatures might be roaming around out there. But we *do* know that none of the local fauna are likely to be dangerous this close to Terran habitations. If something comes at us, feel free to shoot it, but we're not going to hunt down everything we see move."

Kair didn't argue further, but he continued to stare off to the side.

Hadrak ignored that; his entire attention was focused on the two scouts he had sent ahead. Bindar and Dundat had reached the cleared area adjoining the unidentified structure; Hadrak could tell by the bright sunlight reflecting from their armor suits, brighter than any sunlight ever seen back home on Mars. The two were looking around warily.

Then Bindar gave the "all clear" sign, and Hadrak relaxed slightly.

"Come on," he said, waving the whole squad forward.

Together the other five advanced, Hadrak in the center, Di and Kair on the left, Aif and Huzi on the right. They marched out into the parking lot, stopped, and stared at the house.

"It's bigger than it looked from the air," Hadrak remarked.

"It's big," Slithree Di agreed. "Should we get started, sir?"

"No need to rush in unprepared," Hadrak said. "Take a look around, troopers, and tell me what you see."

"An Earth building," Ghettal Aif said. "One we can't identify, too big for a personal residence but with no other obvious function."

"What else?" Hadrak said, gesturing.

"The vehicles," Di said. "You mean the vehicles."

"Exactly," Hadrak said. "Four of them in this area. Notice that the damaged one, while inert, is still smoking."

"Then there are Terrans here," Kair said.

"Where?" Aif demanded.

"Presumably, inside the structure," Di answered.

"We must assume so," Hadrak agreed. "And while none of the vehicles have military markings, it's quite possible the Terrans here are armed."

"Then we enter with caution," Di said.

"We still go in?" Aif asked plaintively.

"Of course!" Hadrak said. "No one ever said the structure was abandoned."

"I hoped it was," Aif muttered.

Hadrak ignored him and waved Di forward. "Blow the door in," he said.

"Should we see whether it will open first?" Di asked.

"No," Hadrak said. "There might be booby traps. We will blast our way in."

"Your will," Di said. He lifted his KA-77 assault weapon, shifted the selector, looked at the front of the structure—then paused. "Which is the door?" he asked.

"That one," Hadrak said, pointing. "The Terrans almost invariably align their doorways with the floor."

Di nodded. "I shall remember that." Then he aimed and fired.

The missile struck the big double door dead center and detonated on impact; shattered glass and splintered wood flew in all directions.

"Come on," Hadrak said, taking the lead with his own KA-77 at the ready.

The seven Martians jogged up the steps, across the porch, over the smoking ruins of the door, and into the cavernous front hall of Gelman Mansion.

There they stopped dead.

For several seconds no one spoke, then Ghettal Aif asked, "What *is* this place?"

"I don't know," Slithree Di said.

"I don't like it," Tenzif Kair said.

Hadrak didn't like it much, either, but he wasn't about to say so.

"What did you expect?" he barked. "They're *Terrans*! Of course their structures are alien!"

"This isn't anything like the projections in the briefings," Aif protested.

"Intel/Div can't cover everything."

Aif looked as if he were about to debate that, then let it drop. "Now what?" he asked.

Hadrak had to admit that that was a fair question. He looked around again.

They were in a hallway some twenty feet wide and fifty feet long, and at least thirty feet high; a vast, red-carpeted stairway ran up the center to the rear, forking halfway up and then leading to balconies on either side, whence other staircases continued up to a third level. The walls on all sides were covered in some dark vegetable substance; the windows at each end of the room were made of colored glass, so they could not be used to see out of, and the light they admitted was dim and multicolored. The warm daylight spilling in through the ruined door was far brighter.

And the place was full of *things*, on all three levels, but Hadrak could not identify any of them with certainty. He did not see anything he recognized as any sort of machine or tool. There were no computer screens, no communications devices, no tables or counters or work spaces, no beds ... one object might have been intended for sitting on, but seemed absurdly ornate for that purpose. Instead there were ... *things*. Things sitting on the floor, things hanging on the walls, things suspended from the ceiling, things stacked atop each other—artificial things, such as carvings and assemblies of various sorts; natural things, such as plants growing in containers, or the pelts and plumage from exotic Terran animals; and things Hadrak could not even begin to identify.

Hadrak stared at it all, his eyes adjusting easily to the gloom of the interior, and as he did, he wondered how Terrans could see in such a place when the door was closed. Their world was so bright and hot that he would have thought they would be as blind as tunnel-snakes in a room like this one.

Perhaps they kept it artificially lit even in daytime; the intricate tubing-and-crystal structures that hung from the ceiling and pro-truded from the walls might be lamps of some sort. Hadrak was fairly certain that humans could, in fact, see in here, and did not find their way by feel or instinct, because there were objects hung on the walls that appeared to be crude visual representations of Terran faces, created by smearing pigments onto a surface. Surely, these would not have been present unless the Terrans were able to see them.

A thought struck him. Perhaps this mysterious structure was some sort of temple, and these were meant to be seen by gods, rather than by mortals. Then the low level of the light presumably wouldn't matter.

The flat, colored depictions of Terran faces were not the only things in the hallway Hadrak took to be attempts at art; a dozen grooved cylinders stood along either side of the chamber, and atop each such cylinder was a rendering, in some hard white substance, of all or part of a Terran body.

Perhaps these were military trophies, he thought. Each one seemed to include a head, though how much of the rest of the Terran was in-cluded tended to vary; perhaps these were created to commemorate victories over notable foes. Perhaps there were the skulls of dead enemies inside each trophy, or perhaps that white material was the crushed bones of the dead.

Or might these be offerings to the bestial gods of the Terrans?

That did seem to make the most sense—and not much about this chamber did. Primitive religions could produce manifestations that didn't make much sense to more civilized cultures, and this place was *full* of things that didn't follow any logic—the hollowed-out leg of a large animal, for example, stood by one wall with several hooked things sticking up out of it, and water was running endlessly and uselessly from a pipe into a stone bowl in one corner. How could anyone, even Terrans, waste water like that?

The more he thought about it, the more convinced Hadrak became that this structure was a temple complex.

That was interesting; perhaps they could gain some useful insight into the Terran mind by studying their absurd, barbaric religions.

Right now, though, he and his troopers had a duty to perform. They had been sent to investigate this place and determine whether it posed any threat to the Martian invasion. They knew there were Terrans in here; they would have to locate and neutralize those Terrans, and perhaps interrogate them about the nature of this place before exterminating them.

There were eight inside doors opening off this room on this level alone, and presumably more on the upper levels, along those balconies. Hadrak frowned. If they stayed together in a single group, they could be searching forever, with the Terrans dodging around them, but there weren't enough of them to spread out and cover the entire building. He'd have to make some sort of compromise.

"All right," he said, "we'll take this one level at a time, and one side at a time. Bindar, Dundat, you take that one." He pointed at the closest door in the right-hand wall. "Aif, Kair, you take the next one. Di, Huzi, you have the third. And I'll take the right-hand door in the far end. Scout out half a dozen chambers or passages, then regroup back here. If you see any Terrans, we could use prisoners for interrogation, but don't take any unnecessary chances—shoot to kill if they're armed and look dangerous."

There was a quick chorus of, "Your will," and then the squad scattered.

8

IN HIDING

Katie Winters watched, fascinated, as Steve slid aside the panel that hid the lever that worked the secret door.

"Wow," she said. "A real secret room?"

"Just like in the movies," Nancy said.

Bud nodded. "That's probably where old man Gelman got the idea," he said.

"Could be," Steve agreed as he pulled the lever. With a click, the adjoining panel popped out slightly—the door was spring-loaded, and when the latch was released it sprang open an inch or two automatically, revealing a hand grip.

Bud grabbed the handle and swung the camouflaged door wide, revealing the comfortable little room within.

The room itself was small and windowless, but it extended chimneylike up five full stories into one of the rooftop turrets, and a skylight provided natural illumination. The walls were white plaster, rather than the usual dark wood paneling, so the place was actually rather bright and cheerful.

A square staircase wrapped itself around three walls on each floor, and Bud knew there was at least one exit on each level, two on each of the first two floors—and all of them except the fifth-floor doorway onto the roof were concealed from the outside. The regular

44

tour came through here and used this as a shortcut from the first floor to the third, then worked up to the fourth and all the way back down using more visible stairs.

Two comfortable armchairs, a tea table, a small bookcase, and an ancient parchment-shaded floor lamp stood on a gorgeous Oriental rug in the secret room, but it was far less cluttered and ornate than most of the mansion.

It was, however, seriously crowded with so many people in it. Bud did a quick head count as everyone clambered in through the secret door—three kids, ten adults, thirteen people in all.

Steve was just pulling the door shut when they heard the blast.

"What was *that*?" Tiffany yelped.

"I don't know," Steve said. "Maybe I better go see . . ."

Bud caught him with an arm across the chest. "Don't be stupid, man," he said. "That was the Martians! They probably just blew in the front door."

"That lovely door with all the beveled glass?" Susan Rubens exclaimed. "How could they do that?"

Betsy Winters made a noise halfway between a snort and a bitter laugh. "They can do a lot worse than *that*," she said. "They did in Toppwood."

"It was locked," Bud said. "I'll bet they tried it and decided not to let the lock stop them."

"Uh . . . shouldn't we all be *quiet*?" Marcie asked. "What if they hear us?"

"Yeah, shut up, everyone," Tony said.

A hush fell over the group—for a few seconds. Then Bobby charged up the stairs yelling, with his brother Sid in close pursuit.

Half a dozen adults shouted at them to be quiet.

"He tickled me!" Sid protested.

Stan Rubens, at the foot of the stairs, started to say something to his sons, but Bud shoved past him and barreled up the stairs. He grabbed the two boys by their shirtfronts, one in each hand, and lifted them up to his eye level.

The two boys stared at him in sudden, silent terror.

"You listen to me," Bud said through gritted teeth. "This is not a game. This is not a drill. This is all our lives on the line here. You make one more noise, either of you, and I'll break both your necks." He remembered his own childhood, when the most important thing in the world, more important than life, death, or even *Star Trek*, was making sure that his older sister didn't get away with anything—the only way to keep them from harassing each other had been to separate them. He added, "One of you is going up to the third floor, and the other one is staying down with the grown-ups, and if I catch you looking at each other, I will personally rip your heads off and stuff them down your throats, and then throw you *and* your parents out there for the Martians to skin you alive and eat your livers. You understand me?"

"Yes, sir," the older boy said.

"Good." He lowered the two kids to the landing. "Then you go on up to the third floor, and your brother goes down. And I'll send some of the others up, too—it'll be less crowded that way."

Bobby took off up the stairs, sneakered feet flying, while Sid hurried back down to his parents.

"You were kind of hard on—" Stan began.

"Shut up," Bud said, cutting him off.

He pushed past to inspect the door and make sure that Steve had closed it properly. He had. And everyone was quiet; as Bud had intended, his little speech had worked on everyone, not just the two boys.

"Marcie," he said, "why don't you go upstairs and keep that other kid company?"

Marcie nodded and went.

"The peepholes are over there," he said, pointing to a space under the stairs, opposite the door they had entered by. "There's a sliding panel. They look out through the mirror in the formal dining hall." He spotted Katie, and after what had just happened with the boys, he decided to keep her out of trouble as much as possible. "You look," he said. "There's a bench you can stand on."

Katie nodded, found the bench tucked under the staircase, and pulled it into position. She climbed up, discovered the sliding panel was already open, and peered through the eyeholes set in the wall.

"I see a big room," she whispered. "There's a long table and a lot of chairs, and fancy cabinets along the walls . . ."

"Do you see the Martians?" Nancy whispered back.

"Uh-uh," Katie replied. "Just the—" She stopped. "The door just opened," she said. "And—"

She stopped again, and almost fell off the bench as she pulled away from the eyeholes.

"The Martians," she said. "Both of them. Right there."

"What'll we do if they find us in here?" Susan wailed quietly.

"We ought to have weapons," Bill Edwards said. "If there are only two of them, and thirteen of us, we ought to be able to defend ourselves."

Steve shook his head. "I wouldn't trust any of those antique guns," he said. "Even if we could find ammunition, which I don't know where any is, none of them have been fired in the last fifty years. Some of 'em are just showpieces, not real guns at all, and I don't know which are which."

"Aren't there any other weapons?" Bill asked.

"Yeah, what about that armor, and them swords and stuff?" Tony demanded.

Steve frowned. "Yeah, there are swords," he said. "Any of you know how to *use* one?"

"What about the big axes?" Stan asked. "Anyone can use those, right? You just chop."

"The halberds?" Steve asked.

"Is that what they're called?"

"Maybe we should have a couple of 'em," Bud said. "Old lady Gelman can't object—not after those Martians blew in her front door. It might make everyone feel a little better."

"Okay, okay," Steve said. "I'll go get them." He looked around, trying to figure out routes—this wasn't just a matter of following the established path of the guided tours.

"The south gallery," Bud suggested.

"Yeah. Second floor," Steve said, heading for the stairs.

"Through the ballroom to the courtyard balcony," Bud suggested.

"That should work," Steve agreed. He leaned over the stair railing and asked Katie, "Are they still there?"

Katie climbed back up on the bench and took another look.

"They're still there," she reported. "They're looking in closets."

Bud glanced up, and Steve, but neither man said anything. Both of them knew that one of the secret entrances to the room they were in was in the back of one of the china closets, but there was no point in frightening anyone. The Martians weren't likely to find it.

The important point was that if both Martians were in the dining hall, they weren't on the second floor or anywhere near the ballroom, the courtyard balcony, the south gallery, or any of the connecting rooms and passages.

"Go on," Bud said.

Steve nodded and quickly let himself out through one of the second-floor exits, into the musicians' alcove of the ballroom.

9

FIRST BLOOD

"All patrols report," Quisaz Hadrak barked into the communicator in his helmet.

"We have proceeded through two rooms and are now in a passageway," Bindar replied. "Everywhere, we see incomprehensible Terran artifacts. I theorize that this place is some sort of bizarre warehouse."

"I think that might be correct, sir," Kair said. "At first I thought otherwise, since we seem to have found a conference room, but there are several cubicles here filled with these strange shiny disks."

"Disks? Some sort of data storage, perhaps?" Hadrak asked.

"I don't think so, sir. They aren't flat, and they come in a variety of sizes and patterns. Some appear to be handmade, and many are highly ornamented."

"Are they metal?"

"No. Some appear to be fired clay, while others are vitreous."

Hadrak was baffled by that, and moved on to his third team.

"Di," he said, "report."

"Yes, sir," Di replied. "We are in a complex of small rooms and passageways whose nature and purpose we cannot determine. We have seen no sign of indigenous life."

Hadrak frowned. "Where *are* those confounded Terrans?" he muttered to himself.

For his own part, he had passed through a stone-paved room and emerged into a sunlit courtyard—*too* sunlit; he had retreated into the shade again, and looked it over.

There were at least a dozen exits from the courtyard—doors and stairways and passages on all sides. He had no way to choose which one he should take, which was why he had paused and called for reports.

He looked around the courtyard again, at the colonnades and balconies, at the flowers and fountains and statuary—not that he recognized the flowers, fountains, or statuary for what they were; to him they were all incomprehensibly alien.

And he glimpsed movement.

Startled, he turned and looked up at the balcony to his right, just in time to see a Terran vanish into the doorway at the far end.

"Damn!" Hadrak muttered as he looked for some way to climb up to that level of the building. He had missed his chance at a clean shot.

At least he had spotted one of the natives, though.

"Di, Huzi," he called, "come here at once! Double back to the room we entered through, and then turn to your right and go through the first door."

A moment later the other two joined him in the courtyard, both of them blinking in the bright sunlight. The dimness of the interior had been comfortingly homelike; this harsh glare reminded them that they were on a strange, as-yet-unconquered planet.

"What is it, sir?" Di asked.

"One of the Terrans," Hadrak explained. "I saw him up there but didn't get a clear shot. The three of us ought to be able to corner him."

Di looked thoughtfully up at the balcony. "Chances of an ambush, sir?"

"Ambush?" Hadrak said. "This place is so big, they probably don't even know we're here!"

Di was not entirely convinced, but when Hadrak took the lead, he followed promptly enough. The three troopers charged up one of the nearest staircases and trotted along the balcony into the south wing.

Steve was completely unaware of his pursuers as he made his way through the tangle of rooms and passageways to the south gallery, where sunlight streamed in through a dozen tall windows and glittered from a dozen polished suits of medieval armor, each on its own mahogany stand, with a brass plaque revealing its provenance. Gleaming rows of swords hung on the long north wall, divided into groups according to age and nationality—Ebenezer Gelman had liked to think of himself as a scholar as well as a collector. At either end of the gallery, glass display cases held ancient wheellock and flintlock muskets.

Stands of pole arms stood in each of the north corners and beside every third suit of armor, each stand holding six assorted weapons—thirty of them in all, ranging from a twelve-foot poleax to something that looked like a sword with a six-foot hilt, which Steve had been told was called a glaive.

Most of them, though, were halberds—seven-foot poles tipped with an axe blade and a spike.

Steve had never handled any of them; Mrs. Gelman didn't allow that, and he hadn't wanted to get fired. The tour guide job was a good, steady gig that paid pretty well without being particularly strenuous. Now, though, he stepped over the velvet ropes and pulled a halberd from the nearest stand.

And almost dropped it. The halberd, he discovered, was heavy— the head was solid steel, not aluminum or hollowed out like many modern implements. And iron strapping that reinforced the shaft added a few pounds, as well.

He hefted the weapon, then looked at the others.

He had planned to bring back four or five of the things—one for himself, one for Bud, and the others for Bill and Stan and maybe Tony. Now he reconsidered. The one he held must have weighed ten or twenty pounds; five of them could be a hundred! He wasn't about to haul a hundred pounds back with him.

Three halberds, maybe.

Some of them looked lighter than the one he held, but they also looked more fragile, with metal tracery instead of solid chunks of steel in the heads. Steve was afraid that if he took one of those it might get broken, so despite the weight, he chose the three that looked sturdiest—massive, serious, businesslike weapons, nothing ornamental about them.

He lifted them up onto one shoulder—the traditional way of carrying these things was the only one that made any sense—and turned to go.

And as he did, he heard footsteps in the distance.

He frowned and looked about nervously. Who the hell was that? He'd left all the others back in the secret room . . .

The Martians. It had to be the Martians.

And they were heading this way.

"Oh, crap," he said, trying to think where he could hide.

There weren't any secret rooms in this wing, so far as he knew—though no one was sure that old man Gelman hadn't had a few surprises somewhere that no one else knew about. He remembered the Martians checking every china closet in the main dining hall, and decided hiding *anywhere* probably wasn't a good idea.

But if the reports were right, there were only two of the Martians; maybe he could dodge them, somewhere in the maze of rooms, and double back past them.

They were approaching the west end of the gallery, where he had entered; now he headed for the east end.

The double door in the east end of the gallery opened into a tapestry-draped hallway; beyond that, Steve remembered, was a Gothic rotunda, where a stone staircase spiraled up into one of the towers and down toward the cellars—but that had been closed off, the big iron-bound oak doors locked, because the stairs had no railings and were considered too dangerous for tourists.

Steve steadied the halberds with one hand and reached for his pocket, then remembered that he had left the big ring of keys on the desk back in the guides' lounge.

He tried the door anyway, but as he had thought, it was locked.

So he wouldn't be using the rotunda to go up to the third or fourth floor and cut back that way.

There were six guest bedrooms opening off the tapestried hall, though, three on each side, with connecting doors between them; if he ducked into one of the middle pair and the Martians spotted him, he would be able to cut through into one of the other rooms and escape. If there were only two of them, the invaders wouldn't be able to cover all three doors.

He hurried to the second door on the left and into the bedroom beyond, a room lined with red velvet wallpaper and decorated in cream-colored antique lace.

The openwork lace bed curtains meant he couldn't hide in the big canopy bed, and hiding under it would be too confining—if they found him there, he'd have no chance at all. Instead he tucked himself into the corner between the connecting door and the side of a big gilt-trimmed Belle Epoque wardrobe, and waited. Two of the halberds he leaned up against the wardrobe; the third he held onto, its butt resting on the floor but both his hands gripping the shaft tightly.

He could hear the metallic footsteps of the Martians in the hall beyond the door.

Quisaz Hadrak stepped cautiously through the door from the long gallery into the hallway.

This structure remained inexplicable. The displays of primitive weaponry could fit either the warehouse theory or the temple theory, but either one took some minor stretching to accommodate everything they had encountered so far. Why would a culture capable of building nuclear weapons warehouse those barbaric blades? What sort of religion would display them?

And now the walls of this hallway were covered with cloth that had crude two-dimensional images sewn into it—images that seemed to have faulty coloring and included a disproportionate number of the reproductive organs of plants. What could be the religious significance of that? Or what value could these draperies have that would justify storing them thus?

He pushed the matter aside and concentrated on more urgent business. The Terran was not in sight. Had it heard them approaching?

Would it even know that there were hostile entities anywhere in the area? Perhaps it was merely going about its business.

Di stepped through the door, with Huzi close behind, and the three of them studied the hallway.

"Seven more doors," Di said.

Hadrak heard the comment over his helmet communicator, of course, but it occurred to him to wonder how audible it would have been outside their helmets. Could the Terran have heard it?

The Terran wouldn't have understood the words, of course, since they were in Martian, but still . . .

"No unnecessary chatter," Hadrak ordered. "Di, try that one." He pointed at the heavy metal-and-vegetable-fiber door that was the only one not standing open.

Di obeyed. "Locked," he replied.

The Terran might have passed through and locked it behind itself, in which case they would have to blast through it, but Hadrak was reluctant to make unnecessary noise.

"We'll check the others," he said. "First this side, then the other." He proceeded to the first door and peered into the room beyond.

He immediately spotted the connecting door to the next chamber.

"Di," he said, "stay here while we check the next." Di nodded, and took up a guard position at the first door.

At the next, Hadrak again spotted the connecting door to the next room.

"Huzi, you go on to the next one," he said. "Then we'll all move in slowly, and if it's anywhere in here, we'll have it trapped."

A moment later the three Martians were positioned at the three doors; at Hadrak's signal they all advanced into the bedchambers.

Steve peered cautiously around the corner of the wardrobe and saw the Martian in the doorway. He sucked in his breath; the thing was hideous! That face, with the red eyes and needle teeth and bulging skull, was a nightmare.

He twisted around and peered through the door into the next room. A Martian was in there, as well!

That was both of them, then—if he could reach the third bedroom undetected, he could slip away. He gripped the halberd—he'd have to leave the other two, he couldn't manage all three and move quickly enough, but he wanted to hang on to one of them anyway.

The Martian had moved into the room and was approaching the bed—it hadn't noticed him yet. It reached up and grabbed the lace curtains, studying them—this was his chance!

Moving as quickly and silently as he could, holding the halberd out before him, Steve dashed into the third bedroom—and came face-to-face with a *third* Martian.

Both of them screamed; then the Martian raised his weapon, and Steve swung the halberd in a great swooping arc.

"You're not supposed to be here!" he bellowed. "There were only two of you!"

The axe blade smashed full-force into the Martian's helmet, and a web of cracks appeared, but the blade didn't penetrate beyond a tiny sliver. The Martian staggered sideways under the impact.

"Help!" Huzi shrieked. "It's armed! It's hitting me!"

Hadrak untangled himself from the framework with the peculiar mesh draperies and hurried to the connecting doorway in time to see Steve raising the halberd for a second swing, vertical this time.

The spike on the back of the halberd stuck into the ceiling and caught there, showering plaster dust, but Hadrak knew that would only hold the weapon for a second or two, at most. Although he would have preferred to have captured a Terran alive for questioning, he had no choice. He fired, his KA-77 set on incendiary.

And almost missed; he hadn't taken time to aim properly. The beam only struck the Terran's garments.

Steve's shirt burst into flame, and he released his hold on the halberd as he screamed and dropped to the floor, rolling on the thick carpets, trying to extinguish the fire.

Hadrak fired again, and this time hit his target squarely; Steve's chest exploded in a fiery gush of scorched flesh. He flung his arms wide in one final spasm, then twitched and lay still.

Meanwhile Huzi had staggered back, unable to recover, and now slumped against the wall. "Sir?" he gasped.

"Huzi?" Hadrak called. "What's wrong?"

"Don't know," Huzi said. "My chest . . . can't breathe . . . *aieee . . .*"

A chill ran down Hadrak's spine as the scream built in intensity. He knew what had happened.

The creature's weapon had cracked Huzi's helmet, and the toxic gases of Earth's atmosphere—the fluorocarbons, the acids, the sulfur compounds, all of them just traces to the Terrans, but intensely lethal to Martians—had poured in. Unless they could get Huzi to a med-unit in a matter of seconds, he was doomed.

And there was no med-unit in the area.

"Hold on, Huzi," Hadrak said. "Try to relax. I'll get help."

Tenzif Kair was their med-rep; perhaps he would be able to do something, if only to ease Huzi's suffering. But Kair was at the far side of the structure.

And then Huzi's death cry stopped, and it didn't matter any more.

Just then the halberd tore free of the ceiling and fell to the floor with a thump.

10

HIDE AND SEEK

"**W**hat's keeping Steve?" Marcie asked fretfully, creeping slowly back down the stairs, looking nervously from side to side.

"It's a long way back there," Bud said. He didn't bother ordering her back up to the third floor; Bobby seemed to be happily involved in some game of his own invention up there.

"Is it?"

"Sure. The south gallery's all the way at the back of the house."

"Maybe he shouldn't have gone."

"Hey, stop worrying, will you? He'll be fine." Bud glanced at Katie. "Any sign of the Martians out there?"

"Nope." Katie shook her head. "They're long gone."

Bud frowned, and looked around at the others. "It has been a while," he said.

"Yeah, he should be back," Nancy said. "I mean, if everything's okay, and the Martians have left, shouldn't we get out of here and head back for civilization?"

"If the Martians are gone, sure," Tony said. "But if they've gone, where the hell is Steve?"

"We shouldn't have sent him alone," Stan said.

"Bud," Bill Edwards said, "maybe you and I should go have a look, see what's keeping him."

"I'll come along," Tony said.

Bud looked from Bill to Tony and back again. "Okay," he said.

"I'll stay here and guard the women," Stan said.

Susan simpered; Betsy snorted; Marcie and Nancy looked at each other in disgust, but didn't say anything. Tiffany looked at Stan, then turned to Tony and said, "Can I come along with you guys, hon?"

"Better you should stay here," Tony said.

Tiffany pouted, but didn't argue. Bud grimaced.

"Come on," he said as he led the way up the stairs to the second floor.

"**H**ow many more are there?" Di asked as he looked down at the smoldering ruin of Steve's chest. The blackened ribs protruded gruesomely. "Was he the only one?"

"I don't know how many there are," Hadrak said. "That's one of the things we were supposed to find out. There were four vehicles out front, I believe."

"Then there are at least three others, and perhaps a dozen or more."

"So it would appear," Hadrak agreed.

"There are only six of us, sir. If there are a dozen of them, and they're all as determined as this one . . . well . . ."

He didn't finish the sentence, but looked meaningfully at Huzi's armored corpse. They had performed an abbreviated version of the traditional death ceremony, consigning Huzi to his ancestors, which made the loss seem more real; often, in combat situations, there wasn't time for the little ritual, but this time they had taken the few moments necessary.

They were leaving the body where it lay, however, since they had no way of getting it to anywhere more fitting.

"Yes," Hadrak said.

He looked around the bizarre room, with its mysterious furnishings.

"Di," he said, "we were sent here to determine whether this structure might have any military value, or whether it might pose a threat. Well, I don't think it has any military value—the most advanced weapons we've seen here have been little more than big pointed sticks. There doesn't appear to be a computer or a firearm or a vehicle in the place."

"Bindar thinks it's a warehouse, sir."

"I heard," Hadrak said. "My own theory, however, is that this is a temple of some kind. I believe that the fanaticism displayed by this Terran in attacking an armed Martian while wielding nothing but a barbed pole is indicative of religious fervor. I think that—" He pointed at the canopied bed, "—is an altar of some sort."

Di considered this, then said, "You could well be right, sir."

"I find it significant that we have now ventured deep into the complex without meeting serious resistance. Our only hostile encounter has been with a Terran we pursued and cornered. I think we can safely report that this place is of no importance and go on our way."

Di hesitated for significantly longer before replying, "If you wish it, your will."

"You disagree?"

"Well, sir," Di said, "I would have preferred to have questioned one of the natives, rather than relying on circumstantial evidence."

"As would I," Hadrak acknowledged. "However, when cornered, this one attacked viciously, and we had no choice but to kill it. I see no reason to think our experience would be any different with the others, and the cost to our own side was too high for me to wish to repeat the experiment."

"An excellent point, sir," Di said.

"Then shall we get out of this place, before all these bizarre Terran artifacts drive me mad?"

"Your will," Di said.

The two turned and marched out into the hallway and back toward the south gallery. As they walked, Hadrak used his communicator to contact the others.

"We've seen enough," he said. "We're leaving. We'll regroup on the pavement out front."

Bindar, Dundat, Aif, and Kair acknowledged the order.

"Has anyone seen any sign of the other Terrans?"

No one had.

They trudged on.

Bill Edwards leaned around a door frame and peered into the passageway beyond.

"No sign of 'em," he said. "Or of Steve."

"The Martians're probably back in the kitchen somewhere," Tony said. "And Steve might've ducked out a back way."

Bud had noticed the odd way Bill perpetually held his hand to the front of his jacket, as if he were always about to reach for something concealed there. But he didn't say anything.

When they were halfway down the passage, Bud stopped dead and grabbed Bill and Tony by their shoulders. "Listen!" he hissed.

The other two men stopped and listened. Ahead, in the distance, they could hear footsteps.

"It must be Steve," Tony said.

"There're two of them," Bill said, his hand actually slipping under his jacket this time.

"So he ran into José," Tony said. "That's what took so long—they stopped to chat."

Bud said, "Steve was wearing Nikes."

Tony listened, and even he couldn't deny that the heavy tread they heard was not anyone wearing Nikes.

"It's the Martians," Bill said. "Back off!"

All three men retreated rapidly down the corridor, moving as stealthily as they could.

"Over there!" Bud whispered, pointing. "We can hide in the sauna!"

"There's a *sauna*?" Bill said, startled. "It wasn't on the tour!"

"Used to be," Bud replied. "Maybe Steve skipped it."

"Who cares?" Tony said. "Let's just get in there!"

All three men ducked quickly into a small room lined with redwood and furnished only with steam vents and redwood benches. Bud carefully closed the door behind them.

The door had a little window, perhaps eight inches square and etched with an Art Nouveau bouquet; Bud took up a position looking out through the glass.

He watched as the two Martians marched by, green armor gleaming, those hideous domed heads plainly visible through the bubble helmets.

"They're back!" Katie called softly.

Marcie and Nancy whirled immediately. "Where?" Nancy demanded.

"In the dining hall, of course," Katie said. "That's the only place I can see from here!"

"What are they doing?" Betsy asked. "Have they spotted you?"

"They aren't looking this way at all. They're just marching straight through, back toward the front hall," Katie reported.

The women glanced at one another.

"Maybe they're leaving," Susan suggested.

"Maybe they have some kind of scanner and spotted the guys and are going after them," Marcie said.

"You think so?" Susan asked uneasily. "Maybe someone should warn the men."

"I'll go!" Bobby shrieked from his place up on the third floor—he had been waiting at the top of the stairs, listening to everything that went on below. Now he charged down the stairs at full tilt and barreled out through the doorway that Steve and the others had used.

"Bobby, no!" Susan called, but it was too late. The boy was gone.

"I'll get him!" Sid called, and started up the stairs in pursuit—but his father grabbed him by the arm before he was three steps up.

"You will *not*," Stan said. "You'll wait here with the rest of us. We can't have everyone running all over the place looking for each other!"

"But Bobby—"

"Bobby's older. He'll be fine . . . I hope."

"Stan, are you sure?" Susan asked.

"Of course I'm sure," Stan blustered. "He'll run into the others and they'll all be back here safe and sound in a few minutes. Don't worry."

Katie looked up at her mother and whispered, "He's dead meat, isn't he?"

"Let's hope not," Betsy replied. "After all, there are just the two Martians, and they might have been leaving."

"We only *saw* two Martians," Katie corrected her. "There might have been more who got here afterward."

Betsy didn't answer that; instead she looked over at the remaining Rubenses, Stan and Susan and Sid, then gave her daughter a quick hug.

11

CAPTURED!

Hadrak and Di paused at the central courtyard, arguing which way to go.

"We came up those stairs," Di pointed out.

"True," Hadrak said, "but I would like to take a different route back, and see a little more of this place. Perhaps we can learn more of just what its purpose might have been."

"Are you certain we won't become lost? This structure is not arranged according to any logic that I can see."

"I think we'll manage," Hadrak said. "If we have to, we can always blast our way through a wall."

"Well, you're in command," Di said doubtfully.

"This way, then," Hadrak said, indicating the passage that led through the courting gallery to the ballroom.

At that moment Bobby Rubens was standing in the center of the ballroom, trying to remember which way to go. There were so many doors opening off this big room! And he hadn't been paying very close attention during the tour, so he wasn't sure which way the men had gone. They had been heading for the south gallery, but where was that?

Then he heard footsteps off in the distance. He smiled; *there* they were! Now he could run out and meet them and bring them back in triumph. He trotted toward the sound.

A moment later, while Bobby was still a few feet from the doorway, the Martians rounded the corner.

They spotted him immediately, of course. Bobby froze, staring up at the monsters in their gleaming spacesuits.

"A small Terran!" Di said. "And unarmed!"

"Grab him!" Hadrak shouted, leaping forward. Only after he had done so did the possibility of a trap, with the small Terran as bait, occur to him.

The boy whirled to flee when he saw the two Martians coming for him, but he had gone no more than two short steps when metal-gloved alien fingers closed on his arms.

Bobby screamed, but only briefly before Hadrak's other hand slapped across his mouth, cutting his upper lip and stifling his cries.

In the secret room Marcie looked up suddenly. "Did you hear something?" she asked.

"Maybe," Betsy said warily.

"It must be the others coming back," Susan said.

"Unless it's the Martians," Katie suggested. "It didn't sound human to me."

Susan shuddered. "My boy's out there!" she said.

"He'll be fine," Stan murmured reassuringly.

Hadrak held the Terran's arm with one hand and its mouth with the other and looked around the big room. There were no signs of a trap. Still, caution won more wars than folly, as the old proverb had it. "Back that way," he said, jerking his head toward the courtyard.

Di nodded, and together, hauling the struggling Terran between them, the two Martians retreated to the balcony. There, they paused to regroup. Di tucked their captive under one arm, clamping its arms to its sides, and used his free hand to take a handy cloth covering from a small nearby table and stuff it in the prisoner's mouth to quiet it.

Hadrak had collected both KA-77s—he had dropped his in his lunge for the Terran—and now led the way down the stairs. As they made their way along the crooked path back to the entry hall, Hadrak called ahead to the others.

"The four of us are safely outside the structure," Kair reported. "The vehicles are still here—none have arrived or departed."

"We'll be out in a minute," Hadrak said. He glanced at Di's burden; the Terran was still struggling. Stubborn creatures!

"Destroy the vehicles," he ordered. "We don't want them pursuing us out of revenge for defiling their shrine, or whatever."

"Your will," Kair replied. He signaled the others.

Ghettal Aif chose the battered, smoking one; Bindar took the small black one, Dundat the big white one, and Kair himself the big boxy one. They fired almost simultaneously.

In three cases the resulting explosion was satisfactory, but nothing special; Kair's incendiary round happened to hit the minivan's fuel tank, however, and the resulting fireball was quite impressive.

The four stared in pleased surprise.

"How'd you do that?" Aif asked.

"I don't know," Kair admitted.

"Let me try again," Dundat said, taking aim at the smoking ruin of the Lincoln. His first shot had been toward the front, since he had recognized that as where the engine was; now he aimed toward the rear, since that was all that was left. It was also where the fuel tank was located, and a second impressive fireball was achieved.

Bindar took two more shots to locate the fuel tank in the Toyota; Aif shot the Chevy almost to pieces before managing a decent explosion.

The four Martians were cheering this final pyre when Hadrak and Di finally emerged, Di still lugging a struggling little Terran under one arm.

Hadrak looked over the flaming wreckage and grimaced. "I hope you all had fun," he said.

"Your will," the four chorused.

"Good," Hadrak said. Then he turned to Di. "Put the Terran down, but hold onto it."

Di obeyed, keeping a firm grip on the boy's arm but setting him on his own feet. Bobby promptly snatched the cloth from his mouth and bellowed, "Let me go!"

Of the six Martians, Hadrak had received the most extensive language training, and he hadn't paid as much attention as he should have, so it took him a few seconds to figure out exactly what the Terran had said. It was, fortunately, speaking the local language the squad had been taught, and not one of the hundreds of others the Terrans used.

Hadrak checked to make sure his external speaker was operating, thought hard on his lessons, then said, "Tell us wanted information."

"No!" Bobby shrieked. "You let me go! You're bad!" He kicked hard at Di's armored leg; fortunately for Di, the armor was braced to compensate for Earth's higher gravity and the blow did no damage.

"It appears to be irrational," Di remarked.

"Yes," Hadrak agreed, frowning. Then he switched back to English.

"Tell us wanted information," he said. "Then we let you go."

Fluid oozed from the Terran's eyes. "What?" it said.

"You tell us stuff," Hadrak said. "Then we let you go. You don't tell, we hurt you." His lessons were coming back to him, and he was fairly certain he was getting his point across. He signaled to Di, who squeezed the Terran's arm harder.

The Terran squirmed, looked up at Di, then at Hadrak. "What stuff?" it asked.

"Tell us what this place is," Hadrak said. "Who is here? Why?"

"This place?" the Terran asked, waving its free hand at the structure.

"Yes."

"It's Gelman Mansion," the Terran said.

Hadrak frowned. "What is Gelman Mansion?"

"This is!" the Terran said, trying again to pull its arm free.

That wasn't very helpful, Hadrak thought. "It is temple?" he asked.

The Terran stopped struggling and stared at him. "Temple? No, it's not a temple!"

That was a disappointment; Hadrak had been so sure of his analysis. "Warehouse?" he asked.

"Right there!" the Terran said, pointing. "The house is right there!"

That didn't seem to be an appropriate answer, and Hadrak tried again. "Is this place a warehouse?" he asked.

"It's a house," the Terran said, looking confused.

That didn't make sense. Hadrak knew what a "house" was—an independent dwelling unit for a small cluster of Terrans. This building wasn't a house; it was far too large.

"Too big," he said.

"Sure, it's big," the Terran agreed. "It was built by some crazy old millionaire. Let me go!"

The word "millionaire" was not in Hadrak's rather specialized vocabulary, but after some thought he did manage to dredge up "crazy." Without the noun, he wasn't sure exactly how insanity fit into the explanation. The preposition "by" gave him some trouble, as well.

Was this built *for* an insane Terran, or had it been built *by* an insane Terran?

The latter didn't seem to make much sense; why would a lunatic have been permitted to build such a structure? Why would it have been preserved? Why would there be several Terrans in it now?

Hadrak was tempted to conclude that what the prisoner meant was that this was a refuge for insane Terrans, but that didn't quite match what it had said.

It didn't really matter; the important point was that the building wasn't anything relevant to the Martian conquest of the planet. Religion or insanity didn't matter, so long as the place wasn't military.

He wanted to be sure of one or two details, though.

"There are humans here?" He wasn't sure Terrans called themselves Terrans, and their word "human" seemed more appropriate.

"You bet, monster! There's my dad and my mom and Mr. Edwards and a whole bunch of others, and if you don't let me go, they'll get you!"

"There are soldiers?"

The Terran blinked and brushed its disgusting head filaments away from its eyes. "Soldiers?" it said. Then it said, "Yeah! Yeah, sure, there are soldiers here with big guns, and they'll blow you away if you don't let me go soon!"

Hadrak sighed. "It has reached the point of lying in hopes of benefiting its own circumstances," he said. "It's of no more use to us; kill it, and let's go on and get out of here."

"Let it go, Di," Dundat said. "I'll take care of it."

Di released the Terran; it looked quickly around at the six Martians, then turned and ran for the porch.

Dundat's death-ray caught it square in the back, and it tumbled twitching to the ground, sprawling on the front steps of the mysterious building.

"Let's go," Hadrak said, waving the squad toward the road.

12

THE SEARCHERS

Bud opened the door cautiously and peered out.

"Looks like the coast is clear," he said, swinging the door wide.

Just then the three men heard a distant explosion.

"What the hell was *that*?" Tony exclaimed.

A second explosion sounded, and a moment later a third, and then a fourth.

That was all.

The three men looked at one another.

"What do we do now?" Tony asked. "We look for that Steve guy, or do we go back and see if the Martians found the rest of us?"

"Look for Steve," Bud said. "Come on."

"Wait a minute," Bill said. "I don't like leaving the rest unguarded when the Martians are back in that direction."

"So go, if you want," Bud said. "Those Martians aren't gonna find any secret panels, and if they do, what're you gonna do about it? But Steve might be hurt somewhere, and I'm gonna find him."

Bill hesitated.

"I wanna know what it was that blew up," Tony said. "You think that was the Martians did that?"

"Of course it was the goddamn Martians!" Bud said. "But I'm gonna find Steve first, and *then* worry about it! You coming or not?"

He stared at the other two for a second, then turned and marched on toward the south gallery.

Bill and Tony looked at each other, then shrugged and followed.

"Never thought I'd let myself be bossed around by some fat biker," Tony muttered.

"Yeah, well, life's full of surprises," Bill muttered back. "I never figured I'd be palling around with someone like you."

Tony threw him a glance. "What's that supposed to mean?"

"Oh, come on," Bill said. "You come here in that suit, in a fancy car, with a showgirl on your arm who calls you Tony the Boot . . . not real subtle, y'know?"

"Hey," Tony protested. "I'm a legitimate businessman! 'Tony the Boot' is just a nickname on accounta I'm as polished as a soldier's best boots."

"Yeah, sure."

They walked on in silence, and a few seconds later rounded the corner into the south gallery.

"No Steve," Tony said.

"He must've gone back by a different route," Bill suggested. "He's probably waiting back there with the others right now."

Bud frowned. He was looking at the stands of pole arms.

"Three halberds are gone," he said. "So he got this far, anyway."

"Sure, he got here," Tony said. "And like Bill said, he must've gone back by another route. Maybe he saw those Martian geeks coming and dodged up or down a floor or something."

"Maybe," Bud said, clearly unconvinced.

"Well, where else could he be?" Bill asked.

"Anywhere," Bud said.

"So what're you gonna do, then?" Tony asked. "Search the whole damn house?"

Bud snorted. "You'd need a whole damn army to search this place!"

"I think we'd better go back," Bill said.

"Yeah," Bud said. "I guess so."

Together, the three of them turned and headed back the way they had come, back toward the secret room.

As they walked, though, Bud was worried; the Martians *had* an army. He'd only seen two of them, but more might have arrived, and they could have caught Steve.

Steve had gotten as far as the gallery. If he'd encountered Martians just about anywhere along the way, he would have been able to double back to the secret room along an alternate route, just as Bill and Tony thought he had. But what if Steve had been *in* the gallery when the Martians found him? Bud wondered. The Gothic rotunda that was the main connection to the rest of the south wing was kept locked, and without it the hallway of guest rooms was a dead end. That's why it wasn't included in the tour on busy days. Steve might have been cornered there.

That possibility had Bud worried.

They hadn't heard anything while they were in the gallery, though. And there were those explosions earlier—somewhere toward the front of the house. Presumably, that meant the Martians had been somewhere toward the front.

What had those sounds really been, anyway? Was someone fighting the Martians out there?

Maybe they were fighting amongst themselves. He hoped so.

There were no sounds of fighting now, though—at least, not that they could hear from in here. But then, it took a lot to penetrate this deep into Gelman Mansion.

They found no sign of Steve anywhere on the long walk back to the secret room.

The door was closed, and neither Bill nor Tony could find it; Bud, working from old, faded memories, found the right wall sconce to pull and the right panel to push to get back into their little sanctuary.

Half a dozen worried faces stared up at them the minute they stepped inside.

"Did you find them?" Susan Rubens asked.

"Them?" Bud asked back.

"That kid Bobby went out looking for you," Nancy explained. "To tell you guys that we saw the Martians backtracking through the dining room."

Bud, Bill, and Tony looked at one another.

"We didn't see him," Bud said. "Didn't find Steve, either."

Susan's face sagged and she began to sob quietly.

"I gotta say, I don't like this," Tony said. "First that kid José from the snack bar goes off and we never see him again, then Steve, now this kid Bobby."

"It's easy to get lost in a place this size," Bill said. "They'll probably turn up."

"Did you guys hear those noises?" Marcie asked. "Like explosions?"

"We heard 'em," Tony acknowledged. "Any of you folks know what they were?"

No one did.

"I don't like this not knowing," Bill said. "If it was just two Martians, how do we explain all this?"

"Maybe they have, you know, psychic powers," Katie suggested. "Maybe they can teleport, and find people telepathically. So whenever they knew someone was alone, they'd teleport there and kill him, and then teleport the body away so we wouldn't find it. But they're not strong enough to attack us when we're in a group like this."

Marcie shuddered.

"That doesn't explain the explosions," Nancy said.

"Maybe that was the sound of them disintegrating the bodies," Katie said.

"Yeah, right, kid," Nancy said. "Why would that sound like bombs going off?"

Katie shrugged. "How should I know?"

"Besides, I counted four explosions," Marcie said.

"So they got someone we didn't know about."

"Oh, shut up," Nancy growled.

"I'm hungry," Sid announced suddenly.

Everyone turned to stare at him.

"Well, it *is* after lunchtime," Stan said apologetically.

"Yeah, it is," Bud said. "And I'm hungry, too."

"So what do we do about it?" Betsy asked.

"They're going to keep us trapped here until we starve!" Marcie shrieked.

"No, they aren't," Bud said. "Shut up, Marcie. There's the snack bar."

"I'm not going out there," Marcie insisted.

Bud sighed and looked around at the others.

Stan looked embarrassed; Susan wouldn't look at him at all.

"We don't all have to go," Nancy said. "Some of us can go get some food and bring it back here."

"Yeah," Bud agreed. "That would work."

"And maybe we can see what the hell is going on out there," Nancy added.

"Y'know, I'll bet that's where José is," Bill said. "He wouldn't know where we were hiding; we didn't leave a note or anything. And maybe Steve went to tell him."

"Could be," Bud acknowledged.

"Sure!" Stan said. "Gotta be!"

"Okay," Bud said, "so some of us are making a run to the snack bar while the others wait here. Who's coming?"

"I am," Nancy said. "I'm tired of being cooped up in here."

"I'll come," Bill said.

"I'm in," Tony said. "Tiff, how about you?"

Tiffany looked uneasy, but said, "Sure, Tony."

"That's five of us; that should be plenty," Bill said.

Bud nodded, and headed for the exit nearest the snack bar.

13

ATTACK OF THE GIANT WASPS

"Those big plants make me nervous," Aif said, as the six Martians walked along the entry road toward the highway.

"I like them," Kair said. "They keep the sun off. Don't you like them, sir?"

Hadrak didn't answer; he had no opinion on the aesthetics of the giant plants the Terrans called trees, and he was concentrating on something else.

"Do you hear something?" he asked.

The others stopped and listened nervously.

"Yes," Di said, "I think I do."

"Like machinery," Dundat said.

"More like chewing," Bindar said.

Dundat and Di laughed at that.

"Chewing?" Di said. "What could chew that loudly?"

"Those," Aif said, pointing.

The others turned to see what Aif was pointing at, and froze.

"Oh, no," Hadrak said.

They were staring at a dozen huge beetles—sixty-foot beetles that were systematically chewing their way through the forest, devouring entire trees in seconds.

"There are things like *that* on this horrible planet?" Bindar said.

"Not ordinarily," Kair told him. "Those are one of Technical Division's secret weapons."

"I didn't see anything like that on the transports!" Bindar protested.

"Of course not," Di said. "You must have slept through the briefings, Bindar. Those are Terran creatures called 'insects,' which have been mutated by our biogenetic modules. Ordinarily they're tiny creatures—you could step on one and not even notice."

"*We* made them?" Bindar asked. "On purpose?"

"Tech/Div did, yes. They're supposed to be a terror weapon against the Terrans."

"Well, they scare *me*," Aif said.

"Tech/Div built controllers," Di explained. "To direct them against the Terrans and keep them from harming us. We have one with us." He held up a small device.

Hadrak grimaced. "I wouldn't put too much faith in that, Di," he said. "The rumor on board the transport was that those controllers don't work. Tech/Div had never had an opportunity to conduct field trials—it might have alerted the Terrans if they had run tests in Earth's atmosphere."

Di turned and stared at his superior, then looked down at the controller, then up at the approaching beetles.

"Oh," he said, turning even paler than he usually was. He reached down and twisted a dial.

Nothing happened.

"That's full repulsion," he said. "Those things should be turning and fleeing from us."

The beetles were not fleeing; in fact they were coming closer. One of them had stepped out on the road a hundred yards ahead.

"Retreat," Hadrak ordered. "Get out of their path!"

The six Martians turned and trotted back down the road, toward the house.

As they moved, Hadrak heard a loud buzzing somewhere overhead. Thinking it might be a Martian craft coming to their rescue, or perhaps a Terran weapon, he looked up—and gasped in horror.

It was another insect—a gigantic wasp. And unlike the beetles, it was clearly coming for *them*. Its tapering black abdomen was curled under, directing a stinger the size of a javelin toward them.

Hadrak looked down at the KA-77 in his arms, then up at the erratic, fast-moving target, covered in chitinous armor that could probably resist anything short of a direct hit.

"Run!" Hadrak shouted.

The six of them ran.

As they fled, Hadrak had a thought and managed to gasp out, "Di . . . that controller . . . it might be working backward . . . luring them toward us . . ."

Di heard, and flung the useless controller as far to one side as he could.

It made no difference. The beetles were still devouring everything in their path and drawing steadily nearer, and the wasp was still buzzing closer.

As the Martians reached the parking lot, the wasp dove for its attack. The immense stinger speared through Ghettal Aif's armor with a clearly audible crunch. The Martian flung his arms wide and had time for one brief scream before he died.

The wasp landed atop the corpse, clutching at Aif's armored form with its six legs. Its head bent down, mouth parts working, and after a moment's struggle Aif's helmet cracked open.

By then the others had turned and raised their weapons. Fiery death-rays flashed out, lashing at the wasp. The insect writhed, buzzing madly, and took off, rising into the air, still clutching Aif's corpse in its grasp.

The barrage continued, and the wasp's flight faltered; finally, when Di put a high-explosive round through one of its wings, the insect tumbled back to earth.

Di and Dundat ran up and blew its head off, making certain it was dead. Dundat began the death ritual for their departed comrade while the body was still wrapped in the wasp's twitching legs.

The insect was clearly dead—but the buzzing hadn't stopped, Hadrak noticed. Puzzled, he looked around . . .

And saw an entire *swarm* of giant wasps approaching from the south—at least a dozen, perhaps more.

"Get inside!" he ordered, his voice cracking with urgency.

The others turned and saw the swarm. Dundat hesitated, reluctant to abandon his comrade's last rites half finished, but then his own survival urge kicked in and he joined the others in rushing headlong for the porch.

The five of them made it safely into the vast, cluttered entry hall, where they turned and stared out through the blasted remains of the big front door.

"Where did those all come from?" Bindar asked.

Di said, "According to the status report we got just before boarding the transport, a reconnaissance flight over the highway out there spotted four small, unidentified vehicles this morning during the initial assault. The pilot destroyed three of them, but the fourth escaped into the foliage and the pilot called in a barrage of biogenetic modules to finish it off. The assault team that supplied the modules was running under quota, so they launched a triple barrage rather than the requested single." He frowned. "It would seem that we've just seen part of the result. There are probably a lot more of those things roaming around out there."

Dundat growled. "Well, I hope that at least they got the Terrans they were intended for!"

Hadrak muttered, "The way things have been going, somehow I doubt it." He stared out at the sunlit parking lot and the forest beyond, and watched the fast-moving shadows that slid across them.

"Well, sir," Kair said, "now what?"

"Now we call in and tell them the situation and ask for pickup right here," Hadrak replied.

"I'll do that, sir," Di said—he was the equipment officer, and carried the long-range communicator.

"Go ahead," Hadrak said. He stepped cautiously back toward the doorway.

The dead little Terran was still lying on the steps—and as Hadrak had feared, a wasp had noticed it. The creature landed atop the tiny corpse, probing at it.

And then the wasp looked up and saw the Martians inside the house.

"Shoot it!" Hadrak bellowed, raising his own weapon.

Bindar, Dundat, and Kair looked up and immediately opened fire. The wasp resisted for a moment, but then it crumpled.

Hadrak shuddered. "We need to block this entranceway," he said. "Use all this Terran junk—build a barrier!"

"Your will." The three began hauling statuary and potted plants up toward the opening. Hadrak watched, then looked out again.

There were more shadows than ever—wasps were circling overhead, lured by the sounds of activity, or perhaps by the presence of their dead comrades.

Hadrak turned to see Di using the long range communicator. Di lowered the device and looked unhappily at his commanding officer.

"The campaign is going badly in this sector," he reported. "They're meeting much stiffer resistance than anticipated. And the wasps are believed to be dangerous to our ships—since I said there were wasps in the area, they won't send a transport without a fighter escort. They can't spare a transport *and* escort for a pickup for at least a planetary rotation or two—possibly as many as four. Until then we're on our own."

"Four *days*?" Hadrak demanded in disbelief.

"Four days—four Terran rotations," Di confirmed.

Hadrak stared out at the wasps and at the growing pile of debris in the doorway.

"If we can get ourselves clear of the wasps and other arthropods," Di offered, "they might risk sending in an unescorted transport. For that they'd only need about two hours' notice. Maybe."

"Wonderful," Hadrak said. "Just wonderful." He looked around at the dark paneling, the looming balconies, the dim stained-glass windows. "So we've lost two of our men, our own Tec/Div's screw-up has trapped us here for maybe four days, in a madhouse full of lurking, fanatical Terrans . . .

"Why am I not surprised?"

14

STRANGE DISCOVERIES

"What's that buzzing?" Nancy asked.

Bud looked up. "I don't know," he said.

"Maybe the Martians tripped an alarm somewhere?" Bill suggested.

Bud frowned. "When I worked here, we didn't have any alarms that buzzed."

"So maybe they added one," Tony said.

"Maybe," Bud said, not entirely convinced.

They were in the mansion's combined snack bar and gift shop—a fair-sized room which had once been a scullery where some of the endless supplies of china in the Gelman cupboards were washed after every meal. It now held three small metal and plastic tables, a dozen chairs, a well-equipped commercial kitchenette, a counter, a cash register, and several shelves of cheap souvenirs. The room's only window looked out on an air shaft; the door at one end opened into a kitchen passageway that had been their way in, and the door at the other end led back to the old service entrance, now the tourist entrance, where they had first come into the house.

They had found no trace of José, Steve, or Bobby in the snack bar, but they did find plenty of food. Nancy had the hot-dog cooker running, but it would be another ten minutes before the

79

dogs were ready. Meanwhile, the others collected an assortment of chips, soda, and candy bars, and began to take the edge off their appetites.

"I think I'm gonna go take a look around out front," Bud said.

The others all looked up at him, with expressions ranging from startlement to terror.

"There might be Martians out there," Tiffany said.

"There might be Martians in here," Bud retorted. "That kid back there, the girl, saw them in the house; probably Steve did, too."

"Katie," Nancy said. "Her name's Katie."

"I don't care if it's Ermintrude the Magnificent," Bud replied. "She saw Martians through the peephole, so we know they got inside, so it probably isn't any safer in here than it is out front."

"Suit yourself, then," Nancy said, annoyed.

"Be careful," Tiffany said.

"You might want to look out a window before you open any doors," Bill said.

"I was planning on it." Bud pushed out to the entryway, glanced at the closed door to the outside, then hurried down the little passage to the guides' lounge.

He had half hoped he might find Steve or José here, but there was no sign of them. He did spot Steve's master key ring sitting on the desk, though, and pocketed it quietly. That might be useful. Then he crossed to the window and peered out.

The first thing he saw was the smoldering wreckage of Tony's white Lincoln.

"Oh, crap," he said. He leaned over to one side and could make out the remains of the minivan and the Toyota, as well.

That explained three of the explosions. The fourth must have been either the Winterses' Chevy or Steve's old Ford. Bud leaned over a little farther, hoping to get a glimpse of the Chevy.

He couldn't see it; it was too far around the corner, over at the far end of the parking lot.

But he could see a giant wasp.

He blinked, rubbed his eyes, and stared, but the monstrosity didn't vanish the way a good hallucination should. It continued to stalk about the parking lot, looking entirely too real.

It was considerably larger than any of the destroyed vehicles, Bud noticed.

Then another insect landed, and another, and he realized what the buzzing was.

A swarm of thirty-foot wasps.

This had to be something the Martians had done, Bud told himself; it couldn't be a coincidence that on the day of the invasion, these monster bugs showed up. Had the Martians brought these things with them?

Bud had a vague memory of having once read somewhere that in lower gravity, things might grow larger. And Mars, he remembered, had lower gravity than Earth.

So these must be Martian wasps, he decided. It was therefore safe to assume that they were hostile—otherwise, why would the invaders have brought them?

Besides, if they were anything like Earth wasps . . . weren't wasps carnivorous? Didn't they eat other, smaller insects? To those things out there, a human being would probably look pretty tasty.

Up until now the plan among the people holed up in the secret room had been to wait until they were sure the Martians were gone—maybe until nightfall, so they could move under cover of darkness—then head out and try to find someplace safe.

Did wasps sleep? Because Bud now had no intention of going out there as long as those things were active. The "maybe wait until nightfall" had just become "by night, definitely."

And heading out had just become a lot more difficult. At least three of the cars were so much scorched scrap metal, and Betsy Winters had said her Chevy was dead, as well. That left Steve's old Ford in the employee lot—maybe. The Martians might have destroyed that, too. There had definitely been a fourth explosion; either they'd blown up the Chevy, not realizing it was already defunct, or they'd found the employee lot and gotten the Ford.

Bud hoped it had been the Chevy—though they obviously couldn't fit everyone in the Ford, and somehow he doubted that if it came down to a vote, the others were going to choose an overweight biker over a bunch of women and kids when it came to assigning seats.

Besides, they weren't necessarily going to take the Ford anywhere, even if it was still there. Steve presumably had the keys—*those* weren't on the ring he had just snatched. Bud had never hot-wired a car, and didn't think he'd care to try it for the first time with killer Martians and hungry thirty-foot insects in the area.

On the other hand, old Ebenezer Gelman had been a collector. He'd collected *everything*—statuary, armor, art . . . and classic cars. The twelve-car garage in the basement was one of the more popular parts of the standard tour.

Bud wondered how many of those antiques down there still ran—and how many of the people here could drive them, since there wasn't an automatic transmission in the bunch. Hell, he wasn't sure *he* could drive the ones with chokes, throttles, spark-advance levers, and the like.

Then he corrected himself—there might be one car down there with an automatic. Mrs. Gelman's pink '59 Cadillac might have one. He wasn't sure what sort of shape it was in, though.

He also wondered whether the Martians were actually gone. Blowing up the cars seemed like something they'd have done on the way out, so maybe they really had left. He hoped so.

But if they had, where was Steve? And little Bobby? And José?

Maybe the wasps had gotten them somehow. Could those things get into the house?

Or maybe there were *other* Martian critters around. He looked around the room uneasily.

He decided that the time had come to let the others know what was happening. He marched back down the passage to the entrance hall and pushed through the door to the snack bar.

"It's me!" he called as he stepped in—and found himself looking down the muzzle of a big, mean-looking handgun that Bill Edwards had pulled out. Behind Bill, Nancy held a bread knife she'd found somewhere in the snack bar's supplies.

"Sorry," Bill said, putting his pistol away. "We're a bit jumpy, I guess."

Bud noticed that while Bill, Nancy, and Tiffany had all been staring at him as he entered, Tony had been staring at Bill, and more specifically at Bill's gun.

"What the hell are you doing with that thing?" Tony demanded.

"Nothing," Bill said. "I've got a permit, okay?"

"You son of a bitch!" Tiffany shouted. "You could've just *shot* those two Martians, and we wouldn't have lost Steve and that kid!"

Bill looked embarrassed. "You're assuming their armor isn't bulletproof," he said. "I'm not so sure. And what if I'd missed one of them? The other might have called in an air strike and killed us all."

"Still might've been nice if you'd let us know you had it," Nancy said. "So, you a cop, or what?"

Bill looked around at the four hostile faces, then threw up his hands in disgust. "I'm a gun dealer. It's a sample, okay? I had a free morning and thought I'd stop in at the local tourist trap. *I* didn't know the damn Martians were going to invade!"

For a moment the other four stared at him. Then Bud shrugged. "Okay," he said. "What the hell. Meanwhile, I've got some bad news, boys and girls."

"What?" Nancy asked. "The Martians still there?"

Bud shook his head. "Didn't see 'em," he said. "But those explosions we heard? That was the Martians blowing up all the cars out front. And they left another little extra—giant wasps."

"Giant what?" Nancy asked.

"Wasps. Bugs. Big black ones that sting."

"What're you talking about?" Tony said.

"Come look for yourself," Bud said. He wasn't surprised the others were having trouble believing it; hell, he was having trouble believing it himself.

Nancy glanced at the hot-dog cooker, but decided it would be okay to leave it unattended for a few minutes. "Lead on," she said.

In the entryway Bud paused; trying to crowd the five of them up to the tiny window in the guides' lounge would be awkward.

"Maybe we should try this way," he said, pointing to the door labeled TOUR STARTS HERE. That would take them to the small parlor, where a bay window would give them a good view of the entire parking lot and front lawn.

"Is that where you went before?" Nancy asked.

"No."

"Then you go first."

Bud hesitated. She might have a point, he thought; what if something out there saw them through the windows and smashed its way in? What if there were Martians already in there?

It was still bright out—still mid-afternoon—and the windows faced north, so the light would make it easy to see out, hard to see in; that wasn't a major concern. There might well already be something unpleasant waiting for them in the parlor, though.

Well, there was one way to find out; he pushed the door open, very slowly and carefully, and looked through.

Nothing. Or rather, Tiffany lamps with beaded shades, red velvet settees, oval portraits hanging on gaudy white and gold wallpaper, Victorian walnut end tables—but no Martians or monsters. The door on the far side, leading to the reception room, stood slightly ajar, as did both doors at the back—Steve, or someone, had been sloppy, as those were supposed to be kept closed.

He latched the door open from habit and stepped through, restraining himself from taking up a position behind the little stand where the guides sold tour tickets. He couldn't resist closing the door to the reception room, though. Then he stood in the center of the parlor and beckoned for the rest of the party to join him.

"There," he said, gesturing at the windows.

The others trickled in and stood, staring.

Bud noticed immediately that the Chevy was a burned-out skeleton, just like the other three; that meant that if any car had survived out there, it was Steve's Ford.

The trees on the far side of the parking lot seemed to be thinner than they ought to be, and Bud thought he could see movement out there, though he couldn't tell what it was. Was something destroying the forest?

There were three live giant wasps in sight, all of them on the ground. Two of them were picking at something over on the front steps; the third was over by the entry road, picking at something there.

"Oh, my God," Nancy said, clapping a hand to her mouth. She pointed at the two by the steps. "Look!"

The five of them all turned to look, and Tiffany promptly screamed and collapsed into the nearest chair, burying her face in her hands.

Bud winced at the scream.

"So much for little Bobby," Tony said. "Poor kid."

"I feel sick," Tiffany said, not looking up.

Bud didn't blame her, but he wished she hadn't let out that shriek.

They still couldn't really see what it was the wasps were picking at, but they could all see the torn shirt that dangled from one wasp's mandible, and they all knew where they'd seen that shirt last.

"What about the other one?" Bill said, turning to peer out at it.

"Steve or José, I guess," Bud said as he looked in that direction.

The other wasp was much farther away, but the angle was such that none of the porch or the railings were in the way, so despite the distance, they could see what the wasp was standing over.

They could all see the metallic green gleam of armor.

"That's not Steve," Nancy said.

"It's not José, either," Bill said.

"It's a goddamn Martian!" Tony said. "I don't believe it!"

"And a dead wasp," Bill added.

"I'll be damned," Bud said.

The four of them looked at each other, puzzled.

"The wasps aren't on their side?" Tony asked.

"Maybe they lost control of them," Bill suggested. "Or at least that one—it killed the Martian, and the other Martian killed the wasp."

"Maybe that Martian was a traitor," Nancy said, "and the wasp was *ordered* to kill him."

"Then who killed the wasp?" Bud asked. "And look over there— is that another dead one on the porch?"

The others turned and looked, but the angle made it hard to be sure whether the wasp on the porch was dead or just motionless.

The consensus was that it was dead. They looked at each other, baffled.

Tiffany uncovered her face and took a look at the dead Martian and the two dead wasps. She shuddered. "Now what?" she asked.

For a moment no one answered. Then Bud shook himself, took one last look at first the Martian and then Bobby's shirt, and turned away.

"Now we eat lunch," he said. "I'm hungry, and those hot dogs must be ready."

15

THE FOG OF WAR

"**F**our days," Slithree Di said. "What are we supposed to do until then?"

"Wait," Hadrak said.

"What will we eat? Where will we sleep?" Bindar demanded.

"We'll eat our emergency rations," Hadrak said, "and sleep wherever is convenient. Maybe on those altar things on the second level."

"Emergency rations?" Bindar said with distaste. Hadrak ignored him.

"And what about the Terrans?" Kair asked. "We'll have to post guards if we don't want them killing us in our sleep."

"I say we should just exterminate them all and be done with it," Dundat said.

"If we knew how many there are, so we could be certain of getting them all, I'd agree with you," Hadrak said.

"We should have asked that one before we killed it," Bindar said, pointing toward the blockaded entrance.

For a moment all five of them looked out over the barricade at the two wasps that were still picking at the little Terran's remains. The Martians had struggled frantically to build that pile up high enough to block the giant insects, and were reasonably sure they had succeeded—the remaining opening between the heap and the door frame averaged little more than a foot in height.

They had stripped virtually all the statuary and furniture from the first level of the hall in constructing their makeshift rampart, but it seemed to have worked.

"It had started lying," Hadrak said. "We couldn't trust anything it said."

No one said anything, but Dundat's expression was openly disbelieving. The others weren't quite so obvious, but Hadrak didn't see any signs of support for his position.

"All right," he said, "next time we capture a Terran, one of *you* can question it."

"It did mention three designations," Kair said. "Specifically, 'Dad and Mom and Mr. Edwards.' And it said there were many more."

"I would guess," Di said, "that those three exist. I doubt there are very many more, or surely, even in a place this size, we would have seen more of them."

"I believe 'Dad' and 'Mom' are terms of endearment reserved for one's parents," Hadrak said. "The term 'Mister' denotes respect toward an adult male."

"Then there are at least three adults."

"Yes."

"Perhaps—"

Kair never finished his sentence; he was interrupted by a scream.

The Martians all looked, startled, in the direction from which the sound had come—toward the open door that Bindar and Dundat had used in their initial reconnaissance.

"What was that?" Bindar asked.

"You tell us," Di replied. "You and Dundat searched that area."

"We found nothing that would make such a sound," Dundat said.

"Was that perhaps a Terran distress cry?" Kair asked.

"I believe it was," Hadrak agreed.

"What did you find in there?" Di demanded.

"A series of chambers," Bindar answered. "There were no Terrans in them—just more of these artifacts." He gestured at the barricade.

"Did you establish a terminus?" Hadrak asked.

"No, sir," Dundat said. "They seemed to go on forever, and they branched off repeatedly, including a stairway and a connection to the conference chamber that Aif and Kair explored. We penetrated perhaps eighty feet, no more."

"Let us take a look, then," Hadrak said. "All of us; there's no reason to separate."

With Hadrak in the lead, Dundat close behind, and Di guarding the rear, the five of them marched through the door into a good-sized chamber. Like most of the others they had seen, it was paneled in dark wood, but here four large windows in the north wall provided plenty of natural light—each was bordered in colored glass, but with two wide panes of clear glass, one above the other, in the center.

More statuary, paintings, and potted plants adorned the room, though in somewhat less profusion than in the grand entrance hall. A short passageway, two doors, and a staircase opened from the side opposite the windows; in the far end were two more doors, the left-hand one standing open, the right-hand one tightly shut.

Dundat frowned. "We did not leave that space separator in that position," he said, pointing at the right-hand door.

"You're certain?" Hadrak asked.

"Absolutely," Dundat said.

"I agree," Bindar added.

"Then Terrans have been here!" Kair exclaimed.

"Or perhaps there is a security mechanism at work. That sound we heard might have been an alarm," Di suggested.

"I never heard any alarm that sounded anything like that," Bindar said.

"How many Terran alarms have you heard?" Di countered.

"It's more likely that sound was made to lure us into a trap!" Bindar retorted.

That possibility had not completely escaped Hadrak. He remembered how he and Di charged forward to capture the little Terran, and only afterward had considered the possibility of a ruse. In that case there did not appear to have been any deception involved, but that didn't mean there wasn't in this new situation.

"Spread out," he ordered. "Kair, into the passageway over there. Dundat, on the stairs."

Puzzled, the others obeyed.

When the five of them were scattered so that no imaginable booby trap or lurking Terran could possibly take them all out at once, Hadrak barked, "All right, Bindar, blast it open!"

"Your will!" Bindar said. He aimed his KA-77 at the center of the door and fired.

Bud had just taken his first bite of hot dog when they heard what was unmistakably the blast of some sort of weapon. His head spun to face the door to the entry hall.

"Damn," he said.

The others had frozen at the sound; now Tiffany asked, "Is it wasps?"

"I don't think so, babe," Tony said. "I think them Martians are back."

"They must've heard the bimbo scream when we were in the front room," Nancy growled, nodding toward Tiffany.

"Not necessarily," Bill said. "They might just be—"

"*Screw* what they might just be!" Bud shouted. "Just grab everything and let's get the hell out of here! Back to the secret room!" He followed his own advice, snatching up his hot dog and cup of Dr Pepper and heading for the door.

Nancy had prepared a tray of hot dogs to take back to the others; she grabbed that and followed close on Bud's heels. Tony had stuffed a bag with chips, candy bars, and half pints of milk, and was close behind.

Tiffany didn't bring anything but her purse, but she, too, hurried.

Bill hesitated, thought about cautioning the others against rushing off wildly, then decided there wasn't time to argue. He trotted after them.

All he carried was his 9mm pistol.

"We didn't leave that one open," Bindar said, pointing. "In our haste, we didn't discover how it could be made to stay open; it kept closing by itself when we looked here before."

"That device at the top closed it," Dundat confirmed.

"And now it holds it open," Di said, pointing. "See how that locking device slides along the bar?"

"Then Terrans *have* been here," Hadrak said.

"Unquestionably," Di said. "And unless some deception has been attempted, they presumably departed in that direction."

Hadrak looked at the other two doors. "Bindar, Dundat, are those as you left them?"

"Affirmative," Dundat said. "I would say the angles are identical."

"Let us proceed, then," Hadrak said. "Di, take the lead."

Di obeyed; in the next room the five again paused and looked around.

The doors here bore signs—the first that the Martians had encountered anywhere inside the building.

"You should have reported these labels," Di said reprovingly.

"We had no opportunity to report them," Dundat replied stiffly.

"Which way did the Terrans go?" Kair asked.

Di frowned. "I have no idea," he said. "Bindar, Dundat, are these portals as you left them?"

The two looked about carefully.

"Yes, they are," Bindar said.

"However the Terrans departed, this time they did it without leaving any indications," Dundat confirmed.

"Other than the permanent signs," Kair pointed out. "Perhaps those might give us a clue."

The others all studied the signs.

" 'No admittance,' " Hadrak read. "That would indicate that those areas were interdicted. 'Snack Bar,' squiggle, 'Gift Shop'—that would be a dispensary of food and . . . 'Gift Shop'? That ought to mean a business establishment that distributes its merchandise without charge. Another inexplicable Terran custom, perhaps."

"Did you say food, sir?" Bindar asked.

"*Terran* food," Hadrak confirmed. "Didn't you look in there before?"

"No, sir—this was as far in this direction as we got." He looked at the snack bar door. "Terran food?"

The Martians looked at one another doubtfully.

"I'm hungry," Bindar said, "but I don't know if I'm *that* hungry."

"We might as well take a look," Dundat said. "Maybe that's where the Terrans are—perhaps they're eating a meal."

"And we might find something we can eat," Kair said.

"We'll try it," Hadrak said. He pushed open the door and the five of them advanced, weapons at ready, into the snack bar.

There were no Terrans. There were, however, paper plates, half-eaten hot dogs, plastic cups . . .

"They were here," Kair said.

Di pointed. "Some of those machines are still in operation," he said. "That one is generating significant levels of heat."

"It would seem they left hurriedly," Hadrak remarked.

"They must have heard us coming," Dundat said.

"There's only one other exit," Bindar pointed out.

"Come on," Hadrak said.

The five advanced into the corridor beyond the snack bar. Here, for once, the walls were not paneled or papered; they were plain white. Open doors along the right gave the Martians glimpses of a large, airy, well-lit, high-ceilinged room equipped with shelves and sinks, a room that any human would have recognized instantly as a kitchen. On the left a swinging door with a round window set in it opened into a short passageway.

"I recognize that," Kair said. "Aif and I got as far as that passage in our own investigations." He frowned. "Poor Aif," he added.

"Where does it lead?" Hadrak asked.

"To that large room with the many chairs and the several storage compartments," Kair said.

"And from there," Di said, "the Terrans could have passed into the central hallway, with its many doors and stairways."

"If they went that way, we'll never catch them," Bindar said.

Hadrak looked down the white-walled corridor. It ran easily another hundred feet, with several more doors on either side. The Terrans could have gone anywhere.

"Blast it!" he said.

Bindar, either startled or misunderstanding, fired several rounds from his KA-77 down the corridor, stopping only when Hadrak raised a hand.

The wild shots had torn long gouges in the corridor walls and shattered the door at the far end into blackened kindling. The echoes rattled back and forth, deafening the entire squad. Clouds of plaster dust sprayed in all directions before settling slowly to the tile floor.

Hadrak resisted the temptation to shout at Bindar; instead he shrugged and turned away, back toward the snack bar.

"They're gone," he said. "At least for now. Now, let's take a look at those Terran foods and see if anything might be fit to eat."

16

SCENIC VISTAS

"It's us!" Bud called as he worked the concealed latch; he didn't want anyone thinking that he and the others were Martian invaders. "We're back!"

As the panel swung open he saw several worried faces looking out at him.

"You were gone so long!" Marcie said. "We were worried!"

"Hot dogs!" Nancy said, displaying the tray. "Took a while to cook!"

"Food!" Katie yelled.

"Ssshhhh!" Tiffany said. "Martians might hear!"

Katie instantly fell silent, and no one else spoke until the five were back in the secret room and the panel was back in place. Bud noticed that someone had turned on a lamp; the light from the skylight was fading. The afternoon was more than half over.

Nancy distributed the hot dogs quickly.

"So what happened?" Betsy asked. "Did you see any Martians?"

"Did you see my brother anywhere?" Sid asked.

The five exchanged glances.

"Stan, c'mere a minute," Tony said, beckoning.

Worried, Stan followed Tony to a quiet corner under the stairs while Bill explained, "We heard Martians moving around in the house, but the only one we actually saw was dead, lying on the ground out front. But we saw something that might be even worse than the Martians."

"What?" Katie demanded.

"Giant wasps," Bill replied.

The others stared at him blankly.

"What do you mean, giant wasps?" Susan asked, nervously eyeing her husband's conversation with the black-haired man in the expensive gray suit.

"I mean giant wasps. Wasps big as a car."

"That's crazy," Marcie said.

"And invaders from outer space aren't?"

"Well, they're crazy, too," Marcie said. "This whole thing is crazy. I think I'm having a nightmare or something, and I'll just wake up back at the Motel 6 with Lenny."

Bud shook his head. "Lenny's dead, Marcie. You know that."

"But it's crazy!" Marcie insisted.

"I wanna see the giant wasps," Sid said.

Bud looked around for Sid's mother, but she had gone to join the conversation under the stairs—Tony and Stan were presumably explaining to her what had become of her elder son, and Bud didn't want to interrupt that. He looked up at the skylight, and in doing so, noticed the landings on the upper floors.

"Maybe we could go up to the fourth floor and take a look out the windows up there," he said. "We haven't seen or heard anything of the Martians above the second floor." He didn't suggest using the fifth-floor door to go out on the roof, where they could get a *really* good view, for a couple of reasons—it was kept locked, and he didn't particularly want to admit yet that he'd swiped the keys. Furthermore, if they went out on the roof, they'd be too vulnerable to attack by those giant wasps Sid wanted to see, too likely to be seen by any Martians prowling the area—and in the case of the kid, too likely to fall off and get killed.

Just then Susan started sobbing, and Bud decided not to wait for a consensus.

"Come on," Bud said, taking Sid by the shoulder. "I think your mom needs some time by herself right now."

"I'm coming, too," Katie said.

"Come on, then," Bud said.

Others joined the party as they climbed upward, and Bud found himself leading an expedition of five—Sid, Katie, Betsy, and Marcie.

"Did you guys find Steve?" Marcie asked as they passed the third floor.

"Nope," Bud said. "Didn't see any sign of Steve or José." He didn't mention his personal conviction that Steve was lying dead somewhere in the south wing.

On the fourth-floor landing they paused while Bud worked the concealed door. This one was not part of the standard tour, so it was stiff from disuse; he had to lean on it with his full weight before at last it yielded.

They emerged through the back of an old-fashioned clothes press into a small, dusty bedroom, tall and narrow, which was remarkably plain compared to the rest of the house. A simple single bed with a painted metal bed frame stood against one wall, an ordinary dresser against the opposite, and that was the entire furnishings. Light came from a slanting window high in one wall.

"Hey, we didn't see *this* on the tour," Sid said.

"They can't show everything," Bud said. "The place is too big. So they skip most of the fourth floor. This was a maid's room. Some people think old man Gelman had his secret panel here so he could slip up here for a visit without his wife finding out."

Sid looked blank, but the women seemed to like the theory; Katie smirked, Betsy nodded, and Marcie stifled a snide remark after a glance at Sid.

Bud paid no attention; he marched on into the hall.

"You can't see anything from there," he said, jerking a thumb at the window; it was, indeed, too high to see anything through but sky.

The hall was also simple and mostly unadorned, with faded white and blue striped wallpaper and a maroon runner on the floor. Bud turned north, toward the front of the house, then paused.

"I was thinking," he said. "I'd figured we could go to the solarium on this floor, 'cause with all that glass, it's got the best view—you saw that on the tour, right, Sid? You know what I'm talking about. But that faces out over the ocean, not the parking lot. So maybe we should go up the big tower and get a better view that way."

"No more stairs," Betsy said. "Maybe just a bedroom or something?"

"I saw the tower before," Sid said. "It was pretty cool."

Bud didn't explain that he had originally intended to use the solarium so that they wouldn't be looking down at Sid's dead brother, but then he had realized that they also might not see any of the wasps from there. The tower was set back slightly, so the porch roof would hide whatever was left of Bobby, but they'd still be able to see the dead Martian.

Now he wasn't sure that was a good idea.

"We'll try the solarium," Bud said. The wasps might be all over the place.

No one objected, so he led the way through a storeroom and a small lounge into the solarium.

This was a room that looked as if it might have originally been intended simply as a section of roof, rather than a room; the floor was sheet metal, sloping to a drain, while the roof and one curving wall were white-painted ironwork supporting hundreds of panes of glass. The furniture was also mostly white-painted ironwork—two round tables and a dozen chairs, with several planters holding assorted ferns and palms.

The place was stifling hot—hardly surprising for what was effectively a greenhouse. Bud started sweating almost the instant he stepped into the room.

The view, however, was spectacular. They were on the fourth floor of a high-ceilinged house, and that in turn stood atop a cliff; the waves dashing on the rocks were a *long* way down. They could see the ocean stretching out to the horizon, and to either north or south they could glimpse stretches of deserted beach.

And almost directly in front of them was a giant wasp; Bud couldn't have asked for a better display. The insect was cruising back and forth, as if looking for something, perhaps ten feet below their own altitude and fifty feet out from the wall.

"Jesus," Marcie said, staring.

"Wow!" Sid said.

Betsy shuddered. Katie asked, "Do you think it sees us?"

"I hope not," Bud said, suddenly regretting his choice of the solarium.

All of them except Sid backed off slightly at the idea that the wasp might notice them. Sid, with the normal attention span of a six-year-old, had already grown bored with the wasp and was studying the distant beaches, pressing up against the glass for a better view.

"Hey," he said, "there's a car on the beach down there."

"There is?" Katie asked. Curious, she stepped up to the glass and looked where Sid indicated.

"I don't see it," she said.

"You can't now," Sid agreed. "It's around there where you can't see it anymore."

"Let's go up to the tower," Betsy suggested, catching her daughter's arm.

"Yeah," Bud said. "Come on."

He led the way out a different door than the one they had entered by, along a short arcade to a narrow staircase leading upward.

Bud led the way up two flights; there were windows on two sides on the fifth floor, but on the sixth the tower was free of the surrounding roof and had a view in all four directions. The seventh and highest level was smaller and less comfortable, and he saw no reason to bother with another flight.

From the sixth floor they could see the ocean, the beaches, the forests, and half a dozen giant wasps cruising the vicinity, as well as a maze of rooftops, chimneys, and turrets.

"Wow, is that our car?" Sid asked, staring down at the blackened ruins in the parking lot.

"Yeah," Bud said. "So where's this car on the beach?"

Katie pointed. "There!" she said.

Sure enough, Bud glimpsed what looked like a red and white Jeep or some similar vehicle approaching rapidly from the south, spraying rooster tails of sand behind it.

"Idiots'll bog down if they keep up like that," he muttered. "What's their damn hurry?"

Then he noticed the gray things following the car.

They weren't giant wasps, at any rate; these things were hopping and crawling, rather than flying, and were a washed-out gray color rather than that deadly black.

"Sand fleas," Marcie said.

"What the hell are sand fleas?" Bud asked. He had never paid much attention to bugs.

"They live in the sand," Betsy said. "They're harmless, ordinarily."

"Those don't look harmless," Marcie said.

"No, they don't," Betsy agreed.

"So we're dealing with lots of different giant bugs, not just wasps?" Bud said. "Oh, great!"

"We sure are, mister," Sid said. "Look!"

Bud turned and looked where the boy was pointing.

"Oh, *crap*!" he said.

There were giant beetles out there, devouring the trees, inland and to the north. Bud thought they must be about fifty or sixty feet long. He could see a couple of different varieties, including—he shuddered; his mother had kept roses once—Japanese beetles.

"At least those are vegetarians," Betsy said.

"Are sand fleas vegetarians?"

"I don't know," she admitted. "I don't think so."

"What're they gonna do when they've eaten all the trees?" Sid asked. "Eat each other?"

"More likely they'll just starve," Betsy said. "Most herbivores can't eat meat even if they want to."

"So all we need to worry about are the wasps and sand fleas, and all the beetles are doing is eating all our cover," Bud said. "That's just great." He leaned over and peered down toward the employee lot.

Steve's Ford was there, and appeared to be intact. That was something, anyway.

The Jeep, or whatever it was, had disappeared beneath the overhang of the cliffs.

"You know, they're going to be stuck down there," Bud said thoughtfully. "The two beaches don't connect; it's all rocks down there below the house. You can climb across it at low tide, but you sure can't drive it."

"Is it low tide now?" Sid asked.

Bud studied the beaches. "Yeah, I think it is," he said.

"Then they'll climb across," Betsy said.

"Not if they have any sense," Bud said. "If they're smart, they'll climb up here to the house, same as we did." He indicated Marcie and himself. "The sand fleas won't be able to get up here after them."

"But there are wasps and Martians and beetles up here," Katie protested.

"They don't know that," Bud said. "They might see the wasps, but not the rest."

"But—"

"I'll bet they're going to come up here and walk right into the Martians," Bud said. "At least, unless we warn them."

"But—" Marcie began.

"Hey, *I'm* going," Bud said. "You can come along or not, but I'm gonna do what I can. Maybe one of you should go tell the others."

"Tell them what?" Sid asked.

"Company's coming!" Bud answered as he started down the stairs.

17

NEW ARRIVALS

Mark Harshaw stared at the rocks ahead. He spun and looked at the ocean, then at the approaching sand fleas and at the looming cliffs. He turned off the engine and snatched up his gym bag.

"End of the line," he said. "Everybody out!"

Stacy and Jennifer opened their doors, but Brenda leaned over from the backseat and demanded, "Are you *crazy*? Those things are right behind us!"

"And there are rocks right ahead of us," Mark retorted. "See for yourself. Think you can drive over those?" He gestured.

Brenda looked out the windshield and stared for a few seconds, then said, "Okay, you're right—everybody out!" She dove out after Jennifer.

"Up the stairs!" Stacy called, pointing as she ran.

Mark hesitated, staring up the cliff at the immense structure looming over them. "What *is* that place?" he asked. "I mean, are the people here going to freak when they're invaded by a bunch of college kids in swimsuits?"

"Who cares what it is?" Stacy asked. "Like we have anywhere else to go?"

"This must be Gelman Mansion," Brenda said, slowing to a walk and looking up. "I've heard of it, never been here."

"It doesn't look like the postcards," Jennifer said, stopping to look for herself. "I've seen them in the drugstore, you know?"

"Who *cares*?" Stacy demanded from four or five steps up. "Come on, before those bugs get here!"

Mark had to agree with that; he headed for the stairs at a steady jog.

The three bikini-clad young women were all past the first landing by the time Mark reached the bottom step; Stacy was halfway up, bounding upward like a gazelle. And Mark was just half a dozen steps up when the first of the giant sand fleas took a hop and landed atop the Jeep.

Mark winced at the sound—a tremendous thump that made him think the entire vehicle had been mashed flat. He risked a look back, though, and saw that while the roof had been dented, everything else looked intact, and the sand flea had slid off again.

The sand fleas seemed to lose interest in the Jeep after that, but they were still interested in the humans; a couple of them turned toward the stairs.

Mark decided he preferred to watch from a safer distance and charged up the stairs, gaining on the girls.

Bud trotted into the solarium, intending to return the way they had come, but as he did, the glass wall burst inward in an explosion of broken glass and flakes of rusted iron—a giant wasp had just rammed into it at full speed, breaking its way in as it tried to get at Bud.

Behind him, Marcie and Katie both screamed. All four of the others had followed him and were in the arcade connecting the solarium to the tower.

Bud whirled and herded everyone back down the arcade as the wasp thrashed about, shattering more glass and shredding potted plants. Bud directed everyone through another door as the wasp swung around and thrust its head into the arcade; the giant insect twisted and wiggled, trying to fit its four-foot thorax through a three-foot door frame.

The instant everyone was safely through, Bud slammed the door shut behind them.

He didn't bother locking it; if the wasp could get this far, a lock wasn't going to make any difference. "Come on," he said, leading the party in search of another staircase.

Unfortunately, he didn't remember the layout of this wing very well. The tour had come through here, yes, but it had never been an interesting or popular part of the route, and had been run in the other direction, leading up to the tower, and then to the solarium, and then across and down through the front hall.

Well, they couldn't go through the solarium with the wasp there, and Bud wasn't eager to set foot in the front hall while there were Martians in the house. The secret room was only accessible through the servants' quarters on this level, and those were a maze of hard-to-distinguish corridors and virtually interchangeable bedrooms.

There were two other staircases that Bud remembered—the twisty little stair that the tour came up, and the locked Gothic rotunda that passed through the back of the fourth floor on its way into the round tower at the south corner.

Right now, as he dashed through empty corridors, dusty storerooms, and plain old unused attic, he couldn't remember how to get to either of them.

Those poor fools from the beach were probably going to walk straight into the Martians before he could find a way down.

Bud didn't want that. He wanted to survive, and he figured that the more human beings they had working together, the better his chances.

Of course, just *how* they were going to survive wasn't all that clear. He had no idea how the Martian invasion was proceeding; for all he knew, the people here in the mansion were the only humans left alive anywhere on the planet.

It didn't seem likely, but it was possible.

And if they were all that was left, then they needed to get to someplace safer—someplace with more food, fewer giant bugs, and no Martians.

Even if they *weren't* all that was left, they needed to get to some-place with more food, fewer giant bugs, and no Martians. They couldn't stay here; Gelman Mansion was becoming a deathtrap. That wasp in the solarium had demonstrated there was no permanent safety here. When those beetles out there finished eating the forest, they might start stripping away the mansion—sure, some of it was stone and metal, but plenty of it was wood.

Finally, he spotted a heavy, ironbound door—the rotunda! He groped for the key ring he had taken from the guides' lounge and fumbled for the right key.

Brenda pressed against the stone wall and stared up at the huge wasp hovering fifty feet above her.

"I'm not going up there," she said.

"You'd rather go back down?" Mark asked, pointing down at the beach, where three sand fleas were burrowing at the foot of the steps. "Come on, Stacy and Jennifer must be at the top by now!"

"And the wasps probably got 'em," Brenda said.

"We'd have heard screams," Mark said. "Come *on*!"

Reluctantly, Brenda pulled herself away from the wall and contin-ued upward, glancing uneasily up at the wasp with every step or two.

"Wow," Sid said, "we didn't see *this* on the tour!" He peered down over the edge of the stone spiral staircase—six stories down, all the way down to the mansion's subbasement. The spiral also ex-tended up two flights into the peak of the south tower.

"That's because it's not safe," Bud said. "No railings, see?" He started down the spiral.

The minute he spotted the rotunda door, he decided that he would get out on the second floor, grab a weapon or two from the south gallery, and head on across the back of the house. In the back of his mind the possibility of finding out what had become of Steve rein-forced this plan. As he descended, he flipped through the keys, look-ing for the right one to open the second-floor door.

The others followed.

They emerged safely on the second floor, and Bud took a long, careful look up the hallway before stepping through into the south gallery. He didn't see any sign of Steve, and he didn't remember the house well enough to be sure whether anything had been disturbed.

There were those six bedrooms, though, and Bud suspected he might find something in one of them if he looked—but right now he didn't have time.

He trotted the length of the south gallery, resisting the temptation to stop and arm himself; he'd wasted far too much time on the fourth floor. Whoever had been in that Jeep might already be lying dead in the parking lot.

The four of them paused to catch their breath at the top of the stairs. Mark looked at the house and noticed the heavy brass padlock and white-painted steel bar on the kitchen door.

"Crud," he said. "We aren't getting in *that* way."

"The place looks deserted," Brenda said.

"No, the garden's still tended," Jennifer said.

"Better than the woods," Stacy said. "Look at that mess!"

She pointed, and the others looked across the kitchen garden at the surrounding forest—or what was left of it. Most of the trees had been stripped bare, with whole limbs snapped, twisted, or simply gone. It reminded Mark of the pictures he'd seen of the French forests of World War I after they'd been subjected to months of shelling.

But this had been done in a single day. He didn't know exactly how or why, but he had no doubt that this devastation was a result of the Martian invasion.

He also suspected that whatever had done it might still be close by. "Come on," he said. "Let's keep moving."

"I need to rest!" Brenda protested from her seat on a wrought-iron bench.

"There might be more wasps," Mark said.

Brenda sprang up. "Let's go," she said. "Let's get inside some-where!" She shuddered. "I *hate* wasps!"

They pressed on, glancing upward occasionally to watch for wasps, until they came to the yew alley. Here about half the shrubs were still green, but half were stripped and trampled.

"What *did* this?" Jennifer asked.

"Who cares?" Stacy said. "Hey, look! A car!"

Mark looked through the remains of the yew and saw an old blue sedan.

"Yeah," he said. "So what?"

"So we can use that to get out of here!" Stacy said. "We can head for Brownsburg."

"It's not ours," Mark said. "We don't have the keys. And hell, look at it! It may not even run."

"I can hot-wire a car," Jennifer said.

"It's still not ours," Mark said. "I'm not up for car theft unless it's our last chance."

"Okay, so we'll check inside first," Stacy said. "Let me go take a close look at it, anyway, and see what sort of shape it's in."

Mark shrugged. "I can't stop you." He looked up at the sky, scanning for wasps, but didn't see any. He, Brenda, and Jennifer ducked back into a niche in the wall of the house, between a porch and a bay window, to wait.

Stacy looked both ways, as if watching for traffic along the branch-strewn grass and flagstones of the yew alley, then dashed for the employee parking lot.

She reached the car and tried the door on the passenger side; it was locked. She circled around the back, heading for the driver's door.

As she did, Mark and the others saw the beetle rear up from behind the fieldstone retaining wall on the far side of the little lot.

Jennifer screamed.

"Stacy!" Mark shouted.

"Jesus, girl!" Brenda shrieked. "Get your ass back here!"

Stacy had her hand on the car door handle; she tugged at it, then heard the screams and stood up to look at the others.

They were pointing at something behind her; she turned.

She saw the beetle as an immense gleaming shape the color of old brass, looming up out of nowhere. For an instant she froze in astonishment.

Then the astonishment turned to terror and she tried to run, but it was too late; the beetle lunged forward and snagged her in its gigantic mandibles.

18

THE BEETLE OF DEATH

Bud and the others were just passing the door to the upper smoking room when they heard the screams.

"Oh, crap," Bud said, breaking into a run.

Sid ran after him; Marcie and Betsy, however, stopped dead in their tracks. Katie took another few steps, then hesitated, looking back at her mother in confusion.

"We'll wait in here," Betsy called after Bud, pointing at the smoking room door.

Bud paid no attention as he charged through the music room toward the big windows overlooking the kitchen garden.

No one was in the garden itself, but when he looked to the north he saw what was happening—a Japanese beetle, grown to the size of a semi, was butting against Steve's old Ford, where it had trapped a young blonde in a skimpy bikini.

She must have been in that Jeep down on the beach, Bud thought, and just as he feared, she hadn't made it to the safety of the house.

The beetle reared back, the screaming blonde clutched in its mandibles, and then it bit down.

"Oh, God!" Bud muttered as blood sprayed in all directions, spattering across the gravel lot and the roof of Steve's car. The girl's scream cut off abruptly.

But Bud could still hear other screams.

One had come from behind him, he thought; he whirled, but that one had stopped. He took a step, then saw Marcie signaling to him from the doorway.

"It's all right!" she called. "Katie was just startled!"

Bud nodded and turned back to the window—where he definitely still heard screams.

He blinked and stared. The blonde *couldn't* still be screaming; the beetle had bitten her almost in half. In fact, as Bud watched, the beetle chewed again and the young woman's remains fell in two pieces, legs to one side, head and chest to the other, with only a smear of blood connecting them.

Someone was still screaming, though, and it was definitely someone outside, not any of the companions he had left two rooms back. Had one of the others downstairs—Nancy or Susan, perhaps—gone outside for some reason? Or had there been others in the Jeep, others who were somewhere he couldn't see them?

"Oh, gross!" Sid said.

That was the first Bud realized that the kid was still with him, and looking out the next window over.

"Get out of here!" he snapped. "You shouldn't be watching this— go back with the others!" He reached down, grabbed Sid, and spun him around.

"Hey!" Sid protested, but he went running back toward the smoking room.

Once the kid was gone, Bud reached up and tugged at the window latch. It was stiff from disuse; in fact, it appeared to have been painted over.

The screaming had stopped, he noticed. The beetle was waving about vaguely, not making any hostile moves in any direction, but at any moment it might change its mind.

"Oh, hell," Bud said. He turned and looked around, then snatched up a piano bench. He used it as a battering ram to smash out the window, sending a shower of broken glass and dried wood and putty down onto the path below.

Mark, Brenda, and Jennifer cowered in the niche as the giant beetle chopped poor Stacy in half; Brenda and Jennifer both screamed, long and loud, but to no avail.

When their breath gave out, they stopped; Jennifer began sobbing, deep, racking, gasping sobs, while Brenda just stared in glassy-eyed horror at the severed remains of her friend and the aimless meandering of the bloodstained insect that had killed her.

And then an upstairs window twenty feet to the south exploded outward and something tumbled to the ground amid a million shards of glass.

"What the hell . . . ?" Brenda asked.

All three of them leaned out around the bay window, peering at the wreckage.

"It's a piano bench," Jennifer said, baffled.

"Guess the place isn't deserted after all," Mark said.

Then Bud leaned out the window, and the three got a look at him—unshaven, long-haired, none too clean . . .

"Uh-oh," Jennifer said.

"Oh, come on, girl," Brenda said. "At least he's *human*!" She waved. "Over here, mister!"

Bud heard her and then spotted her.

"Hey!" he shouted. "You okay?"

"For now," Brenda called back. "But that thing just killed our friend!" She pointed at the Japanese beetle, which was wandering off to the north.

"Yeah, I saw," Bud replied.

"Can we get inside?" Brenda said, pointing at the front of the house.

"Not that way!" Bud replied. "There're Martians around front."

"Jesus, and we're yelling like this?" Brenda said, suddenly ducking back in the niche and looking around warily.

"Hang on," Bud called. "We'll find a way to get you up here." He turned and looked around the music room.

A violin case served to smash the remaining glass out of the lower sash, so that climbing in would be easier; then Bud looked for something he could lower for the others to climb.

He spotted the velvet ropes that had kept tourists from plucking at the big harp or plinking on the piano, and grabbed the three longest. It only took a few seconds to loop one around a nearby radiator pipe, then hook the others end-to-end and dangle them out the window.

"Don't let it sway too much, or the hooks might come unhooked!" he called down as he lowered the end.

Down below, the three looked at one another.

"Do we trust him?" Mark asked.

"We got a choice?" Brenda replied.

Jennifer looked around uneasily and didn't say anything.

Finally, Brenda shrugged. "Hey, *I'm* goin'," she said. She took a final look around to make sure no giant bugs were nearby, then dashed for the dangling rope.

As she did she heard a buzzing somewhere overhead.

"Oh, hell," she muttered as she started climbing. She didn't look up.

"Grab hold!" Bud called, reaching out a hand; she glanced up just long enough to grasp it.

Bud hauled the pretty black woman up into the music room, then leaned down and called, "Next!"

"You go ahead," Mark told Jennifer.

Jennifer hesitated, then looked up—and saw a wasp cruising over the house.

She grabbed for the rope and started climbing, and the minute Bud had helped her up through the broken window, Mark followed.

The buzzing grew louder. A moment later the wasp flew past the window, but it made no attempt to enter.

The window was big enough that Bud thought the insect might

have been able to get in if it had tried, but he was relieved it didn't make the experiment.

He turned away and gestured toward the doorway. "This way," he told the three he'd just rescued.

He was at the door of the smoking room when he realized that they'd left the velvet ropes hanging out the window. He hesitated, then shrugged. It didn't matter.

19

CLAWS OF
THE POLAR BEAR

"We'll wait in here," Betsy called after Bud as he broke into a run, followed closely by Sid. She pointed to the smoking room.

Bud paid no attention, but Katie took the hint instantly. She wheeled about and ran into the room her mother had indicated. She wanted to get away from that screaming, and quickly.

The smoking room was fairly large, like most of the rooms on the lower floors, but dim and shadowy—there didn't seem to be any windows to the outside, just stained-glass transoms over several doors. The whole place was lined with cabinets, all with glass or carved wood fronts; Katie glimpsed assorted old books, pipes, jars, tins, and beer steins through some of the glass. The other furnishings consisted largely of half a dozen overstuffed armchairs, a few ancient floor lamps, and an absurdly elaborate Victorian mantelpiece and fireplace.

None of that interested Katie, and she could still hear the screaming far too well; she charged on through into another dim chamber. There, she turned to see what was keeping her mother and that Marcie person—and let out a shriek of terror.

A gigantic white bear was looming over her, forepaws raised and claws spread to strike.

Betsy, who had been ambling through the smoking room in no

great hurry, dashed in to save her daughter; Marcie stopped dead in her tracks and said, "Oh, Christ, now what?"

By the time Betsy reached her, Katie had stopped screaming and felt thoroughly foolish. She realized she'd just screamed in terror at the sight of a slightly moth-eaten stuffed polar bear.

It was a *big* polar bear—this room extended two stories to make room for it—but it was obviously long dead.

"Sorry, Mom," Katie said. "It startled me." She pointed at the bear.

Betsy turned and looked at the animal, which was standing directly behind the open smoking room door, where she hadn't been able to see it as she entered.

"Oh," she said. She let her breath out in a rush. "I can see why," she said, then giggled nervously. "It's okay," she called back to Marcie. "Katie was just startled."

Marcie untensed somewhat.

"Tell Bud, would you?" Betsy called. "He must've heard the scream."

Marcie wasn't so sure that Bud had heard anything over the racket coming from outside—a regular chorus of shrieks seemed to be continuing out there—but Marcie returned to the other end of the smoking room long enough to signal to Bud that everything was okay.

Then the three females gathered in the polar bear's room—they had no idea what name the room might have, or what purpose it was intended to serve.

The room was almost a perfect cube, roughly twenty feet on a side; the polar bear occupied the center of the south wall, between two doors, and faced an elaborate confection of a fireplace and mantel—the carved stone fireplace front blended into a wooden tangle of miniature columns, knickknack shelves, tiny statuary niches, spires, and even a pair of gargoyles. It was all topped with an immense gilt-framed portrait of a dark-haired woman in a fancy white and gold dress from around the turn of the century. She seemed to be glaring across the room at the polar bear. Seen by itself, the bear appeared to be lunging to the attack, its eyes directed downward at its prey, but in combination with the painting, it seemed to Katie that the bear was looking down, cowed by the woman's stern gaze.

Whatnots adorned all four corners, with assorted bric-a-brac arranged on every possible surface. An Oriental rug covered most of the polished hardwood floor. A writing desk stood against one of the walls, midway between portrait and bear and beneath a small, ornately carved balcony that opened off someplace on the third floor; opposite the desk was a glass-fronted bookcase. Four rickety-looking tables were scattered about; three were empty, while the fourth held a two-foot statue of a nude woman holding an urn on one shoulder. Most of the light came through the French doors behind the third-floor balcony; on the second floor, where Katie and her mother stood, there were six doors in all, two in each side and two in the end with the bear.

The whole place looked dim, dusty, and incomprehensibly Victorian.

"What a weird room," Betsy said.

"The whole house is weird," Katie said.

"True enough," Betsy agreed.

Just then Marcie stepped cautiously into the room. "So what startled you?" she asked.

"That," Katie said, pointing at the stuffed bear.

"Oh, wow," Marcie said when she turned and saw that triumph of the taxidermist's art. "Is it real?" She leaned over and felt the fur on the polar bear's leg. "It *feels* real," she said.

"I think it must be," Katie said.

"Hey!" Sid's voice called. "Where is everybody?"

Marcie beckoned in the doorway. "In here," she called.

Sid dashed into the room. "Wow, you should've seen it!" he said. "There was this woman in a swimsuit and she got chopped right in half by a giant bug!"

The women exchanged glances.

"Ewww," Marcie said.

"So what do we do now?" Sid asked.

"What's Bud doing?" Betsy asked.

"I dunno. He shooed me away before we did anything but look."

They all heard a loud crash then, and the sound of shattering glass.

"We'll stay here," Betsy said.

"**D**id you hear something?" Tenzif Kair asked.

Hadrak looked up from the array of alien food products. "Hear what?" he asked. He hadn't been paying much attention; he had instead been trying to figure out some way to get food into his mouth without exposing himself to the deadly Terran atmosphere. Some of this stuff looked as if it might be quite edible after all—certainly better than the emergency rations in their armor.

"I do hear something, sir," Di said. "A high-pitched wailing of some sort."

"It's probably those confounded insects Tech/Div gifted us with," Hadrak said.

Di frowned. "I don't think so," he said.

"Should we investigate, sir?" Bindar asked.

"Affirmative," Hadrak said. "You go, Bindar; stay in touch by communicator and let us know what you find."

"Just me, sir?"

"Yes, just you! You're a trooper, trained for just such an assignment. Go!"

Bindar reluctantly retrieved his KA-77 from the table he had left it on and marched out of the snack bar. He paused in the entryway, listening.

The sound definitely seemed to be coming from outside; perhaps it *was* the insects, he thought. He hesitated, trying to decide whether to go back through the big room to the barricaded door or to look for a shorter route.

The sound stopped.

Bindar frowned.

Well, he should at least take a look, he supposed, before going back and rejoining the others. He tried the door with the colored glass inset, which appeared to be an exit from the building.

Beyond it was the parking lot—yes, it *was* an exit. He stepped outside and looked around warily.

No giant insects were right at hand; a beetle was moving about off to one side, he noticed, but it didn't seem to be threatening.

Something in the vicinity of the beetle caught his eye, and he leaned over for a better look.

"Sir," he said into his helmet communicator, "I think I see another of the Terran vehicles, one we missed before."

"Where?" Hadrak asked.

"It's around to the side of the building," Bindar replied. "Behind a row of plants—that's why we didn't see it before, I guess. It appears the giant insects have eaten many of the plants, however, leaving the vehicle visible."

"You're sure it's a vehicle?"

"Ah . . . reasonably certain."

"Get a closer look," Hadrak ordered. "See if we might be able to use it ourselves. Would we fit in the seats? Is it armored sufficiently to protect us from attacks by insects?"

"Your will," Bindar replied unhappily. He inched out from the door, KA-77 ready in his hands, scanning carefully for any hostile life-forms.

A wasp buzzed overhead, but it passed on over the house, apparently without having spotted him. The big beetle was wandering off to the north. The area was probably about as safe as it was going to get, Bindar thought. He trotted out toward the vehicle.

It was dark blue, but something red was smeared across the roof and dripping down the glass in places. That puzzled Bindar; was it some venom the beetle had exuded, perhaps? Or wasp excrement?

Then he saw the remains of the Terran—or at any rate, half of them—and realized that the red stuff was human circulatory fluid.

That probably accounted for the screaming, he decided.

"There's a dead Terran here," he said. "I think a giant beetle got it." He trotted around the vehicle and located Stacy's other half; the incision looked entirely consistent with those biting parts the beetle had displayed.

This particular Terran had been wearing considerably less clothing than most, but Bindar remembered that this place was supposed to be an insane asylum, and decided that this Terran must have chosen to dress aberrantly.

"What about the vehicle?" Hadrak asked.

Bindar looked up from the pieces of Terran and studied the vehicle. "I think that's what the Terran was doing here," Bindar said, looking over the smear of blood and the position of the body fragments. He tugged at the car's door handle, twisting and pushing it various ways, but the latch did not open. "It appears to be locked."

"Can you break it open anyway?"

"Sir, I don't know enough of how these vehicles operate, or what security devices they utilize," Bindar replied. "I could get in, of course, but I'm not sure I could do so without disrupting vital systems."

Back in the snack bar Hadrak shoved aside the box of candy bars he had been studying. As nearly as he could translate, the lists of ingredients invariably included additives with whose nature Hadrak was unfamiliar, any of which might prove toxic. That, combined with the Martians' sealed helmets, meant they would not be eating any Terran food during their stay here; they would have to make do with the field rations included in their suits and the water from their condenser purifiers.

It would be unpleasant to do without real food for four days—assuming the wait was actually going to be that long—but not particularly dangerous. Trying to eat alien food, though, or trying to operate a primitive hydrocarbon-fueled internal-combustion vehicle, might prove lethally reckless. They had all seen how easily, and how spectacularly, those machines could be made to explode.

"All right," Hadrak said. "Then destroy the vehicle. We don't want any of these Terrans to use it to flee this place."

"Your will," Bindar answered.

Dundat grumbled, "Why does he get to have the fun all by himself?" but fell silent when Hadrak glared at him.

Out in the little graveled lot Bindar looked around for any enemies, but saw none. He stepped back several paces, well away from the Terran vehicle, then selected the incendiary setting and fired, aiming low and toward the rear.

The Ford exploded satisfactorily. Bindar smiled as he watched it burn furiously.

Then the smile vanished.

He was well away from the house itself—he had gone around to the far side of the vehicle to investigate the dead Terran, and then backed farther away in getting distance to shoot. He therefore had a pretty good view of one entire side of the structure, and could see something that he was fairly certain had not been there before.

A window on the second level of the building had been demolished, scattering debris on the ground beneath, and a purple cord dangled from the opening.

"Sir," he said, "it appears that the Terrans may have escaped." He described what he saw.

"You don't think that was how the Terran you found dead got out there?" Hadrak asked.

Bindar relaxed. "Of course, sir, that must be it," he said. "I wasn't thinking. Certainly, it must have smashed its way out and gotten as far as the vehicle. Perhaps it was the breaking glass that attracted the beetle."

"Most likely," Hadrak agreed.

"Shall I return, then? The vehicle has been disposed of, and the wailing was undoubtedly this Terran's death-cry."

"It wouldn't hurt to take a look inside that broken window," Hadrak said. "Perhaps there were other Terrans assisting the dead one."

"Sir, I—"

"Can you climb that rope, Bindar?" Hadrak said, cutting off Bindar's protest.

Bindar hesitated, then admitted, "Yes, sir, I think so."

"Then do it."

Bindar sighed. "Your will," he said.

20

THE FACE IN
THE WINDOW

The two groups of humans met in the smoking room.

"Thanks for the help," Mark said, holding out a hand for Bud to shake. "I'm Mark Harshaw."

Bud took the hand and gave it a perfunctory shake; he didn't much like Mark's looks. The guy looked like a typical spoiled college kid, with his fancy haircut and Speedo swim trunks, not to mention a body that looked as if he'd spent a lot of hours in a gym.

"Bud Garcia," Bud said. "That's Marcie, and the kid is Sid Rubens."

"I'm Betsy," Betsy said, "and that's my daughter Katie."

"My name's Brenda."

"Jennifer," said the little brunette. "And . . . oh, my God, poor Stacy!"

Betsy looked questioningly at Bud.

"There were four of them in the car," he said. "One of them didn't make it."

"A giant beetle got her!" Sid said. "Crunch! Cut her right in half!"

"Shut up," Katie said, walloping Sid on the side of the head. "These were her friends!"

"*You* shut up!" Sid said, trying to hit her back but unable to reach her head.

Bud was about to intervene, to keep the dispute from turning into an all-out brawl, when they heard the explosion. For a moment everyone froze.

"Oh, crap, what was *that*?" Marcie said.

"Steve's car," Bud said. "Didn't it sound just like the others?"

"Louder," Betsy said.

"There's that broken window just around the corner," Bud pointed out.

"That would account for it," Betsy agreed.

"Uh . . . should we do something about it?" Jennifer asked, eyeing the doorway uneasily.

"What's to do?" Bud asked. "The car's scrap metal by now. Which is too bad; I was hoping some of us could use it to get back to civilization."

It took a moment for this to sink in; then Marcie exclaimed, "We're trapped here! That was the last car anywhere!"

Bud shook his head. "Not necessarily, it wasn't," he said. "Old man Gelman collected cars. Some of them might still run."

"Where are they?" Marcie demanded. "Why didn't you mention them sooner?"

"They're in the basement garage," Bud said. "And nobody asked. Anyone who took the tour saw 'em."

"Yeah," Sid said. "He had some weird old cars, all right!"

"Our Jeep's okay," Mark said. He felt a little ill at ease, standing surrounded by strangers amid Victorian gloom wearing nothing but a swimsuit, but he felt he had to speak up. "Or it was last I saw, anyway. But it's down on the beach with those bugs."

"Well, I wasn't figuring on going anywhere until about midnight, anyway," Bud said. "The bugs should all be asleep by then—and maybe the Martians, too."

Jennifer shuddered. "You saw Martians around here, too?"

"Sure," Bud said. "That's why I hauled you in the window, remember? There's a bunch of Martians downstairs, in the front."

"Then what the hell are we doing inside here in the first place?" Brenda demanded.

"There's giant bugs out there," Bud said. "*That's* what we're doing in here."

"Jesus, I think I'd rather face the bugs than the Martians," Jennifer said.

"You would?" Katie asked. "Why?"

Mark and Jennifer and Brenda exchanged glances.

"You tell 'em," Brenda said to Mark.

Mark shrugged. "Well, we camped out on the beach last night, ten of us from Toppwood Community College. And this morning, when we were getting ready to head back into town, we saw the Martians coming in—their saucers were blasting everything in sight. The whole town was burning. So we stayed holed up on the beach—but then a squad of them came after us there, too. Brenda and Stacy and I hid under some blankets, and they missed Jennifer . . ."

"I hid under some bodies," Jennifer said. "Including my boyfriend."

"Yeah," Mark agreed unhappily. "Anyway, after they left, we crawled out and looked around, and . . . well, it was bad. So we collected what we could salvage in my Jeep, and while we were arguing about where to go, those giant bugs came after us and we headed north . . . and here we are."

"And we saw that beetle kill my roommate Stacy," Jennifer said, "but that wasn't anything near as bad as what the Martians did back in Toppwood!"

"Hey, so how come a Japanese beetle killed her, anyway?" Katie demanded. "Don't they just eat leaves and flowers and stuff?"

"The kid's got a point," Brenda said, puzzled.

"You ever smell Stacy's perfume?" Jennifer asked.

Brenda stared at her. "Sure," she said. "She did slather it on kinda thick, but so what?"

"So I always teased her that it smelled like the stuff they put on Japanese beetle traps to lure the bugs in. She used to just laugh and say she hoped it worked as well on boys as those traps work on bugs." Jennifer sniffled and laughed nervously. "I guess it worked on bugs, anyway," she said.

"Whoa," Brenda said. "I want a bath!"

Bindar looked up at the broken window, then raised his weapon. Hadrak hadn't said anything about clearing the way, but he hadn't said not to, either, and Bindar wasn't going to ask. Sure, it might scare away any Terrans in the area, but that suited Bindar just fine.

He aimed carefully through the hole in the window and opened fire.

Marcie dropped to the floor at the sound; Betsy grabbed Katie and dove for the doorway to the next room. Sid looked around, startled but not scared.

Bud whirled, falling automatically into a crouch. Mark ducked, but stayed on his feet. Jennifer screamed and fell to her knees. Brenda threw herself against a wall.

"What the hell was *that*?" Marcie asked.

"Martian gunfire," Mark told her. "We've heard it before."

To Bud it had sounded more like a slow-running pneumatic jack-hammer than a gun, but he was willing to take Mark's word for it. "Where?" he asked.

"That way," Mark said, pointing toward the door to the music room.

Bud had known that much himself; now he crept toward the doorway, still crouched, and peered around the door frame.

The music room ceiling had been shot to pieces; plaster was strewn everywhere. And the velvet rope that he had carelessly left draped out the window was jerking about—someone, or something, was climbing up it.

"You wouldn't happen to have a gun in that gym bag, would you?" he asked Mark.

Mark shook his head. "A shirt, a towel, a pair of sneakers, and my wallet," he said. "I don't even have clean underwear."

"Then I suggest we get the hell out of here," Bud said.

"Shouldn't we try to unhook the rope or something?" Mark asked, peering around the door frame beside Bud.

Just then a metal-gloved hand reached up and grabbed the window frame beside the rope.

"Nice idea," Bud said. "A little too late, though." Then he turned and ran. "Martian coming!" he shouted as he dashed through the smoking room and the room where the polar bear and portrait faced each other. He continued on into another corridor.

Marcie and Jennifer picked themselves up and ran after him; Mark and Brenda looked at one another, hesitating.

"If we split up, it can't get us all," Brenda said.

Mark nodded, and the two of them started trying other doors until they found one that opened.

"Hey, what about me?" Sid asked, standing in the middle of the smoking room. For the first time he was genuinely scared. Up until now it had all seemed like a game, and there were always grown-ups around to protect him, but now . . . now he had seen that lady get chopped in half, and it was beginning to sink in that Bobby was gone and might not be coming back, and the grown-ups were all running away and they all seemed to have forgotten about him.

"Come on, kid," Mark said, holding the door open for a few more seconds to let Sid through.

Then he slammed it behind him, just as the thumping sound of a Martian weapon began again, louder than before.

Bindar had climbed into the music room, scanned it quickly and seen no Terrans—but he was taking no chances. He had raised his KA-77 and sprayed the room, just to be on the safe side.

Windows and mirrors shattered spectacularly; a chandelier fell, shreds of wallpaper flew, and clouds of plaster dust erupted. A bass viol disintegrated with a deep, deep crunch. In the resulting chaos Bindar missed the sound of running feet.

"Bindar!" Hadrak shouted over the communicator. "What's going on up there?"

"Thought I heard something," Bindar said—truthfully. He had indeed thought, as he climbed, that he heard voices somewhere ahead.

"Did you see anything?" Hadrak asked.

"No," Bindar admitted.

"Well, look around," Hadrak ordered.

Bindar sighed. "Your will," he said.

He didn't *want* to look around. He didn't want to wind up like poor Huzi, his helmet cracked by a Terran lunatic with a giant axe.

At least there weren't any giant insects in here.

Then he remembered the size of the hole in the window, and revised that. At least there couldn't be any *really* big insects in here.

He stepped forward a couple of paces and then paused. He leaned on what he took for a table.

The table made a loud, strange sound, and Bindar jumped away, weapon firing.

In a corridor not too far away, Marcie suppressed a laugh. "Sounds like the big, bad Martian just killed a piano," she whispered to Jennifer.

Jennifer smiled slightly, then asked, "Where are the others?"

Marcie looked around, realizing for the first time that there were only three of them in this party. "Hey, Bud!" she called.

Bud, who had been several feet ahead, stopped. "What?" he answered.

"Where is everybody?" Marcie asked.

"They scattered, I guess." He frowned. "That's bad, isn't it? Look, I'm going to the south gallery for weapons—can you take her back to the secret room?" He pointed at Jennifer. "And anyone else you find?"

"Sure, I guess," Marcie said. "Where is it?"

"Through there," Bud said, pointing off to the left. Then he turned right, breaking into a ponderous run.

"Through where?" Marcie asked—too late. Bud was gone.

"Secret room?" Jennifer asked.

"Yeah," Marcie said. "There are more of us holed up there." She looked around at paneled walls, dusty portraits, and a marble column supporting a bust of Caesar Augustus. She had no idea at all where she was, and had nothing to go on but Bud's directions.

"That way," she said, turning left.

21

THE POLAR BEAR STRIKES!

"I appear to have destroyed a musical instrument," Bindar admitted as he looked at the tangle of wires and broken wood that had been a piano.

In the snack bar, Hadrak sighed. Bindar hadn't given any details about what *sort* of musical instrument had startled him. "Could that instrument have been what made the sounds you heard earlier?" Hadrak asked.

Bindar snatched at the idea. "I believe it could, sir," he said.

"Then there are no indications of live Terrans in your vicinity?"

"None that I can see, sir."

"You might as well come back down here and rejoin us, then," Hadrak said.

Bindar was about to agree when he heard the now-familiar buzz of an approaching wasp outside. He glanced out the window and saw the insect bumbling about over the kitchen garden, working its way closer.

Bindar suddenly had no interest at all in climbing back down the purple rope, exposed to that lumbering monstrosity. "Sir, shall I attempt to find a route back there through the building?" he asked. "Perhaps I'll encounter a few Terrans along the way."

He hoped not, but Terrans were better than wasps. The lunatic with the long axe had gone down a lot more easily than the wasp that had killed Aif.

"Good," Hadrak said. "Do that."

"Your will," Bindar replied.

He looked around the ruined music room. He had done a lot of damage here, he realized—not that it mattered. He doubted anyone would care what had happened to a Terran asylum once the planet was conquered.

In getting here he had come out a door and then around to the side, and then up through the window. He needed to descend one level, and to move back to the northern side of the building, perhaps twenty or thirty feet in from the corner—that should put him back in the little refectory where the others were gathered.

Getting down a level would be the hard part. He could just blast a hole in the floor, he supposed, but shooting out anything he was standing on did not appeal to him. He was unsure just how good the structural integrity of this Terran architecture might be. He would take a look around first, he decided, and see if he could find a stairway or lift.

The north end of the room opened onto a sort of porch, open to the outside air—he looked out at the wasp and decided he didn't want to try that route, or for that matter any route that led past a lot of big windows. An inside route was definitely preferable.

He poked his head carefully through the nearest door and found a small antechamber. He could proceed in three different directions from here—north, south, or straight ahead.

South would take him farther from his goal; straight ahead might work, but he chose north, and turned the corner into a good-sized room—a dim chamber lit entirely by stained-glass transoms over several doors, and lined with cabinets.

One door at the far end stood open, and that was the direction he wanted to go in any case; he marched on through.

The next room was smaller, but had a much higher ceiling; an elaborately-framed opening in the base of the far wall, perhaps intended for ventilation, was surmounted by the largest pigment image Bindar had seen yet, this one depicting a formidable Terran in a peculiar garment that fit snugly above the waist, then flared out absurdly from that point down.

Bindar stepped into the center of the room, looking up at the painting with interest; then he turned to choose an exit.

A high-pitched cry rang out, so loud and intense that Bindar's helmet speakers buzzed with overload. Bindar whirled just in time to see an immense white shape lunging at him. He raised his weapon, but did not have time to fire before the huge white thing slammed into him, knocking him back onto the floor.

He landed hard, and lay there for a few seconds, dazed; he was vaguely aware of movement off to one side, but was unable to concentrate sufficiently to identify it.

Then he came back to himself and found himself lying on his back, staring up at the grinning, fanged, and glassy-eyed face of some great Terran beast. A black-tipped snout was pressed against his helmet; a white-furred body had him trapped beneath its weight.

Bindar froze, expecting to have his armor stripped off and his belly ripped open at any second.

The monster didn't strike, though; it lay there atop him, utterly motionless, staring blankly, hungrily, down at him.

Bindar remembered stories of the old days on Mars, when brave adventurers had fought against various now-extinct fauna. He remembered the tales of the flistigris, the hunting beast that would trap its prey and wait for it to die of fright, only striking a fatal blow when the prey tried to escape. He remembered the legendary venomous kinkoba that only struck at moving targets.

This great white animal, he thought, must be the Terran equivalent. It was waiting for him to move, and then it would kill him.

He held utterly still.

"Is he coming?" Betsy asked, not looking back.

Katie threw a glance over her shoulder. "I don't see him," she said. "Slow down!"

Reluctantly, Betsy slowed to a walk and risked a look back. There was no sign of the Martian.

"I told you hiding behind the polar bear was a stupid idea," she said.

"No, you didn't!" Katie protested, astonished.

"No, you're right, I didn't," Betsy said. "I'm sorry. Now I think I *should* have said it, but you're right, I didn't."

"Twenty-twenty hindsight, huh? But Mom, it turned out okay— we got away. Heck, maybe we even killed that damn Martian! I didn't see him get up."

"Ha!" Betsy laughed bitterly. "If they were *that* easy to kill, Toppwood would still be there!"

"Well, they'd have stayed in their saucers instead of landing ground troops," Katie agreed. She looked back the way they had come, dodging through a series of rooms she hadn't recognized. "Now what?" she said.

Betsy looked around. "Now we try to find our way back to the secret room," she said.

"Oh," Katie said. "How do we do that? We never saw where the entrance is on this floor. Do we go all the way back up to the fourth floor?"

Betsy shook her head. "I wouldn't know the right closet up there if I saw it. No, we stay on this floor and look for secret doors."

"But Mom, we won't *see* them! That's why they're called *secret* doors!"

Betsy shrugged. "Do you have a better idea?"

Katie considered that for a long moment, then said, "Okay, we look for secret doors."

22

BINDAR AND THE BEAST

"**B**indar!" Hadrak's voice barked at him. "Bindar, what's going on up there?"

That jarred Bindar out of the near-hypnotic state he had gotten himself into, staring up at the beast's glassy eyes.

Very glassy eyes, he realized. The monster hadn't moved at all since landing on him, hadn't twitched, hadn't drooled, hadn't blinked . . .

Cautiously, moving very slowly, Bindar closed his hand on the grip of his KA-77 and gradually lifted the weapon up from the floor.

The beast didn't move.

Bindar swung the muzzle of the KA-77 around until it pointed directly at the creature.

The beast still didn't move.

Bindar pulled the trigger.

The weapon flashed, and a shower of sawdust sprayed up into the air above Bindar and the beast.

"Oh, for honor . . ." Bindar muttered. He put down the weapon and pushed, lifting the heavy animal off.

The thing was massive; it took a minute or two before he could slide himself out from underneath, but at last he stood beside it, looking down at the long-dead polar bear.

Annoyed with himself for being so slow to catch on, he blasted the bear's head into scraps before reporting, "I thought I had encountered a hostile Terran beast, sir, but it appears to have been an old hunting trophy."

"A hunting trophy attacked you?" Hadrak asked. "The Terrans animate them somehow?"

"This one was shoved from its place, and landed on top of me," Bindar said.

"It would seem you're having problems with Terran furnishings, Bindar," Hadrak remarked sarcastically. "First a musical instrument, now a trophy . . . What's next? Are you going to be taken prisoner by a food storage unit?"

"Someone shoved it!" Bindar protested.

Then he realized what that meant, and what that fleeting movement had been that he glimpsed from beneath the dead animal. "Terrans!" he said. "There were Terrans hiding here, and they pushed it on top of me!"

"Did you kill them?" Hadrak asked.

"I barely even *saw* them!" Bindar exclaimed. "They moved so fast! They must have been hiding, and then they dropped this huge thing on me, and they were gone before I knew what had happened!"

"Go after them," Hadrak said. "I want any Terrans we can find to be exterminated, so we can sleep in peace."

"Your will," Bindar said. He turned, trying to remember where he had seen those movements.

They must have gone through one of three doors, he decided. He chose the center one of the three, and charged through it in belated pursuit.

"**S**o, kid," Mark asked as he peered around a door frame, "you live around here?"

"We live in Toppwood," Sid replied. "Me and my mom and dad and my brother Bobby. Except I think maybe . . . maybe the Martians got Bobby." He sniffled uncertainly.

Mark and Brenda exchanged looks—or tried to; the room was so dark they could barely see each other. "Are your folks back in Toppwood?" Brenda asked.

"Nope. We came here this morning and took the tour, and then when we finished, the guy in the snack bar told us about the Martians invading, and Steve hid us all in the secret room, except Bobby ran off and didn't come back, and I wanted to see the giant wasps, so we went upstairs and I saw your car on the beach."

"Secret room?" Mark asked.

"Your folks are here?" Brenda asked.

"Mom and Dad are in the secret room," Sid said. "Or anyway, they were when I left."

"Can you show us where that is?" Mark asked.

Sid looked around at the gloom. "I dunno," he said. "I don't know where we are."

"Neither do we," Mark admitted, looking around the dark, stuffy little room, furnished with leather chairs, where they happened to be at the moment. "If we got you to somewhere you recognize, could you lead us to the hidden room?"

"I dunno," Sid said. "Maybe."

"Well, let's just give it a try, shall we?" Mark muttered to himself. He peered around the door frame again.

The room on the other side was huge—the door actually emerged on a balcony, not at floor level, and Mark could see more balconies on the far side, both at this level and the next one up. The big room was only dimly lit by several stained-glass windows—but even that was more than the room they were in could boast.

Any room that big and spectacular must have been included in the tours, he thought. Sid would have to recognize it.

"Come on," he said, beckoning.

Bud hefted the halberd he had selected and gave it a few trial swings. It probably wouldn't cut through that armor the Martians wore, but it should knock them off their feet, he thought. That was something, anyway.

He glanced at the doorway at the far end of the south gallery and frowned.

He probably ought to get back and rejoin the others—they had scattered somewhat when they heard the Martian coming, and gathering them safely back to the secret room would be a good idea. Most of them didn't know their way around the mansion very well.

On the other hand, he'd been wondering for hours what had happened to Steve, and whether he was in one of the bedrooms off the dead-end corridor just beyond the gallery, and here was his chance to investigate.

It would only take a few minutes.

With the halberd clutched in both hands, he advanced down the gallery and into the corridor beyond.

The first bedroom on each side was empty and apparently undisturbed. The second on the right was also untouched.

In the second bedroom on the left, however, the lace hangings on the canopied bed were badly disarrayed. That might just mean that Steve had let the two boys play on the bed, but tour guides weren't supposed to do that, and Steve had seemed pretty conscientious. Bud frowned, and approached the third room on the left cautiously.

He saw the Martian first, neatly laid out on the Persian carpet. Dead, or just sleeping? Its helmet was cracked open, he saw, but he wasn't sure how significant that was—he didn't know whether the Martians needed their helmets to breathe, or wore them for defense.

Then he spotted Steve—or what was left of him.

That was one mystery solved, at any rate. Keeping the halberd ready, he crept into the room, inching up to the Martian.

It didn't move.

He prodded it with the butt of the halberd; it still didn't move. He looked at the thing's face.

The face was pale and tight, while the back of its bulging head looked soft and swollen—the blood must have settled, Bud decided.

Which meant, if it was anything like Earth creatures, that it was really dead.

He glanced over at Steve, lying there in a pool of blackened blood, ribs protruding where his chest used to be, a halberd on the floor at his side.

At least Steve took one of the bastards with him, Bud thought.

Then he looked at the Martian again. There wasn't a mark on the armor anywhere except for the notch cut into the helmet and the radiating web of cracks. Earth air must have killed it, Bud decided.

So Earth's atmosphere was lethal to Martians. That was useful to know.

He wondered whether there was anything else useful he could learn here. Finding a dead Martian like this was really an amazing piece of luck, he realized; the only other dead one he'd seen was the one outside—the one the wasp had been eating. That one he didn't want to approach, at least not when any more wasps might be around. This one, though, he could study safely.

He didn't see a weapon anywhere. That was too bad; if he and the other humans had Martian weapons, they wouldn't need to run and hide all the time, they could fight back.

There must have been a weapon here once—the one that had killed Steve. Its absence meant that this Martian hadn't been alone.

One dead here, one dead out front, one climbing in the music room window—the initial count of two Martians had clearly been wrong all along. The two he had seen approach the house must have just been the advance guard.

He wondered how many there were, then—not *too* many, or they'd have stormed through the whole place.

He wondered whether the Martian's armor might be useful. It wouldn't fit him if he got it loose, he knew that, but there might be some way to take advantage of it. He thought it might fit some of the other people in the house—Marcie, for one, or Katie.

He poked at it, at the connection between armor and helmet, looking for a way to open it. He ran a finger over the chestplate and up the front of the helmet, but found no openings or functioning controls. He grabbed the helmet with both hands and twisted, seeing if it unscrewed.

It didn't; as he strained at it, however, the cracks spread, and the entire top half of the helmet broke off in his hands, exposing the top half of the dead Martian's head.

He tossed aside the broken helmet and cautiously poked at the Martian's head.

It was disgustingly soft.

"Ecchh," Bud said, his face mere inches from the dead Martian's face.

In the snack bar, four Martians jerked upright.

"What was *that*?" Dundat demanded.

23

VOICES FROM BEYOND

"**B**indar!" Hadrak shouted, "was that sound from your vicinity?"

"No, sir," Bindar replied instantly. He had heard the Terran voice as well as the others, but assumed it was something going on downstairs; now he, too, was worried. He looked around, puzzled.

He thought he glimpsed movement up ahead, and had been in pursuit, but now he hesitated. "What should I do, sir?" he asked.

"If that didn't come from your communicator, then just carry on as you were," Hadrak said.

"Your will," Bindar replied. He crept forward, resuming his hunt.

In the snack bar the other four Martians looked at one another, baffled.

"It definitely came over our squad's communications circuit," Di said.

"And we're all here except Bindar," Kair said. Then he added, "except for Aif and Huzi, of course."

Sudden understanding dawned in Hadrak and Di, and an instant later in Dundat. Kair saw their faces, and realized he must have said something important; he thought back, and then he, too, understood.

"Which one is it?" he asked.

"I cut Aif out of the circuit so we wouldn't have to listen to the wasp feeding," Di replied.

"Then it's Huzi," Hadrak said. "One of these Terran madmen has found him."

Two of the others accepted this immediately, including the description of the Terran as a madman—the sound had not been anything any of them recognized as speech.

Kair, however, protested, "Can we be sure it wasn't just a beast of some sort?"

"Terrans *are* beasts," Di muttered.

"Whatever it was that made that sound," Dundat said, "I think we should kill it."

"Agreed," Hadrak said. "Come on, then—this way!" He gestured for the others to follow, and marched out of the snack bar.

The route back across the front of the house to the front hall, back to the courtyard and up the stairs, then through the long weapon-lined gallery, might not have been the shortest or best route, but it was the one Hadrak knew, so that was the route the four of them took, explaining their actions to Bindar as they went.

Bindar was not really listening; he was fairly sure he had finally cornered at least one Terran. He could hear it talking, somewhere in the big room just ahead.

"**I**t's got to be around here somewhere," Marcie said, rapping on one wall of the ballroom and trying to decide whether it sounded hollow. "I wish I knew what the door looks like from this side!"

"It doesn't look like a door?" Jennifer asked.

Marcie shook her head. "No, it'll be disguised somehow. The one I saw downstairs is a wall panel; the one on the fourth floor is the back of a closet."

"Like in the movies, huh?" Jennifer asked.

"Yeah," Marcie replied.

"So maybe, like, a swinging bookcase, or the back of a fireplace?"

"Could be," Marcie agreed. "I thought it was somewhere in here, though. Damn, I wish Bud had told us more!"

"Yeah," Jennifer said. "Hey, what about that area there?" She pointed at the musicians' alcove.

Bud crouched, frozen, and listened to the strange noises coming from the base of the dead Martian's helmet.

Those voices were not human.

He couldn't have said how he knew, but he knew, beyond any possible question—those voices were not human, and that meant they must be Martian.

They weren't speaking any language he had ever heard before, either, but he was fairly sure he was hearing words.

It sounded nasty. He didn't like it.

Then it sank in that he was hearing the dead Martian's comrades speaking over the helmet radio, and that they had started speaking only when he had made his noise of disgust.

The radio must have been left turned on all this time. They must have heard him. And if Martians were smart enough to build spaceships and invade Earth, then they were smart enough to figure out what it was they had heard.

Which meant they might well be on their way to investigate the mysterious noise *right now.*

Taking time to think could be fatal; he snatched up his halberd and ran. He dashed down the hallway so fast that the tapestries on the walls flapped; he stopped at the far end and peered into the south gallery.

No sign of them yet, but he wasn't going to risk going that way, not when the only other exit from the gallery was at the far end, sixty feet away—well, the only exit if you didn't count diving out those windows overlooking the south cliffs.

He tried the rotunda door and found it was still unlocked, as he'd left it after coming down from the fourth floor. That was good. He slipped through, closed the door behind him, and took time to fish out the key ring from his jeans, find the right key, and lock the door.

Then he looked up into the tower, up past the third and fourth floors.

He shook his head. Not that way; there were wasps up there, and no way out of the house. He turned his gaze downward.

The first floor was infested with Martians, but beyond it were the basement and subbasement. Somewhere down there he might even find the legendary José, who he had never seen. And at one end of the basement was the twelve-car garage where the prizes of Ebenezer Gelman's auto collection were kept—along with his widow's favorite Caddy, added after the old man's death.

He headed down the spiral, the halberd swinging out over the empty space in the center of the stairway.

"They should have been back by now," Nancy said from her place in one of the two armchairs.

"Yeah," Tony agreed as he trudged back down the stairs. He had just tried the door to the roof and found it locked. "And I thought I heard stuff earlier—banging and stuff."

"We all heard it," Bill said. "But it's quiet now."

"What's goin' *on* out there?" Tiffany asked. She had claimed the other armchair and curled up in it, catlike.

Tony shrugged. "I dunno, babe."

Susan sobbed loudly. She and Stan were sitting on the floor under the stairs, arms around each other. The sun was setting and the room was almost dark at first-floor level; Tony, his eyes not yet readjusted after his visit to the brighter upper levels, could barely see them.

"Think someone should go looking for them?" he asked.

"Jesus Christ, no!" Nancy snapped. "We're safer here, and splitting up is the *worst* thing we could do! For God's sake, don't you people ever watch horror movies?"

"No," Bill said.

"I have," Tiffany said. "You mean like, there's a bunch of people in an old dark house, and they're okay as long as they stay together, but whenever someone leaves the group, the monster gets him?"

"Right," Nancy said. "Steve went off on his own and he didn't come back, and Bobby went off and got killed . . ."

"And José," Tiffany said.

"Yeah, well, he was gone before I even *got* here," Nancy said.

"We did okay when the three of us went looking for Steve," Tony pointed out.

"And when five of us went to the snack bar," Nancy agreed. "Sure, groups are okay, but no one goes anywhere alone!"

"Bud and the kids weren't alone," Tiffany said.

"Yeah, and that's why I think they might still come back," Nancy said. "But nobody else leaves!"

For a moment after that pronouncement no one spoke; no one really wanted to argue, but there was still a vague feeling that someone ought to do something about the missing party.

Then Tony said, "Jeez, it's dark in here," and turned up the floor lamp—it had been on the lowest of its three settings, doing little more than glow dimly. Now it brightly illuminated the entire first floor of the secret room.

Stan and Susan looked up, startled.

"Won't that show through the peepholes?" Tiffany asked.

Tony turned, startled by the suggestion. "Yeah, I guess it might," he said. "So we'll close them." He crossed the room, leaned across the Rubenses, and pulled the little sliding panel closed.

"What if the light shows through cracks, or something?" Tiffany asked.

"Jeez, Tiff," Tony said, "I'm not about to sit here in the dark all night!"

"I think Mr. Gelman would have thought of that," Bill said.

"What if he didn't?" Susan said. "Where's Sid? Why isn't he back? He's all I have left!"

Stan threw her a glance at that.

"Did you hear something?" Nancy asked.

The others turned to stare at her.

"I didn't—"

"Shhh!"

Silence fell as the six of them listened intently.

"I do hear something," Bill said. "Up there." He pointed to the second floor.

"A sort of tapping," Nancy said. "And it sounds close."

"Probably the plumbing," Tony muttered.

"Let me look," Bill said, mounting the stairs.

"Don't open the door!" Nancy called after him.

"But what if it's the others coming back?" Tiffany asked.

"What if it's the Martians looking for us?" Nancy countered.

Bill hesitated, glancing down at the two women, then at the door to the ballroom.

"Someone's tapping on the wall," he said in a low voice, "but not in the right place—they're off to the side." He pointed to his left.

"Martians!" Nancy whispered loudly. "Bud *knows* where the door is!"

"He does?" Tony asked. "You sure? He wasn't on the tour with us."

"He used to work here," Nancy retorted.

"But that was years ago, wasn't it?" Tony replied. "Suppose he forgot? People do, y'know."

"And Bud may not be with them," Bill said. "Who else was there? That girl and her mother, and your friend—they weren't on the tour, and they never worked here. And Sid's just a kid; he might not remember where the door is, either."

"Bud's with them," Nancy insisted.

"But what if he's not?" Bill argued. "They might've split up, or Bud might've gotten caught and the rest made a break."

Nancy frowned.

"The tapping's coming closer," Bill said.

"And what if it *is* the Martians?" Nancy said.

Bill nodded. "It could be," he admitted. He drew his gun and flicked off the safety. Then he leaned over and put his ear to the door.

On the other side, Marcie and Jennifer were working their way systematically around the alcove.

"I thought I heard something," Marcie said. "Voices somewhere."

They stopped rapping to listen.

On the other side of the panel Bill relaxed slightly.

"I hear them," he said. "A woman's voice, speaking English. Might be your friend Marcie."

"It might be a Martian trick," Nancy muttered, but she didn't sound very convincing, even to herself.

Bill smiled and reached for the latch.

Marcie and Jennifer were about three feet from the secret panel, and Bill had not yet released the latch, when Bindar, who had entered the ballroom a moment earlier and was now scanning the various niches and alcoves, spotted the two women and opened fire.

The first shot neatly decapitated Marcie; Jennifer had time for a single shriek before the second caught her in the shoulder. The impact jarred her sufficiently to stop her screaming; she stumbled, gasping, trying to escape. The third shot went over her head and shattered paneling.

Bill had ducked instinctively the instant he heard the Martian weapon firing; he was well clear when the wood just to the left of the door burst inward about five feet above the landing.

With his fourth shot Bindar finally had the sense to aim low; the bolt caught Jennifer just below her ribs. She fell to the floor, twitching; blood poured onto the polished wood.

Bindar lowered his weapon and approached, intending to fire one more shot to put the Terran out of its misery—but then he stopped dead in his tracks.

His third shot had blown a hole in the wall—and warm yellow light was pouring from the opening. "All honor, sir," he said into his communicator, "I think I've found—"

Then the hole darkened again—not because the light had been turned off, but because a Terran's head and hand were blocking it. Bindar started to raise his KA-77.

A sharp report sounded, and Bindar sensed a projectile passing him at very high speed. The Terran had a weapon!

Bindar dodged to one side.

Bill cursed; his first shot had missed, and now the Martian was warned.

He wondered how many were out there. He'd only seen one, but the ballroom was dim, with several dark recesses, and he couldn't see much of it through that little hole. The light behind him hadn't helped much.

He needed some advantage—perhaps he could surprise the Martians somehow . . .

They still didn't know where the hidden door was, of course. That might be important. Maybe if he threw the door open suddenly . . .

He risked a quick peek through the blast hole.

The Martian was nowhere in sight.

Bill thought he heard a Martian weapon firing somewhere, though—somewhere not all that nearby, but still inside the house.

The one who had blasted the hole couldn't have gone that far. It had to still be somewhere very close at hand.

"Sir, I have eliminated two Terrans," Bindar reported as he stood safely behind a corner, out of sight of the hole in the wall. "However, I appear to have uncovered a place of concealment where at least one more, armed with a Terran projectile weapon, has been hiding. I request instructions."

"We're busy right now, Bindar," Hadrak replied. "Just blast the Terran any way you can."

"Your will," Bindar said unhappily. He stole a quick look around the corner.

The Terran was not visible in the hole; Bindar swung quickly around the corner into a firing stance.

24

BLOOD ON THE STEPS

"**W**ow, someone sure messed *this* place up!" Sid exclaimed as he peered down over the balcony railing.

"I guess so," Mark agreed. He was pleased that Sid recognized the room, altered as it was.

He hadn't seen the place when it was intact, of course, but the chaos below was obviously of very recent origin. Potted palms had been overturned, dirt scattered everywhere, paintings torn from the walls; most of the first floor, from the front door about two-thirds of the way back, had been stripped virtually bare.

And everything that had been collected had been piled in a great heap, blocking the front doors—pedestals and statuary, paintings, carpets, uprooted plants, emptied pots, chairs, tables, coat racks, even an elephant's-foot umbrella stand, had been stacked together apparently at random, forming a seven-foot-high, ten-foot-wide barricade across the front of the room.

What Mark didn't know was *why* anyone had done that. What was out there that justified such a defense?

The Martians?

"Did your people do that?" Mark asked.

Sid looked up at him, puzzled. "Who?" he asked.

"The people you're with," Mark explained. "The ones we're looking for."

"My parents? No, of course not!"

"Then who did?"

Sid shrugged. "The Martians, maybe?"

"Why would they do it?" Mark asked.

"To keep out the bugs," Brenda suggested.

"But they *made* the bugs!" Mark protested.

"A wasp killed a Martian," Sid said. "We saw it. Well, we saw the dead one, anyway, we didn't see it happen, like we saw that lady get chopped in half."

"Shut up, kid," Brenda said, grimacing at the reminder of Stacy's death. She turned to Mark. "See? To keep out the bugs."

"Okay, the Martians did it to keep out the bugs. Where are they, then?"

"I dunno," Sid said.

Mark sighed. "Okay, then, where do *we* go from here?"

"To the secret room, right?" Sid asked.

"Right," Brenda said. "So where is that?"

Sid frowned, looking around. "I don't know where it is on this floor," he said. "Upstairs on the third floor it's behind a bookcase, and downstairs there's a secret panel, and on the *fourth* floor it's in a closet."

Mark and Brenda looked at each other. "It's on more than one floor?" Brenda asked.

"Yeah, it has stairs in it," Sid replied. "It goes from downstairs all the way up through the roof."

"You buy that?" Brenda asked.

Mark shrugged. "Who knows?"

"Okay, so we can get in on either the first or third floors," Brenda said. "Which should we try?"

"I think we'd be more likely to run into Martians downstairs," Mark said. He asked Sid, "Could you find that bookcase on the third floor?"

"I dunno," Sid said.

"Could you *try*?" Brenda asked.

"Sure," Sid said.

Together, the three of them headed for the stairs at the back of the room and made their way up to the third-floor balcony. Then they began looking through doorways.

When they had worked their way all the way around and looked in all nine doorways, Mark asked, "So which one is it?"

"I dunno," Sid said. "I don't remember."

Mark stood, seething, for a long moment. Then he said, "Think you'd remember downstairs?"

"I dunno," Sid said.

"God *damn* it—" Mark began.

"Hey, calm down," Brenda said. "He's just a kid!"

Mark fumed for a moment more, then said, "Yeah, okay, he's just a kid. C'mon, kid, think—where's that secret room?"

"It's on that side," Sid said, pointing to one side of the room.

"Well, that's something, anyway," Mark said. "Think you could find it downstairs?"

"I can try," Sid said.

"Let's go, then," Mark said.

Sid ran for the stairs, while Mark and Brenda strolled along at a more leisurely pace.

"Hey, look at that," Brenda said with a giggle, pointing at one of the statues as they passed.

Mark looked. The statue was a bronze atop a wooden column. It depicted a satyr—an anatomically accurate, very aroused satyr. Mark could barely make it out in the fading light, though; the sun was setting and the stained-glass windows dimming steadily.

"Yeah, yeah," he said. "Come on, we don't want the kid to get *too* far ahead." He took Brenda by the hand and pulled her toward the stairs.

Sid was already halfway down the flight from the second floor to the first.

Hadrak was in the lead as the four Martians burst out of the reception room. They were on their way to kill the Terran who had dared to defile Huzi's remains, but Hadrak was also somewhat distracted by having just received a transmission from Bindar that had cut off in mid-sentence. "All honor, sir, I think I've found—" Bindar had begun.

Then he had simply stopped, and Hadrak wanted to know what had interrupted Bindar. He was not watching his surroundings as closely as usual.

Di had second position, and was so focused on finding his destination in the dimness that it was Kair, in third place, who spotted the boy on the stairs.

"Hey, look!" he said.

Dundat fired first, tearing a chunk out of Sid's side and spinning him around. Di's shot took him squarely in the head, and neither Hadrak nor Kair bothered to follow that up.

The bronze statue flung from the third floor balcony missed Hadrak by inches. He swung his weapon up but could not spot a target.

Just then Bindar's voice came over the communicator.

"Sir, I have eliminated two Terrans," he said. "However, I appear to have uncovered a place of concealment where at least one more, armed with a Terran projectile weapon, has been hiding. I request instructions."

"We're busy right now, Bindar," Hadrak replied as a second sculpture, plaster this time, shattered on the floor at his feet. "Just blast the Terran any way you can."

"Your will," Bindar replied. He didn't sound happy, but Hadrak didn't have time to think about that.

"You're not hitting them," Mark said, pulling Brenda away as she groped for something else to throw. "Even if you did, their armor would probably protect them."

"They blew that kid away!" Brenda protested.

"And they'll blow *us* away if we don't get out of here! Come on!" He pulled harder, and Brenda yielded reluctantly. Together, the two of them ducked out of sight into a darkened corridor.

25

SHOOTOUT!

Everyone in the secret room started when Bill's pistol fired; somehow the loud crack was far more startling than the deeper, less familiar thump of the Martian weapon. Stan and Susan ducked farther back under the stairs, out of sight; Tiffany uncurled abruptly and rolled out of her chair, heading for shelter on hands and knees.

Nancy, on the other hand, snapped to her feet and looked for a weapon. She snatched up the tea table, holding it by one leg.

Tony's reaction was even more extreme; he dashed halfway up the stairs and froze there, waiting for his chance to help.

Bill saw Tony and waved him back down, but Tony ignored that and stayed right where he was.

Bill reached for the latch, preparing to throw the door open and spray bullets out into the ballroom—he had ten rounds left, which he hoped would be enough.

Before he could act, though, the wall burst in.

Bindar had thought about it. If one antipersonnel charge could blow a ten-inch hole in the wall, what could a KA-77's demolition charge do? He had flipped the selector and opened fire.

A KA-77's demolition charge could, it appeared, reduce a couple of square yards of the wooden paneling to scorched kindling and splinters. He could see the Terran, crouched at one side of the newly

149

enlarged hole, its clothing torn, bleeding from a dozen small wounds.

He took careful aim and fired again.

Bill was cursing, dabbing at his shredded and bloodied jacket with one hand while the other aimed the pistol, when the door exploded inward and ripped him to bits.

The pistol dropped, and bounced, rattling, down the stairs, where Tony grabbed it.

Tiffany screamed.

Bindar smiled. He had seen the weapon fall. Even if the Terran was not quite dead, it was disarmed.

The high-pitched cry meant there was at least one more alive in there, but Bindar was fairly sure that had been a fear cry, rather than a battle cry. He had found an entire nest of the Terrans, no question about it, but it appeared he had the upper hand.

He approached the gaping hole in the wall cautiously. He could see the other walls of the chamber that his shooting had revealed, and a staircase going up—he saw no other Terrans, but whoever had screamed was presumably on the next level up, at the top of those stairs. There didn't seem to be enough left of the wall on this side to be hiding anyone on this level.

And the Terran who had shot at him looked indisputably dead—that red stuff they used for blood was all over, and a few pieces of flesh were strewn about.

He stepped up to the opening and leaned inside, looking up, KA-77 ready.

He never thought to look down, never thought that the stairs might run in both directions. He never even saw Tony until it was too late.

The first bullet punched a large hole in Bindar's helmet and grazed his cheek, and the second caught him as he turned, taking him through the eye.

His fingers twitched spasmodically as he died, though, and the KA-77 fired one last time before he crumpled across the sill of the demolished secret door. The blast caught Tony in the right shoulder and ripped through cloth, flesh, and bone.

"Tony!" Tiffany shrieked as Tony stumbled backward down the stairs, collapsing in a heap at the bottom. She stumbled to her feet and ran to his side.

Nancy snatched the pistol from Tony's lifeless hand and charged up the stairs, kicking the weapon out of the Martian's hands and staring out into the ballroom, looking for more enemies.

She saw none. The ballroom was still, dark, and silent.

She stepped through the blasted wall, scanning for more Martians, but saw and heard no sign of any.

Finally, she relaxed; the Martian must have been alone. She turned and headed back to the no-longer-secret room.

That was when she first consciously noticed the two bodies lying in the alcove.

She recognized the headless one by its clothing, even before she located Marcie's head.

"Oh, God *damn* it!" she said, her eyes suddenly stinging. Then she looked at the other one, the one with her side blown apart.

The other one was a stranger in a bikini.

"Who the hell is *that*?" Nancy asked no one in particular.

"Nancy!" someone called. "Help!"

Nancy dashed back through the wall, pistol ready, expecting to find Martians breaking in one of the other doors, but nothing looked any different—Bill's dead body lay on the second-floor landing with the dead Martian sprawled across it, Tony lay at the foot of the stairs with his head in Tiffany's lap, and Stan and Susan were cowering under the stairs.

"What?" she asked, looking around wildly.

"Down here!" Tiffany called. "Tony's bleeding to death! Do you know any first aid?"

Nancy stared, then started down the stairs, cursing. She had assumed Tony was already dead!

She looked quickly at Tony's shoulder, and found that Tiffany had torn off part of her already short skirt and improvised a bandage—but the damage was too extensive; the Martian's blast hadn't just punched a neat little hole through Tony's shoulder, but had torn away pieces of it. Splinters of bone protruded here and there, and bloody shreds of flesh were tangled in the ruins of his expensive suit coat.

Tony coughed. " 'S too late," he said. "Punctured a lung, I'm pretty sure." Blood trickled from his mouth as he spoke.

"Oh, Tony!" Tiffany wailed.

"Hey, Tiff, gotta tell you somethin'," Tony said.

"What is it, Tony?" Tiffany asked, leaning over him. Nancy stepped back, embarrassed, expecting Tony to tell Tiffany that he loved her.

"I'm not really a gangster," Tony said.

"What?" Tiffany and Nancy stared down at him.

"I'm an accountant for an insurance company," Tony said. "Mos' boring thing inna world. But I got the looks and an Italian name, so I dress like I do an' talk ... gets me girls like you wouldn' b'lieve. Got me *you*, Tiff—how else'd an accountant ever get a girl like you?"

Tiffany and Nancy were too astonished to speak.

"Was worth it," Tony said.

Then he died.

26

IN THE DEPTHS

Bud flipped the switch, and light flooded the corridor.

It wasn't much of an improvement; the walls were bare stone. At least he could see there weren't any Martians lurking here.

He had never actually been in this particular part of the mansion before; while he had been allowed to explore a little during his stint as a guide, he hadn't gotten into every nook and cranny of the place. He hadn't bothered with much of the two levels of basement.

The garage exit opened onto a ramp at the very edge of the seaside cliff, a ramp that led up to the parking lot; Bud knew it was at that corner of the house. And he knew how to get to it along the tour route, which came down through the kitchen, past the storerooms, through a lounge and the garage, and then back to the lounge and up to the great hall. That hall occupied much of the seaward end of the first and second floors, and had a fabulous ocean view through a dozen Gothic-arched windows.

He had assumed it would be easy to find his way through the cellars. He now saw he'd been wrong. The doorway from the rotunda had opened into a corridor that headed off at a right angle to the direction he wanted.

At least the lights worked; the power was still on. Bud hesitated to think about that, for fear the electricity *would* be cut off, stranding them all in the dark. On the other hand, wasn't it a good sign that it had lasted this long? Logically, the power should have gone out almost as soon as the Martians attacked, shouldn't it? Wasn't it standard practice to target power plants?

Well, nobody knew what was standard practice for Martians, of course. Still, the fact that the electricity was still flowing presumably meant that human civilization had not yet been completely destroyed.

That was cheering news; if he could just get out of Gelman Mansion and get past the bugs, he might be able to find someplace relatively safe, where Earthmen were still in charge.

If the power *did* go out now, that would be really depressing, not to mention that it would strand him in the dark without a flashlight, or even a candle.

He should have grabbed a candle somewhere, he realized. There were hundreds of them in various places around the mansion, in wall sconces and candelabra. And there were flashlights in the guides' lounge, in case of power failures—but that corner of the house had been full of Martians last he saw.

For now, the lights worked, and he hoped they would continue to work.

He carried the halberd in one hand, holding it easily with the head ahead of him and about two-thirds of the shaft behind him. It wasn't ready to use like this, but it was easy to carry and didn't bump into anything. There wasn't room to swing it in the corridor, anyway.

There were no doors along this particular corridor, which was surprising. Most of the mansion had doors all over the place, leading to rooms, passageways, staircases, closets . . . Here, though, the only doors were at either end of the fifty-foot stone passage.

And as he discovered when he reached it, the one at the other end was locked, just as the one from the rotunda had been. Annoyed, he tried key after key until at last one clicked and the lock opened.

Bud turned the knob, started to push the door open, then froze.

He heard a voice.

He listened intently. He couldn't make out the words, and he didn't recognize the voice as anyone he knew, but something about it sounded familiar, and after a moment he placed it.

It was an announcer's voice. Someone on the other side of the door had a radio or TV turned on.

Bud thought that probably meant a human, rather than a Martian, was on the other side of the door—José, perhaps. He pushed the door open slowly and peered in.

He had never seen the room before, but he recognized it immediately from the descriptions. He'd just found the indoor swimming pool.

Like the rotunda, this had been closed off, deemed unsafe for tourists—the pool was drained back in '43 and never used again; it was doubtful it would even hold water anymore. Old lady Gelman hadn't wanted to worry about tourist kids falling in. Furthermore, the tile walls had decayed to the point that tiles would occasionally fall off and shatter on the floor, and she hadn't wanted any to fall on customers' heads.

And there was also the fact that the mosaic on the north wall, depicting sea nymphs and mermaids cavorting in the nude, might not go over well with the more staid visitors.

The pool was actually in the subbasement, but Bud had found his way onto the balcony across the south end of the two-story natatorium. Now he stepped out on the balcony and surveyed the situation.

There was the infamous mosaic mural—pretty tame, really, Bud thought—and the dry pool, and the broken tiles—some, he noticed, from the ceiling as well as the walls.

And there was somebody who had to be José, sitting in the bottom of the pool, surrounded by stacked boxes, blankets, and gardening equipment. He was curled up on a blanket, listening to a boom box.

Bud couldn't see the details very clearly, since José had no lights on—assuming there were electric lights in here at all, which Bud wasn't sure of. Fading daylight was pouring in from a row of small windows high in the south wall, above Bud's head.

"José!" Bud called. "Is that you?"

The young man in the pool jerked his head around, abruptly turning his attention from the boom box to staring up into the shadows.

"Who is it?" he shouted back.

"My name's Bud Garcia," Bud replied. "I got here after you came downstairs."

"What do you want here, man?"

"Nothin'," Bud said. "I just came down to get away from the Martians."

José got to his feet. "There are Martians upstairs?"

"Yeah," Bud said.

"They comin' down here?" José's voice cracked.

"Not that I know of."

José relaxed slightly.

"Maybe we should, you know, compare notes," Bud suggested. "Maybe work out some way to get away."

"I'm not goin' anywhere," José said. "I been listenin' to the radio, man. It's *bad* out there. They sayin' the Martians been wipin' out whole cities—Boston, and Washington . . ."

"Hey, it's not that great here, either," Bud retorted. "I mean, I gotta tell you, Steve's dead upstairs, and one of the tourist kids, maybe more by now."

"Oh, Jesus," José said. "Stop shouting, then. You come down from there so we can talk. And close that door."

Bud hesitated, then crossed to the stairs at the far end of the balcony and started down.

27

MARCHING TO BATTLE

"**S**hould we pursue them, sir?" Di asked, peering up at the now empty third-floor balcony.

"What about the one who found Huzi's remains?" Kair asked.

"Maybe we should split up," Dundat suggested.

"No," Hadrak said. "We don't split up when we know there are hostiles who might be setting up an ambush." He frowned. "How many of the confounded creatures *are* there, anyway? Bindar said he'd found some. Bindar! Report!"

The four of them waited expectantly. Then Di and Dundat exchanged worried glances.

"He said one of them was armed," Dundat said.

"I know," Hadrak said. He looked at the tiny corpse on the stairs. "One there, and one out front, and the one with the axe, and Bindar said he'd eliminated two—we've killed at least five of them, and the insects got a sixth. Then we saw one or two up there, and Bindar saw at least one more, and there's the one we heard . . ."

"A minimum of nine in all, sir," Di said. "There could well be more. It's a large structure."

"*Too* large," Hadrak said. "Even when there were seven of us, it was far too large to search. Now it's completely impossible. We need to know how many Terrans there are, and *where* they are, if

157

we're to deal with them properly and remain here safely until pickup."

"Perhaps we shouldn't stay," Kair said. "Maybe we should head north . . ."

"And how would we get past those insects?" Hadrak demanded. "We *have* to stay!"

"Perhaps if we had a vehicle, we might outrace the insects," Kair suggested.

"Or we could armor the vehicle," Di added.

"And where would we get a vehicle? In case you've forgotten, we destroyed them all!" Hadrak replied angrily.

"We might have missed one," Kair said. "The Terrans certainly seem to have a lot of them, and if there were nine Terrans here and we only destroyed five vehicles . . ."

"And if we did find one, how could we use it?" Hadrak asked. "Remember when Bindar looked at the one?"

Kair thought for a moment, then said, "Perhaps if we capture a Terran, the Terran could teach us to operate a vehicle before we kill it."

"It's a possibility," Hadrak admitted grudgingly. "But how are we going to capture one? The creatures fight whenever we see them, and we're forced to kill them."

"We caught one before," Di protested.

"True," Hadrak admitted. "All right, then, let's see if we can capture one alive, for questioning."

"Your will. Which way?"

Hadrak looked up at the balconies, then ahead at the door to the courtyard, then over toward where Bindar had last been heard from. The Terran who had discovered Huzi's body had had plenty of time to escape by now; the ones on the third level were alerted; and Bindar might still be alive, but unable to communicate. They could track him through his armor's built-in homing device.

"The second level," he said. "That way. Di, get the scanner running. Let's find Bindar—and that hiding place he uncovered."

Tiffany picked up the Martian weapon and hefted it.

It was heavy, but not as heavy as it looked. It was alien, but the general shape was enough like an ordinary gun that she had no doubts about how to hold it or which way to point it. And the firing stud was enough like a trigger that she was fairly certain what it did.

"You bastards killed Tony," she told the dead Martian. "You're going to pay for that!" She pressed the firing stud.

The blast blew the Martian's head to atoms and gouged a good-sized hole through the floor beneath.

"Whoa, Tiffany," Nancy said. "Careful with that thing!"

"What are you girls doing up there?" Stan demanded from the floor below.

Nancy brandished the 9mm automatic; Tiffany hoisted the Martian death-ray. They looked at each other and smiled in feral understanding.

"We're gonna go kick some Martian butt," Nancy said. "Want to come along?"

Stan looked at the two of them—the busty blonde in the heavy makeup and torn-off miniskirt, the overweight brunette in the tight Levi's and black leather jacket, both holding loaded weapons. He looked at the dead bodies—the man and the Martian up on the landing, the supposed gangster at the foot of the stairs. He shook his head.

"No, thanks," he said weakly.

"Suit yourself," Nancy said with a shrug. Then she stepped through the hole, into the ballroom, and was gone.

Tiffany followed close behind.

"What's going on?" Susan called from beneath the stairs. "What was that noise, and the flash? What happened?" She pointed at the hole Tiffany had blown in the landing. "What's been going *on*?"

"That's a little hard to explain, dear," Stan said.

"Is it safe to come out?"

"I . . . I *think* so."

Susan got to her feet and marched out. She stopped dead when she saw Tony.

"Is he dead?" she asked, clapping a hand to her mouth.

"I think so, dear," Stan replied. "So are they." He pointed up the stairs.

"Oh, my *goodness*!" Susan exclaimed when she saw the mess on the second floor. Then she looked around.

"Where is everyone?" she asked.

"Well, that's Mr. Edwards," Stan said, "and those two young women just left."

"So we're alone here?"

"I'm afraid so."

"Well, that's . . . that's *unacceptable*, Stanley! It's not safe here!"

"It's not safe *anywhere*, Susan."

"Well, it can't be any worse than here! Those monsters killed our *son*, Stanley, and now they've killed that nice Mr. Edwards and that awful Tony . . . We have to get out of this place."

"How? And what about Sid and the others?"

"What do you mean, 'how'? We just *go*."

"The Martians blew up our car, dear."

"Well, then we'll *walk*. It can't be *that* far to somewhere we can get help."

"It's fifteen miles to Toppwood."

Susan hesitated at that. "Fifteen?"

"About that."

Susan let out a huge sigh. "Well, needs must, and all that, Stanley—we'll just have to walk that fifteen miles."

"What about the giant wasps?"

She gestured at the skylight. "It's getting *dark* out, Stan," she said. "Wasps don't come out at night. But we'll want to reach Toppwood before morning, so the sooner we get started, the better. Open the door and let's go."

Stan moved reluctantly toward one of the first-floor doors. "I don't know, hon," he said. "They said that there were those Martians right by the door we came in by. And what about Sid?"

"Sid should have been back long ago," Susan said.

"Yes, he should," Stan agreed.

"Well, we can't very well hope to find him in a place this size, can we? And we can't wait around forever. Either he's with someone else and he'll be okay until we can get back here with the police or the National Guard or somebody, or, let's face it, Stan, he might already be dead, same as Bobby."

"You think so?" Stan said.

"Well, I *hope* not, but we have to be realistic!" She waved at the corpses. "I mean, just look!"

"Shouldn't we . . . I don't know . . ."

"We should save *ourselves*, Stan, and then once we're safely out of this deathtrap, we can get help and come back for the boys."

"All right," Stan said, "but I'm still concerned about those Martians. They might be guarding the doors . . ."

"So we'll go out a window," Susan said. "You're right, the doors are probably being watched. Open the panel!"

Stan nodded, and worked the latch.

It took him a few tries; he hadn't worked it before, and hadn't been watching closely when Steve demonstrated it. Eventually, however, he got it open, and the two of them stepped out into the deserted corridor beyond.

"It's dark," Stan whispered.

"Of course it is," Susan muttered back. "And a good thing, too—it'll make it that much harder for those Martians to spot us."

Stan didn't argue with that. "Which way?" he asked.

Susan peered into the gloom, then pointed. "That way," she said. "Toward the kitchen. There were those big windows over the sinks, and we can climb out those and then cut across the garden into the woods."

Stan could hardly make out the pointing finger, but he followed as Susan marched on.

28

IN THE NIGHT KITCHEN

"**W**ell, he gave a good account of himself, at any rate," Dundat said, glancing around at the four dead Terrans.

"Where's his weapon?" Kair asked as he stared at what was left of Bindar.

"It's gone," Di said. "The Terrans must have taken it."

"There were more?" Dundat asked, looking up. The four of them had not encountered any living Terrans on their way to this "nest" Bindar had discovered; they had come in almost a straight line from the front hall, and until reaching the ballroom with its blown-out wall, they had seen nothing along the way but dim, unoccupied rooms full of bizarre Terran artifacts.

"Obviously," Hadrak said. He had been studying this peculiar tall, narrow room, with its stairs, its skylight, its mismatched and abnormal doors, and the glowing floor lamp, but now he turned to Dundat and waved at the scattered corpses. "Who killed Bindar, if these four were all there were?"

"That one," Kair said, pointing at Tony. "His wounds were fatal, but not immediately so. He could easily have shot Bindar before he succumbed."

"Then where are the weapons?" Di said, echoing Kair's question.

"And who shot Bindar with his own gun?" Kair said. "The blast that took his head off was from a demolition charge fired at least a minute or two after his death; the coagulation of the tissues is clearly postmortem. That dead Terran could have killed Bindar, but I doubt it could have fired that final shot, and if it had, the weapon would still be here. So there were more Terrans. And now they're armed."

"They were *already* armed," Hadrak said. "Bindar said as much before he died."

"Well, now they have one of *our* weapons," Di said. "I think a KA-77 must be more formidable than anything they had before."

"They must have left through *that* opening," Dundat said, pointing at the panel standing ajar on the lower level. Stan and Susan had not bothered to close it behind them.

"Should we pursue, sir?" Di asked.

"Yes," Hadrak said. "Come on." He led the way down the stairs.

Tiffany flicked the switch, and the chandeliers blazed into life, flooding the big front hall with light.

They had not arrived there by a direct route; Nancy had never seen this part of the mansion at all, and Tiffany had only been through once, with the tour that morning. Tiffany had retraced the tour's route, as best she could remember it, from the ballroom to the front hall—though the tour ran in the opposite direction. This involved heading south to the courtyard, down a set of stairs there, and back north into the house on the first floor.

They therefore missed the Martians heading in the other direction.

The two women blinked, standing in the doorway with weapons pointed into the room, ready to fire—but there was nothing to shoot at. There were no Martians; in fact, most of the room had been stripped bare of its clutter of statuary and furniture, so there wasn't much of anything.

"Where *are* they?" Tiffany demanded.

"I don't know," Nancy replied, peering around the door frame at the stairs and the balconies above. "Hey, what—" She stepped into the room, scanning carefully for Martians, and not finding any as she moved far enough forward to see what lay on the stairs.

Poor little Sid's body was sufficiently damaged that it took a moment to recognize him, but who else could it be?

"Murdering bastards!" Tiffany said.

They had found the hall deserted, but there was plenty of evidence that the Martians *had* been here, in the form of the barricade, the smashed statuary, and the pitiful little corpse scattered on the stairway.

"Poor little kid," Nancy said.

"Where'd they go?" Tiffany demanded. "They were here, they killed him—then where'd they go?"

"They followed us to the snack bar before," Nancy said. "Maybe some of them are still there. How do we get there from here?"

"Oh, Jeez," Tiffany said, slumping. "I don't . . . I mean, those were practically at opposite ends of the tour." Then she brightened. "But hey, couldn't we just go out the front door, and then back in at the regular entrance? Then the snack bar's right there!"

Nancy eyed the barricade. "I don't think I want to climb that," she said. "Maybe if we just stay inside, but follow the front of the house?"

"That should work," Tiffany agreed. "Come on!"

With Tiffany in the lead, they charged toward the door to the reception room.

Stan knelt on the tiled kitchen counter and pried at the window latch, but could not budge it.

"It's stuck," he said. "Maybe we should just smash the window."

"No," Susan said, looking around nervously. Some of her earlier assurance had faded. "The Martians might hear if we did that. Maybe we could find a screwdriver or something, to pry it with?"

Stan looked around the unlit kitchen. "Find one how?" he asked. "I can't see a thing in here. Maybe if we put on the lights—"

"There might be Martians outside who would see," Susan protested. "All those windows . . ."

Stan glanced along the row of windows that provided what little light there was. "Well, that's why we're *here*," he said.

"Look in the drawers," Susan suggested, following her own advice and yanking open the nearest drawer.

It was completely empty—not so much as a scrap of shelf paper remained. She tried another, and another, as Stan climbed down from the counter and joined her.

"Nothing," Susan said. "They've all been stripped bare!"

"Well, *that* wasn't the Martians," Stan said. "That must have been the Gelmans, when they cleaned out the place and got it ready for tourists. They probably didn't want to worry about kids getting into stuff."

"Maybe they missed something somewhere, though," Susan said. "Maybe in the cabinets, or the pantries."

"Maybe," Stan said, squinting into the gloom.

"Let's check." Susan headed for one of the several doors.

Stan sighed and followed her.

The first door Susan tried was an utterly bare pantry; the second was a walk-in refrigerator that clearly hadn't functioned in years. Stan found the cellar stairs and a dumbwaiter. All had been stripped clean.

Susan turned to ask whether Stan had found anything, and spotted the rack of cast-iron skillets hanging over the ancient gas stove.

"What about those?" she asked, pointing.

"What about what?" Stan asked, unable to see her hand.

Susan said, "Those frying pans over the stove!"

Stan turned and nearly hit his head on one of the half-dozen skillets. He lifted it down and hefted it.

"Well, if all else fails, this'd be great to break the glass with," he said.

"Could you use the handle to force the latch?"

"Maybe," Stan said, holding the pan in one hand and feeling the end of the handle with the other. "I can try." He headed for the counter.

Susan stood behind him, watching anxiously, though she couldn't see much as he pried at the latch.

"*Heavy* sucker," he muttered as he tried to maneuver the skillet.

He was about to give up when, almost miraculously, the hole in the end of the handle, intended to fit over a hook, snapped onto the little lever that worked the latch.

"*Now* we're getting somewhere!" he said. Using the pan as if it were a crowbar, he heaved.

The latch snapped open.

"There!" he said with satisfaction. "Hold this." He handed the skillet down to Susan.

She took the pan and stood holding it, watching, as Stan heaved at the window.

It still didn't budge, but they could both hear a crackling, and Stan saw paint chipping along the crack between the upper and lower sash.

"It's coming," he said. "It's—"

That was when a light came on somewhere behind them, spilling its golden glow through the open door and the row of windows high on the kitchen's inside wall.

Stan and Susan froze.

Then the light blinked out again.

"What—" Susan began.

Then the light came back on.

"Who would do that?" Susan asked.

"The Martians!" Stan gasped. "Hide!"

"Can't you get the window—"

"Not in time! Hide!" He scrambled off the counter and dove for an open door.

Susan dashed for a nearby door as well, then stopped when she realized she'd been about to hide in the walk-in refrigerator. She had heard too many stories about children getting trapped in abandoned refrigerators to use *that* as a hiding place.

She was still standing beside the open door, hesitating, trying to think of someplace better, the cast-iron skillet in her hand, when Tenzif Kair stepped into the room.

29

THE SHOWGIRL'S REVENGE

As Hadrak rounded the corner of the passage, he put a hand on the wall and felt a small protrusion. Puzzled, he paused and slid his metal-gloved hand over it.

The protrusion shifted. Lights came on at three separate points along the hallway ceiling, illuminating the plain white walls and the gouges where Bindar had fired more or less at random a few hours before. "Ah," Hadrak said, looking at the switch he had bumped. "I see." He flipped it off, and then on again. "Simple incandescent devices," he said, looking up at the ceiling fixtures. "Very good."

"Sir, won't that alert the Terrans to our presence?" Di asked.

"Yes," Hadrak said. "I triggered it unintentionally at first."

"Should you turn it off, perhaps?"

"No," Hadrak said. "The damage is done, and I prefer not to waste necessary battery energy on our night-vision domes." He looked up and down the hallway, and recognized the door to the snack bar. Then he looked back the way they had come, at the concealed panel that had led them out of the "nest."

"*That's* how they escaped us before," he said. "I see." He considered the several directions fleeing Terrans could have taken from the spot where the squad now stood, looked at the wide crack under the door at one end of the passage, the glass panels set high in one wall, and the two side passages; light would have gone into all those places, alerting the Terrans. They would almost certainly have then fled—but it wouldn't hurt to be certain.

"Di, check in the 'snack bar,' " he ordered. "Dundat, look in that corridor. Kair, check in that chamber. I'll try down this way. Just take a quick look, then come right back—and be careful; remember, one of the Terrans has a gun."

"Your will," the others responded, almost in unison. Then the four of them scattered.

And Tenzif Kair stepped into the kitchen.

Susan knew it wasn't a good enough hiding place, but she had no time; she ducked behind the open refrigerator door—not into the refrigerator, but on the other side—as the Martian approached.

This was the first time she'd seen a live Martian up close, but she wasn't interested in its appearance; she crouched back, trying to stay out of sight.

She couldn't resist peeking around the edge of the door at it, though.

It swung its oversized head back and forth inside that big clear helmet, scanning the kitchen—and it swung the barrel of its big fancy gun back and forth, as well. It peered into a pantry, then into the empty refrigerator.

Then it grasped the edge of the refrigerator door and started to pull it. In a second it would be looking right at her.

Susan panicked; she shrieked, and swung the cast-iron pan in a great swooping arc, smashing it down onto the Martian's transparent helmet. Iron rang, and something cracked. The Martian staggered back, caught off guard.

Susan came charging out of her hiding place like a whirlwind, pushing the Martian back, keeping it off balance, shoving it first one way and then another, finally giving it one big shove that sent it tumbling into the refrigerator, its armored arms and legs flailing wildly as it fell flat on its back.

It landed with a metallic clang. Then Susan slammed shut the refrigerator door and threw a terrified glance at the door where the

Martian had entered. She could hear alien voices and the tread of armored feet—the thing had companions who had heard the commotion and were coming to investigate!

She threw herself across the kitchen, bounded up onto the counter, and swung the frying pan like a baseball bat, shattering the window; no need for secrecy now!

She smashed the pan from side to side, knocking out more shards of glass, then dove through the hole, enlarging it further. She landed on the graveled walk outside and then picked herself up and ran, vanishing into the darkness beyond.

Hadrak heard the scream and spun about. Another Terran distress cry! One of the others had found something!

He charged back into the passageway, KA-77 at the ready. "Di! Dundat! Kair! Report!"

"I haven't found anything, sir," Dundat replied.

"Nothing here," Di said. "Regroup?"

"Get back here, all of you!" Hadrak shouted.

A moment later Di emerged from the snack bar, and Dundat ran up the corridor to the dining hall. The three Martians almost collided in the passageway—but Kair was nowhere to be seen.

Then they heard the sound of shattering glass.

"In there!" Hadrak shouted.

The three of them charged into the kitchen, weapons raised.

Kair didn't know what had hit him; he had been making a cursory inspection of the room, looking behind an open door, when suddenly something had slammed down on his helmet with incredible force—he felt the impact on his shoulders and heard the helmet crack. His night-vision dome had failed instantly, leaving him half blind and off balance, and then a berserk Terran had repeatedly rammed into him, forcing him back into this little metal-walled room lined with empty wire shelving, knocking him off his feet.

He sat up, groping in total darkness. He had heard his helmet crack! Hadrak was shouting over the communicator, the signal barely penetrating the metal walls, but Kair ignored that; he had more urgent concerns. If he didn't patch the cracks immediately, Earth's toxic atmosphere would kill him. He thought he could smell the acrid stench of it already.

He found his medical kit, and working entirely by touch, extracted a wound-sealant applicator. He felt for the cracks in his helmet, being as careful as possible under the circumstances not to apply any pressure that might worsen the damage.

He located a spot where the helmet's surface wasn't smooth, and began spraying the wound sealant, wishing he could see what he was doing.

When he was reasonably sure he had done all he could, and the supply of sealant began to run low, he put down the applicator—and realized that he had dropped his weapon somewhere.

He groaned. Now there were *two* Terrans in possession of KA-77s!

Hadrak scanned the room quickly, then stopped dead in his tracks, baffled.

Tenzif Kair was nowhere in sight. Neither were any Terrans. A window had been smashed out, but that didn't account for Kair's absence.

"Look!" Di shouted.

Hadrak looked, and saw Kair's weapon lying on the tile floor beside a closed door. He frowned.

If the Terrans had caught Kair off guard and killed or disarmed him, surely they would have taken the weapon! He looked at the shattered window. Had one of the giant insects broken in and snatched Kair, perhaps?

But they had heard a Terran's distress cry *before* they heard the window shatter.

"Pick that thing up," Hadrak ordered, and Dundat hurried to recover the KA-77.

Just then Hadrak heard a faint groan over his communicator.

"Kair?" he asked. "Where are you?"

"I'm locked in a small dark room," Kair replied. "Just off the large room you sent me to check."

"The door," Di said, pointing.

"Open it," Hadrak ordered.

Dundat obeyed, and the three of them discovered Kair sitting on the floor of the refrigerator, the front of his helmet entirely covered with something white and opaque.

Just then they heard a faint, distant scream from somewhere beyond the broken window, a scream that was abruptly cut short. The three standing Martians exchanged glances.

"The enlarged arthropods," Dundat said.

The others nodded.

"They aren't here," Tiffany said as she pushed open the door of the dark, deserted snack bar.

"Shhh!" Nancy ordered.

Tiffany turned to look at her, startled. "Why?" she asked. "What is it?"

"Look at the other door!" Nancy said, pointing at the crack beneath it.

Tiffany looked, and saw the light, both literally and figuratively. She and Nancy exchanged glances.

"Maybe we can catch 'em by surprise," Tiffany said.

"If it's really the Martians," Nancy said. "It might be Bud, or the Rubenses, or someone."

"Or it might be the Martians," Tiffany said stubbornly. "Why would anyone else have come back here?"

"*I* don't know. I'm just saying don't shoot until you're sure."

"Okay, okay!" Tiffany hesitated. "You ready?"

Nancy checked her pistol—six rounds left in the magazine. That ought to do, she thought.

"Yeah," she said. "Let's go!"

Side by side, guns ready, they burst through the door into the brightly-lit passageway—and found it empty.

"Damn!" Tiffany said under her breath.

Just then they heard a faint, distant scream that was abruptly cut short.

"Shh!" Nancy said, indicating the open door to the kitchen—the scream had come from that direction.

Tiffany nodded.

Silently, the two of them crept up to the kitchen door.

"**W**hat *is* that stuff?" Dundat asked as Di scraped delicately at the white gunk covering Kair's helmet.

"Wound sealant," Kair explained. "My helmet was cracked, and it was dark—I did the best I could."

"You did fine," Di said. "We just need to clean off enough for you to be able to see."

Hadrak left the clean-up to the others as he crossed to look out through the demolished window.

"I'd wondered whether Terran insects might be dormant after dark," he remarked. "Judging by that scream, it would appear they are not."

Dundat glanced over at Hadrak, then strolled toward him, saying, "Perhaps we should investigate? Carefully, of course."

Hadrak turned to reply just in time to see the two Terrans appear in the doorway.

"Look out!" he shouted, grabbing his weapon.

Tiffany and Nancy made the mistake of both choosing the same target—the most obvious one, the Martian in the middle of the room. A 9mm bullet spanged off Dundat's armor an instant before the blast from the Martian weapon shredded the armor and tore him in half.

Di and Kair cringed at the distinctive roar of a demolition charge; Di dropped his scraping tool and snatched up a weapon.

Hadrak had no time to think; he fired at the first target he saw, and only too late did he realize that he had chosen the less dangerous Terran. His shot punched through Nancy's neck and shoulder, a little to one side, tearing away half her lower jaw and spraying blood and tissue across the hallway behind her. The cauterizing effect of the blast prevented any great spray of blood, but the result was still messy, and almost instantly fatal; Nancy toppled over and was dead by the time she hit the floor.

But Hadrak saw the muzzle of the captured KA-77 swing over to aim directly at him. He stared at it, as time seemed to distort and slow; his own muscles refused to work as he tried to aim his own weapon and fire first.

Then Tiffany pressed the firing stud.

Nothing happened.

Hadrak and Tiffany both stared at her weapon, neither of them comprehending at first what had happened.

"Oh, crap," Tiffany said.

And Hadrak understood.

The Terran had been using demolition charges. A KA-77 only carried so many of those. And poor, stupid, ignorant creature that it was, it didn't know how to work the selector.

"Di!" Hadrak called. "Seize it! The charge ran out!"

Tiffany was still fumbling with the weapon, trying to make it work, when Di and Kair grabbed her, one on either side.

Once again the Martians had taken a live captive for questioning.

30

ESCAPE?

Stan dove through the nearest doorway, and only realized when his shins slammed into the lower edge that he had dived into the dumbwaiter.

He didn't change course; it was as good a hiding place as any. He crammed himself into the tiny lift and pulled the door shut behind him—or as far as he could, at any rate; there was no handle on the inside, so he was unable to pull it shut tight. He hoped the remaining inch-wide crack wouldn't show.

The inside of the dumbwaiter was extremely cramped and uncomfortable, but he tried to ignore that. He heard his wife scream, and then a series of thumps and bangings, culminating in a tremendous smash of breaking glass—and then the sound of armored feet and alien voices.

The Martians were in the kitchen, no doubt about it.

He wondered what had happened to Susan. Had she escaped? He couldn't tell.

The dumbwaiter was *horribly* uncomfortable; he shifted, but it didn't help much.

The door wasn't completely closed, so he slid a hand out to steady himself as he adjusted his position.

His finger pressed against a button set in the wall beside the dumbwaiter.

The dumbwaiter jerked, and began to move downward.

At first Stan started to panic and grabbed for the door—but just then the Martians began shouting, and something roared as if a bomb had gone off, and Stan decided that getting out of the kitchen any way possible, including by riding a dumbwaiter down into the cellars, sounded like a *fine* idea.

The last trace of light vanished and he sank into utter darkness.

The descent seemed to last for hours, but at last the dumbwaiter bumped to a stop. Stan felt for a door and found one, but could not push it open. He struggled with it for several minutes, feeling the entire time as if he would smother if he didn't escape soon, before discovering at last that it slid *up*.

He pushed it up, and heard a latch click; he tumbled out and landed heavily on a hard, cold floor, where he lay in the darkness, breathing deeply and feeling his muscles relax.

At last, when he felt somewhat calmer, when the stiffness brought on by being jammed into far too small a space had passed, he sat up.

He couldn't see a thing. He was sitting on a concrete floor, by the feel of it, but he was in utter darkness and silence. By the feel of the air, he didn't think he was in a large room.

His wife was lost, probably dead. One son was dead for sure, and the other might be. He was on his own.

He knew he ought to feel stricken, overcome with grief, but all he actually felt was a sense of relief; for once he didn't have to worry about his family. He could take care of himself, and do what he pleased without worrying about what Susan thought.

Of course, right now he had no idea what he wanted to do.

After a time he shrugged, got to his feet, and began groping his way cautiously along.

Susan ran headlong across the garden, panting. The night was moonless so far, but the stars were bright, and a faint orange glow lit the sky far to the south, so she was able to see more or less where she was going.

She saw what appeared to be an open gate in the far wall, and steered for it—and suddenly ran smack into something, something that felt at first like thick vines or thin branches. She tried to push her way through, but her hands and legs stuck to the things, and the more she struggled, the more entangled she became.

"What the heck is *this*?" she asked no one in particular. She twisted around, trying to see where she was and what had caught her, and found herself staring at a living nightmare, a round black face with eight glittering, faceted eyes. She started to scream.

The spider threw a loop of web around her head, filling her mouth with sticky silk and cutting the scream off short.

Brenda kicked at some of the scorched sawdust and said, "Will someone tell me what the hell this polar bear was doing here, and who blew its head off?"

"I have no idea," Mark replied. He wasn't looking at the remains of the bear; he was looking through a doorway into the next room.

They had been wandering about, occasionally going up or down a floor, hopelessly lost, for several minutes. At first they thought the Martians were close behind, but seeing no sign of pursuit, they gradually calmed down and began risking the use of electric lights.

They were startled when Brenda flipped the latest switch and found an immense stuffed polar bear lying on the floor of the room they had just entered, with a hole through its chest and its head disintegrated, so that it was bleeding huge quantities of sawdust.

Now Mark was looking into the next room. "I think I recognize this," he said.

Brenda looked up.

"This is almost where we came in," he said. "Through that door and to the right, and there's the broken window, I think."

Brenda stepped over the bear's head and crossed the room to look over Mark's shoulder.

"I believe you're right," she said.

For a moment the two of them stood there, contemplating the

smoking room. Then Mark said, "You know something, Brenda? I think it's time we got out of here."

"Care to explain that?" she asked.

"I mean I think it's time we left," Mark said. "We came in here to get away from the giant bugs. Well, it's dark out, and wasps don't come out at night, do they? Most bugs don't. I'll bet the sand fleas are gone. And it's not exactly safe in here with those Martians blasting anyone they find. *I* think we should head back down to the beach, get back in the Jeep, and go somewhere else."

"Hm," Brenda said.

"I'm gonna do it," Mark said. "You coming?"

"What about the others? What about Jennifer?" Brenda asked.

Mark hesitated. "Well, we can send help for them once we get back to civilization," he said.

"If there still *is* any civilization," Brenda said.

"Well, do you have a better idea? You want to spend the rest of your life sneaking around this place, dodging Martians until we starve to death?"

"No," Brenda said.

Mark took that for agreement. "Come on," he said.

He led the way through the smoking room and around the corner to the music room. There, he started across the room.

Brenda paused in the doorway and looked around, then froze. "Mark!" she called in a harsh whisper.

He stopped and turned questioningly.

Brenda pointed to the other end of the music room.

A giant wasp was crouched there, curled into sleeping position.

"They don't stay out at night," Brenda whispered. "You were right. They find somewhere to nest!"

"It's asleep," Mark hissed back.

"I'm not settin' foot in there," Brenda said.

"Fine!" Mark said. "Be like that. I'll go get the Jeep and come around by the road; you try to find Jennifer and anyone else who wants a lift out of here, and find a way out that doesn't take you past our friend Mr. Wasp over there, and I'll meet you out front."

"You do that," Brenda said, retreating.

Mark hesitated, took another look at the wasp, then dashed for the window, clambered over the sill, and began to lower himself down the rope.

"**O**kay, Mom," Katie said. "Now what?"

The two of them, having given up on finding the secret room, and seeing no point in running around aimlessly, had been resting quietly in a sitting room overlooking the courtyard. They had occasionally glimpsed lights or movement in the distance, and heard screams and explosions, but had no desire to investigate any of them.

"It sounds as if there's a lot going on," Betsy said thoughtfully. "There must be Martians all over the house."

"Martians or giant bugs," Katie agreed.

"So it's not safe anywhere here."

Katie said, "It probably isn't safe *anywhere*, period."

"But it's bound to be better somewhere than it is here. So I think it's time we got out of here."

"How?" Katie asked. "The Martians blew up our car, and I'm not about to walk anywhere with those bugs around!"

"Bud said there was a whole collection of cars somewhere, didn't he?"

"What, you want to *steal* one?"

Betsy nodded. "I think so, yes."

Katie stared at her mother in astonishment.

Betsy looked back. "These are special circumstances," she said. "We *need* a car, and no one is using any of these, they're just sitting there. If we *don't* steal one, the chances are pretty good the Martians will destroy them all anyway."

"Wow," Katie said. "My mother, the car thief." She shook her head in amazement. "And you drove like a maniac getting us here this morning."

"I do what I have to," Betsy said. "I always have, ever since your father left."

"Okay, so we steal a car," Katie said. "How?"

"Well, we have to *find* them first," Betsy said, getting to her feet and straightening her blouse. "Did you see a garage anywhere?"

"No," Katie said. "Didn't that Bud guy say it was in the basement?"

"Oh, that's right," Betsy agreed. "Then we need to get to the basement." She looked out the window at the courtyard, where no fewer than four staircases led from various balconies and arcades down to ground level—and where light from several stained-glass windows spilled out into the night. "We can get down one level out there," she said. "From there I guess we'll just have to keep looking until we find something."

Katie got up. "I hope we do better this time than we did looking for the secret room," she said.

Bud and José sprawled comfortably in the bottom of the dry swimming pool, surrounded by boxes and various collected supplies. The radio was still on, but José had lowered the volume so they could talk.

"I tell you, man, we gotta get *out* of here," Bud said. "The whole house is full of bugs and Martians."

"The whole *world* is full of bugs an' Martians, man," José retorted. "I been listenin'. The Toppwood stations are gone, man—nothin' left. Brownsburg's still on the air, but they been callin' for help, askin' everyone to come up there and join 'em—they say they're holdin' off the Martian attack, they got the Army and everythin', but I'm not buyin' it. Down here I got food, I got supplies, I got everythin' I need, and I don't see no Martians or giant bugs or nothin'."

"What food?" Bud asked.

José waved at the boxes. "Stock for the snack bar, man. Canned soup—*lots* of canned soup. Candy bars an' stuff. And I didn't forget to bring a can opener, either."

"How you gonna cook soup?"

"You don't need to cook it, you can eat it cold. It just tastes better hot. And anyway, I got gas heat, used to heat the swimming pool." He pointed at a metal panel set in the side of the pool. "Open that up, turn it on, you can cook anythin'."

"As long as they're pumping gas, yeah," Bud admitted. "What about water? You gonna go upstairs for that?"

"Don' have to. This is a *pool*, man." He pointed at a coiled hose hanging on the wall. "I got food and water, I got blankets if the heat goes out, I got all kinds of tools, I got goddamn chain saws if they bust the house down and I hafta cut my way out. I can live down here for *weeks*, man."

"And what happens if the Martians come down here? You find a gun somewhere?"

José shook his head. "No, I didn't find no gun. They come down here, then I'm screwed, maybe. Or maybe we see if the chain saws can cut that armor they wear."

"I dunno, man," Bud said. "I think I'd rather get the hell out of here and go up to Brownsburg, join up with the folks there."

José shrugged. "You go ahead, if you want to."

"I was figuring on using one of the cars from the garage."

"You think they still run?"

"I sure as hell hope so."

"You get one runnin', I won't stop you takin' it."

"Think you'd come with me, maybe?" Bud asked. "I could probably use a hand."

José shook his head. "I tol' you, man, I'm stayin' here until this whole thing blows over and the Martians go home."

Bud sighed and got slowly to his feet. "I hate to say it, José, my man, but somehow I don't think these Martians are planning to leave anytime soon."

"Yeah, well, we'll see," José muttered.

"So," Bud said. "Which way to the garage?"

31

TIFFANY UNDER TORTURE

Di checked the wrist clamp one final time, then stepped back and looked at his handiwork.

Tiffany hung suspended from the railing of a second-floor balcony in the mansion's front hall, her stockinged toes dangling two feet above the polished oak floor. She spat at Di's face, leaving a small wet spot on his helmet.

"It keeps doing that," Kair remarked. "Do you think it has any significance?"

"Who knows?" Hadrak said. Then he switched to the Terran's language.

"Answer our questions and we will not kill you," he said.

"Liar!" Tiffany shouted.

"That would seem to display a definitely negative attitude," Di remarked.

Hadrak sighed. "Very well, then," he said in his own language. Then, in English, he continued, "If you do not believe me I have no way to—" He groped for the word. "—to *convince* you. I must find other ways to make you answer. If a promised positive incentive does not work, we will try a negative incentive. If you answer our questions, we will stop hurting you."

"Bastards!" Tiffany said.

Hadrak gestured to Kair, who stepped forward, his medical kit in his hands. He knelt and reached for Tiffany's foot.

Then he noticed the panty hose stretched between her toes—she had lost her shoes somewhere.

"Sir, do Terrans have webbed feet?" he asked.

Hadrak blinked, and struggled to remember the details of the orientation lectures.

"No," he said.

"In that case, this Terran is wearing some sort of protective covering."

"Remove it," Hadrak ordered.

Kair tried to get a grip on the slippery nylon; his armored gloves were not really suited for this sort of thing. At last he managed to pinch the material tightly and tug at it.

The panty hose stretched out until several inches of brownish nylon dangled from Tiffany's foot, but it did not come off. Kair groped upward, looking for the other end of this strange garment.

Tiffany squirmed and kicked at him. Kair caught her foot and twisted it, and she stopped.

"Pervert," she muttered as Kair pushed her dress up to her waist and finally located the waistband of her panty hose. He dug his fingers under the waistband and began working the garment off, inadvertently taking her panties with it.

"Interesting," he said as he removed the hose and tossed them aside. "This would appear to be a female. I was under the impression that virtually all Terran warriors are males."

"That was my understanding," Di said. "What makes you think this one is a warrior?"

"It killed Dundat, did it not?" Kair asked.

"All the same, I do not believe it to be a warrior," Hadrak said. "I think it was driven to irrational behavior by our actions here. Since it had Bindar's weapon, it was presumably present during the confrontation when Bindar died; perhaps the display of violence drove it berserk."

"Or perhaps one of the dead Terrans there was its offspring," Kair suggested. "I have heard that Terran females of various species will exhibit abnormally fierce behavior when their young are threatened. Very well, I withdraw my suggestion that this is a warrior. All the better, then, for our questioning."

"I hope you murdering freaks aren't discussing what you saw under my skirt," Tiffany muttered. "Bad enough hanging here with my ass bare without hearing you compare notes."

"We will continue the interrogation," Hadrak said.

Kair lifted a field surgeon's cutting tool from his kit. He dialed the anesthesia setting to zero, and the cauterization and blood vessel sealant to maximum. Then he applied the blade to the underside of Tiffany's left big toe.

Since he was not very familiar with Terran anatomy or the sensitivity of human toes, and since he was working at an awkward angle with his vision still somewhat limited by the wound sealant on his helmet, he cut deeply into the flesh.

Tiffany screamed. "Bastards!" she shrieked. "Let me *go!*"

"Answer our questions," Hadrak said calmly.

"All right, all right," she said. "*Ask* your damn questions! Don't cut my toe off!"

"Good," Hadrak said. "Tell us how many Terrans are in this structure."

"How many people are in the mansion, you mean?" Tiffany asked. "How should *I* know?"

Hadrak signaled to Kair, who applied the blade to a second toe.

"Stop! Stop! Let me think!" Tiffany yelped.

"You may think," Hadrak told her.

Tiffany struggled to do so.

There had been seven people on the tour that morning—herself and Tony, Bill Edwards, and the Rubenses. Steve and José worked here, which made nine. The three bikers had shown up, and then the mother and daughter—fourteen.

And then there had been that dead brunette who Tiffany hadn't seen before, whoever she was and wherever she'd come from.

"Fifteen," she said. "Except you killed most of them."

"Fifteen," Hadrak said. He looked at Di.

"It could be accurate," Di said.

"Then how many remain?" He turned back to Tiffany. "Fifteen alive, or fifteen both alive and dead?"

"Both," Tiffany said. "I don't know how many you killed."

Di counted off deaths.

"Her partner in the attack that killed Dundat," he said. "Four in or near the stair chamber where Bindar died. The one Bindar found dead outside. That one." He pointed at what was left of Sid. "The one we questioned." He pointed at the barricade in the front door. "The one who broke open Huzi's helmet. Nine dead. That leaves six—five of them still loose."

"One of them cracked *my* helmet," Kair said.

"That one must have gone out the window," Hadrak said. "Four still loose in the building, then."

"The fifth could have doubled back," Di suggested.

"True," Hadrak said.

"And this assumes the Terran is telling the truth," Di said.

"Oh, I think she is," Hadrak said.

"This assumes she *knows* the truth," Di said.

Hadrak glared angrily at Di.

"Sorry, sir," Di said.

"Four or five more," Hadrak said thoughtfully. "That's not so bad, then." He switched back to English. "Tell us about the other survivors," he demanded.

"What about them?" Tiffany asked, looking fearfully down at the tool in Kair's hand. She could not see just what it had done to her feet, and was trying to figure out how it could hurt so much, and feel as if her toes were being sliced off, without getting blood all over the floor.

"Who are they?"

"I don't know who you've killed," Tiffany said. "Not all of them, anyway."

"Then tell us about everyone you do not know to be dead." Hadrak was becoming more comfortable with the Terran tongue; the grammar was strange, but not overly complex.

Tiffany tried to oblige. "There's Steve," she said. "You probably got him. And I haven't seen José since this morning, before you even got here. Betsy and Katie and Bud all went off to look at something; they had Sid and Marcie with them, though, and you got those two." She looked toward the pitiful heap on the stairs.

"That was Marcie?" Hadrak asked.

"No, that was *Sid*," Tiffany said. "You got Marcie upstairs, outside the secret room."

"You know about those four," Hadrak said. "You know about your comrade in your attack on us. You know about the small one on the stairs. That is six. You have also named Steve and José and Betsy and Katie and Bud. This is eleven. Who are the other four?"

"There was Bobby. The others told me that a wasp was eating him out front."

"Very good," Hadrak said. "Three more."

"Bobby's parents. Susan and Stan Rubens."

"Is that not four? Bobbeez, Parents, Susan, and Stanrubens?"

"No, Susan and Stan were Bobby's parents."

"Ah. And Rubens was the third?"

"No, that's their last name. Their family name."

"Then that is two. Who is the last?"

Tiffany had lost track of who had already been named, and had to think for a minute. Stan, Susan, Bobby, Sid, Bud, Nancy, Marcie, Steve, José, Tony, Bill, Betsy, Katie . . .

There was the mystery girl who had been with Marcie, and she started to say something, then realized that that was one of the six dead ones the Martians had listed.

"Me," she said suddenly.

Hadrak stared at her, and felt his face muscles tighten with embarrassment.

"Yes," he said. "Of course. Then the ones who are unaccounted for are Steve and José and Betsy and Katie and Bud and Susan and Stan. Do you know where any of them are?"

Tiffany started to shake her head, but found it was more effort than it was worth while hanging by her wrists. "No," she said.

"Are any of them skilled as warriors?"

"Um . . . not that I know of. Bud might be pretty good in a fight, I guess."

Di had been listening to all this, and suggested, "Perhaps this 'Bud' was the one who killed Huzi."

"I had thought as much myself," Hadrak agreed. He asked Tiffany, "Are Bud's head filaments pale and short?"

"His hair, you mean? It's black. Curly. Kinda greasy."

"Not the same one, then," Di muttered.

"This 'Bud' is still out there, then," Kair said.

"Tell us about Bud," Hadrak ordered.

"I don't know anything about him," Tiffany said. "He's a biker, showed up at the front door after one of your flying saucers shot up his buddies. He's a big guy, seems nice enough."

Hadrak drew a blank on several of the words the prisoner used, and decided it didn't matter.

"What are you people doing in this place?" he asked.

"Hiding from *you*!"

Kair and Di exchanged glances.

"You attacked us," Hadrak pointed out.

"You killed Tony!"

"I *told* you she was avenging her offspring!" Kair said.

"The others—are they planning to destroy us?" Hadrak asked.

"How should I know? I haven't seen them in hours."

"Are they planning to escape from us?"

"Probably."

"How? On foot?"

"I don't know."

"Are there any more vehicles here?"

"I don't know," Tiffany said.

But she had hesitated before she said it; all three Martians had seen it.

"Are there any more vehicles here?" Hadrak repeated.

Tiffany didn't answer.

Kair had run out of toes on her left foot and was working on the right when Tiffany finally broke down and told them about the garage full of old cars.

When she had told them everything she knew, including the workings of ignition, brake, accelerator, transmission, and steering wheel, she hung there, weeping, while the Martians looked at one another.

"What do we do with her now?" Kair asked.

"Well, she *did* kill Dundat," Di said.

The two of them looked at Hadrak.

"Suit yourselves," he said.

"I *am* curious about Terran anatomy," Kair said. "We damaged all the others."

"She's all yours," Di said.

Tiffany looked up as Kair approached. She spluttered through her tears, "You said you wouldn't kill me if I answered your questions!"

"And you called me a liar," Hadrak replied. "You were right."

Tiffany stared at him for a moment—but then Kair used a cutter to slit her dress up the front, and she paid no more attention to Hadrak as she struggled to escape Kair's attentions.

She couldn't.

She screamed for a long time before she died.

32

ON THE BEACH

Mark crept across the garden as quietly as he could. The sleeping wasp had been encouraging, but there might still be other menaces awake out here.

There were huge moths fluttering overhead, and he heard glass break as one bumped against a window somewhere, but they didn't seem to be a threat. He didn't know what, if anything, moths ate, other than stored clothing, but these weren't moving toward him.

He wished he had shoes; the area below the broken window he had used as his exit was liberally strewn with shards of glass, and even when he had gotten clear of that with only a few superficial scratches, he found himself walking on rough gravel or prickly plant stubble.

Light was spilling from some of the mansion's windows, and he had spotted something glimmering palely on the other side of the garden. He knew he should probably have ignored it and just headed for the stairs, but he was curious—and besides, he told himself, what if it was some new enemy lurking over there, something that might wake up and pounce while he was on those long stairs with nowhere to dodge?

So he slipped silently past the flower beds and hedges, and finally got a good look at what he had seen.

It was a silvery bundle hanging in some sort of netting—a bundle as big as a person. He picked up a stick and poked at it.

It swayed gently; it obviously didn't weigh as much as a person.

A sudden movement glimpsed from the corner of his eye caught his attention, and he looked up and saw the spider.

Everything fell into place. The netting was a web, the bundle some poor person who had stumbled into it, and it was as light as it was because the spider had already sucked out most of the juice.

He turned and ran, just in case this particular spider was a species that didn't necessarily wait for its prey to become entangled.

At the top of the stairs he stopped, panting—he wasn't about to try running down those stairs in the dark. He might fall and break his neck.

Or there might be another spiderweb across the steps.

He frowned, and took a moment to find a good, strong stick that he could wave in front of himself as he walked. Thus prepared, he started down the steps.

The staircase was in the shadow of the house and cliff, so he was in almost total darkness once his head sank below the level of the garden wall. He waved the stick around until his arm and shoulder ached, then switched hands and continued; he listened intently for any sound of approaching enemies, either Martian or insect, but all he could hear was the pounding of the surf far below.

Or at least, at first that was all he could hear; when he was about a third of the way down he thought he heard screaming somewhere in the distance.

He shuddered and kept going.

As he descended, various uncomfortable thoughts ran through his head. What if the sand fleas had smashed the Jeep after all? What if the Martians had found it and destroyed it?

What if the keys weren't there? He was fairly certain he had left them in the ignition when he and the girls bailed out and headed up the cliff, but what if his memory was playing tricks on him? What if they had fallen out somehow?

How much gas was left in the car? He had filled it up about three days ago, but he wasn't sure how much driving he'd done since then—especially that long, panicky drive up the beach from Toppwood. The Jeep didn't get very good mileage in sand. He kept telling himself everything was going to be fine—he'd left the keys in the car, the sand fleas hadn't hurt it, there was maybe half a tank left—but he couldn't stop worrying.

As he neared the bottom of the stairs, he peered out into the darkness, trying to see the Jeep there on the beach.

He spotted it at last, but it seemed farther away than it ought to be. In fact, it looked as if it was several feet out in the water, and moving.

That couldn't be right. It had to be some sort of optical illusion. Either that or someone else had come down here and moved it.

He kept telling himself that right up until he stepped off the bottom step into cold saltwater.

The splash startled him so much he staggered and almost fell, catching himself on the railing at the last possible instant.

He stared down at his foam-covered feet, then out at the Jeep.

The tide had come in.

He had parked the Jeep at the very edge of the water at low tide, and now the tide had come in, and the Jeep was *floating away*!

Just then a wave broke over the Jeep, and when it was gone Mark saw that the vehicle was floating a bit lower in the water.

It was also drifting farther out to sea.

"No!" Mark shouted, splashing his way down the flooded beach. He lost his footing and tumbled facedown into the surf, then struggled to get up.

When he finally regained his feet, the Jeep was a hundred feet offshore, and he located it just in time to watch it sink into the brine.

He stared at the spot where it had gone down—the waves broke over it, making it easy to spot even in the near total darkness. Wild schemes for salvaging it, for swimming out and somehow driving it back to shore, ran through his head.

Then sanity returned.

The Jeep had sunk in six or seven feet of saltwater. The battery would be shorted out, the carburetor ruined—at the very least! There was no way it would be fit to drive ever again, short of being hauled out, dried out, and subjected to a thorough restoration.

He tried to tell himself that the wetness in his eyes was just spray.

He stared for several minutes before he finally turned around and started back up the stairs. He was perhaps halfway up when he heard the distinctive whine of an approaching mosquito.

33

A MOMENT'S PEACE

Brenda sat on the floor in the corner, her legs stretched out on the thick Oriental carpet, and wondered what was going to become of her.

Just twenty-four hours ago she had been partying on the beach with her friends, and all had been right with the world. A student at a respectable, if minor, college, she had friends, her family was safe and well, her grades were okay, and she had enough money to get by, though most of it was loans she'd have to pay back eventually.

Now she was lost and alone in this strange old mansion. Most of her friends were dead, the rest were missing, and she had no idea what had become of her family. Grades and money seemed completely unimportant, and she had no idea where her next meal was coming from, or even whether she would live to see the sun rise. Crazed aliens and hordes of giant insects were trying to kill her; there was a thirty-foot wasp sleeping just a few rooms away.

She had closed the doors, of course. She'd always hated wasps. Still, she knew the wasp was there. She wasn't ever going to forget what she'd seen when she went wandering through this huge old house—she wouldn't forget seeing poor little Sid blasted, or even the way the Martians had carelessly stacked up what must have been tens of thousands of dollars worth of antiques in the doorway.

She wasn't going to forget some of the things around here that had nothing to do with the Martians, either. As if the whole world outside going mad wasn't bad enough, she had kept coming across signs in this place that the world had *always* been mad, and she just hadn't been paying attention—such as the huge stuffed polar bear in the next room, with a scorched hole in its side and its stump of a neck spilling sawdust everywhere.

Or maybe it was just Ebenezer Gelman who had always been mad. She supposed that was it. That she could handle.

The Martians were another matter.

She'd grown up with her mama telling her that she could overcome anything, that the world was going to do its best to trample her down and she had to keep her head up no matter what came her way. But somehow she didn't think Mama had had a Martian invasion in mind.

She wondered what had become of all the others. Where was Jennifer? Was Mark okay? Would he get back to the Jeep, and if he did, would he come back for her?

She could almost hear her mother's voice saying, "You rely on yourself, girl, don't you ever rely on some man to take care of you. Especially not some white man."

She supposed she should take that to heart and *do* something, but she really didn't know what. Where *was* everybody? That girl Katie and her mother, and the biker and that Marcie . . . they'd all vanished, so far as she could tell. Even the Martians seemed to have vanished—though there had been those screams a while ago.

She shuddered. Whoever had been screaming had taken a long time to die.

Whatever had happened to that screamer, Brenda didn't want it to happen to her.

It was all just too much to deal with. She lay down on her side and curled up into a ball and just wished it would all go away. The quiet and the dark and her exhaustion caught up to her, and she fell asleep.

"**T**his is ridiculous," Betsy said, flopping into a dusty armchair. "There must be stairs to the cellars *somewhere*."

"Well, we haven't found them," Katie said. "Maybe in the kitchen?"

"So where's the kitchen?"

"*I* don't know."

"Neither do I. It's probably full of Martians."

"And where's everybody else? I haven't heard or seen anything since that screaming stopped."

"They're probably all in the basement—or dead." She wondered who it was who had been screaming, but didn't say so aloud.

For a few seconds they were silent; then Katie said, "Mom, I'm hungry."

"So'm I, honey. Not much we can do about it."

"Maybe go find that snack bar? Get a hot dog or something? And wouldn't that be near the kitchen?"

"And full of Martians."

"Mom, *anywhere* might be full of Martians. The basement garage could be full of Martians. Couldn't we at least take a *look* at the snack bar? Sneak up real quiet?"

Betsy let out a sigh. "If we can find it," she said. "Let's go."

Bud flicked on the lights and smiled at the sight.

All the cars were still there, paint polished to a fine sheen, brass and chrome sparkling.

Of course, that didn't mean any of them would run.

Assuming they did, though, he began considering which one to take.

The Model A Ford was too small and rickety; he wanted to fit in as many of the survivors as he could find. Bud had always wondered why Gelman had ever bought anything that cheap in the first place; it was clearly out of place in the collection.

Maybe it had actually been for one of the servants. He shrugged and moved on down the gleaming row of cars.

The '31 Packard touring car was too open; he wanted some protection against any giant bugs that might come along. He doubted any car would be able to resist a concerted assault by wasps or beetles, but he wanted some chance of surviving a casual encounter. The Rolls-Royce Silver Ghost was unacceptable for the same reason.

The Duesenberg J was perhaps the most beautiful machine Bud had ever seen in his life, and solidly built, with room for six or seven people if they squeezed a bit, but that big custom V-12 was intimidating.

The Locomobile was out; Bud had no intention of driving anything with eight wheels. They were likely to need to do some maneuvering, and those things were notoriously hard to steer.

The Hispano-Suiza was a possibility; so was the Bugatti Royale. The Bugatti was awfully big and heavy, which was good from the point of view of safety, but Bud wondered what sort of mileage that thing got—would they be able to cover the thirty miles to Brownsburg without refueling?

At least gas was available. The glass tank on top of the antique gas pump in the corner was full to the top. That was only about ten gallons, and he didn't know if there was any more to be had, but ten gallons ought to be enough.

The Pierce-Arrow was another serious contender. The Auburn was too small and open. The Cord was a possibility, but borderline—if there were as many survivors around as Bud hoped, it would be cramped.

And that left Mrs. Gelman's Cadillac.

That was the obvious choice, as far as Bud was concerned. Sure, it might be fun to drive a museum piece, but a 1959 Cadillac was a *real* car, one he was almost familiar with. His Cuban grandfather had had a '62 Caddy once. (His Mexican grandfather had never owned a car in his life.)

And the Caddy had been driven far more recently than any of the others, and had the best chance of still being in running condition without needing a major overhaul. Even after her mother died, old lady Gelman had taken it out for a spin two or three times a year, right up until she moved to Florida year-round in 1988. As Bud understood it, all the other cars had been mothballed since 1943.

That additional forty-five years was a big difference.

Bud ran a hand over the Caddy's sleek side and up the arch of one tail fin. That gaudy pink was a stark contrast to the sedate colors of the other cars—black, blue, tan, even yellow or red, but nothing like that postwar pink.

Now if only the car still ran.

There was a lot to be done here; he'd need to check the engine over carefully. The oil and fuel must have been drained; he'd need to top off everything he could and gas it up. He'd need to make sure there was a working battery, and that the tires were sound.

He'd need to either find a key or hot-wire it, too. Maybe break in, if the doors were locked.

It would have been so much simpler if Steve's Ford hadn't been destroyed.

And he wanted to collect as many of the survivors upstairs as he could, and make another attempt to talk José into coming along.

His talk with José had settled one question, though—where to go once he was out of here. The radio reports had made it pretty clear that Brownsburg was his best bet; there was organized human resistance there holding its own against the Martians and looking for help. Thirty miles away.

He crossed over to the garage door and peered out one of the little windows.

The moon was coming up, and he could see the ocean glittering in the moonlight. The driveway came out the garage doors, then made a right-angle turn up a ramp. At the top it made another right-angle turn into the parking lot in front of the house.

On three sides of the driveway nothing but a low fieldstone wall, scarcely more than a curb, separated it from a sixty-foot drop down the cliffs onto foam-splashed rocks. Old man Gelman's chauffeurs must have hated that, especially with the bigger, less maneuverable cars.

The Locomobile was *definitely* out.

He could hear something outside that he eventually identified as the whine of mosquitoes; the open-top cars were all definitely out, as well. While 1959 had been a really prime year for Cadillac convertibles, Mrs. Gelman's was a hardtop.

He turned and popped the Caddy's hood.

Stan opened the door carefully.

The door had been locked once, but someone had pried it open; he could feel the bent metal and splintered door frame. That probably meant someone had been here recently—someone human, as the Martians would have blasted the lock, instead of prying it. If the break was old, someone would have found it and cleaned it up.

And there was a light under the door.

The broken lock and the light didn't *necessarily* mean there was someone on the other side, but that did seem like the way to bet it.

"Hello?" he called softly, ready to jump back and slam the door if he saw or heard any sign of Martians or giant bugs.

"Yeah, who is it?" someone answered.

Stan let his breath out. "Me," he said, stepping through.

He blinked in surprise at what he saw.

He was in a huge room that seemed to be completely covered in crumbling tile; he had just emerged from a balcony that ran across one end. A central section of the lower level was sunk even lower, but it was several seconds before he identified the pit as an unused swimming pool.

This was partly due to the peculiar lighting. The only illumination in the room came from the faint moonlight spilling through a row of windows high in the south wall, and from a little reading lamp down in the pool. A young man sat beside the reading lamp, amid a veritable fortress of boxes and miscellaneous material, and most of the light fell on him or the surrounding cardboard barricades.

The man looked vaguely familiar.

"José?" Stan asked.

"Yo," José replied. "Who're you?"

"Stan Rubens. I took the tour this morning." He stepped forward to where José could see him.

"Oh, yeah," José said. "Weren't you the guy with those two kids?"

"Yes, that was me," Stan acknowledged.

"So where are they? They with you?"

Stan shook his head. "The Martians got them," he said.

"Wife, too?"

"I don't know," Stan admitted. "She went out a window and didn't come back. They might've gotten her, I'm not sure."

"Or maybe the bugs did," José suggested. "I been hearin' about the bugs, man. Heard 'em buzzin' past the windows this afternoon."

"Could be," Stan said, sidling farther in and closing the door behind him. He looked around at the vast, empty chamber.

"So, José," he said, "you're alone down here?"

"Why you askin', man?"

"Oh, I . . . you know, I was just curious."

"Don' be curious, man, or I might think you're a Martian spy."

That caught Stan by surprise. "You think they have spies?" he asked, startled. "You mean, spies disguised as ordinary people?"

"I think they might, yeah," José said. "How else did they catch everyone off guard like they did? How'd they screw up our radars and missiles 'n' stuff if they didn't have spies helpin' them out? How else'd they make the TV stations go on and off the air the way they did?" He shook his head. "That's why I came down here, man, 'stead of stayin' up there with the rest of you; I didn't think I could trust no one."

"Is *that* it? Wow. We thought they'd killed you."

"Nobody killed me, man—not so's I noticed, anyway." He grinned. "Or maybe they did and I'm a Martian spy now, hey? Think of that?"

Stan laughed weakly.

"Hey, man, I'm sorry 'bout your kids," José said, turning serious again. "Two boys, right. Martians got 'em both?"

"Yeah," Stan said. He didn't mention the possibility that Sid might still be alive; he didn't believe it, and it was simpler to accept that both his sons were dead.

José looked up at him for a minute, then said, "Hey, man, don' look so scared. I'm no Martian and you ain't, either. Come on down and have a Milky Way or somethin'." He held up a candy bar.

Stan hesitated, looking into the shadowy corners of the big room.

He didn't see any lurking Martians, or other monsters, and he didn't believe José's scare stories about spies—or even if he did, he knew *he* wasn't a spy, and he didn't think José was, either.

What José was was safe, tucked away down here with whatever was in those boxes.

"Yeah, okay," he said. His stomach growled when he thought about the candy bar. Without consciously intending it, he began to hurry.

"Thanks!" he called.

34

DRAINED OF BLOOD

Mark staggered up to the rope and flung away his ichor-smeared stick.

He had swatted the mosquito, but not before it had lunged at him and plunged its sucking proboscis into his side. He'd had to beat at it for what had seemed like hours, though he knew they were only seconds, before he had managed a lucky blow that snapped its neck. He yanked himself off that hideous proboscis and fled without bothering to finish the creature off; he hoped it suffered horribly before dying.

He had lost a lot of blood; he knew that. The mosquito had sucked out what had seemed like gallons before Mark managed to pull away. What was perhaps worse, the damn bug's venom was keeping the blood from clotting; Mark was holding the hole in his side shut with his hand, but he could feel blood seeping out between his fingers.

Now he would have to climb the velvet rope back up to the music room, sneak past the sleeping wasp . . . it was almost more than he could contemplate, and he was tempted to just lie down right there in the garden and die.

He couldn't let himself do it, though. He had come this far, and to give up now and die of a lousy mosquito bite would be just too much. He took a deep breath and grabbed the rope.

He fell from halfway up on the first try, landing on his back in a welter of broken glass; he winced, but was already in such bad shape that it didn't really hurt that much more than the pain he was already feeling.

He picked himself up and tried again, and this time managed to sprawl through the window into the music room, landing heavily on the edge of a rug, half on the thick wool and half on bare wood.

The wasp in the other end of the room stirred; he could hear the clicking of chitin as it shifted. It didn't wake, however.

He couldn't get to his feet; he lay on the floor for a moment, gathering his fading strength, then began crawling.

"Brenda," he whispered.

No one answered.

He reached the door, planning to crawl on through—and his hand hit wood.

The door was closed.

Gasping, he pulled himself up the door frame, reaching for the knob. He twisted it, and the door opened; he fell through and landed with a thump.

Brenda started awake. Something had disturbed her, she knew, but she didn't know what. No one was screaming; she didn't hear any insects buzzing, or weapons firing. She was sure she had heard *something*, though.

She stood up and peered around, but the room was almost totally black; she couldn't see a thing.

Then she heard another thump, fainter this time, and identified a direction.

Something was moving around out there. She wondered whether it might be the wasp.

Or maybe it was Mark, returning.

She hesitated, then decided to take a look. She opened the door cautiously and crept through.

She found Mark lying semiconscious in the hallway outside the music room, hand clamped over a bloody wound. She could see a trail of bloodstains, black in the moonlight, stretching back across the music room to the window.

"Oh, crap," she muttered. She looked around for something she could use as a bandage, and spotted a table scarf.

A few minutes later Mark was slumped in an antique crewel-upholstered chair, bandaged but still weak, blood still seeping from his wound and the cuts on his back.

"Thanks," he murmured.

"No problem," Brenda said. "What happened to the Jeep? And what happened to *you*?"

"Mosquito got me," Mark said. "Jeep floated off—the tide came in. God, I feel stupid!"

Brenda sat back on her haunches and thought it over. "So you parked at water's edge at low tide," she said finally. "Yeah, that was stupid—but hey, none of the rest of us noticed, either; don't feel *too* bad."

Mark looked down at the bandage and saw that it was already swollen thick with blood. "Christ," he said, "I'm bleeding to death."

Brenda looked worried. "I tied it tight as I could. It ought to stop."

Mark shook his head. "No," he said. "Mosquitos inject this stuff to stop clotting, so they can suck more blood—and the one that bit me was fifteen feet long. I might as well be a goddamn hemophiliac now!"

"What can we do about it?"

"Nothing. I'm gonna die. *Damn* it!" He looked down at the wound, then up at Brenda.

"Give me a hand up," he said. "If I'm gonna die, I'm at least gonna try to take one of those Martian assholes with me!"

"If you're quite finished," Hadrak said, "I think it would be appropriate to locate the Terran vehicles and carry on with our departure." He glanced at the barricaded front door, where they could all hear the flapping of gigantic wings; this place was clearly unsafe and becoming more so. There were insects fluttering at the colored windows, as well, and they had all heard glass straining and cracking as the creatures battered at them.

"I'm done," Kair said, stepping away from what was left of Tiffany. "Interesting creatures."

"She said the garage was 'downstairs,' on the side of the structure facing the sea," Di said. "We are on the ground floor, and the sea lies in that direction." He pointed. "Shall we proceed?"

Hadrak looked at the three doors and chose the center one. "That way," he said.

The three of them marched on, through the center door and into the maze of rooms beyond.

A moment later Betsy leaned out of the south door in that wall and peered around.

When she caught sight of Tiffany's dangling, eviscerated corpse, she sucked in her breath, but did not turn back. Instead she leaned out farther and looked more carefully.

"The lights are on, but I don't see anyone alive," she said at last.

"What do you mean, 'anyone alive'?" Katie asked, pushing up past her mother.

She spotted Tiffany immediately.

"Oh," she said. She swallowed hard. "I guess the Martians *were* here," she said.

Betsy nodded. "Come on," she said.

The two of them dashed diagonally across the front hall and into the reception room.

A moment later Brenda and Mark emerged onto the second-floor balcony, Mark leaning heavily on Brenda's shoulder. They paused at the railing and looked down.

"Oh, my God," Brenda gasped when she saw Tiffany.

"Who is that?" Mark asked.

"I don't know," Brenda said. "It's not Jennifer or any of the people we met here."

"Get me downstairs."

Brenda looked at Mark. "What exactly are you planning to do, Mark? You can barely walk! Soon as the Martians see you, they'll blow you away."

"That's better than dying of a goddamn mosquito bite," Mark muttered. "Come on!"

They staggered on. On the stairs Brenda insisted on staying far to one side, to avoid passing any closer than necessary to Sid's remains.

She had her doubts whether Mark's wound was actually fatal; he seemed to be regaining strength. She wasn't ready to argue with him yet, however. He was absolutely set on doing *something*, though she wasn't clear on just what he intended, and he wouldn't listen to anything she said.

As they bumped down off the final step, she asked, "How do you plan to *find* the Martians?"

"I'll find them," he said. Then he stood, looking at the half-dozen doors, trying to choose one.

"**I** can't believe what a disaster this has been," Kair said. "With all due honor, sir, I hope that the rest of the invasion hasn't been anything like our mission."

"As do I," Hadrak agreed. "Four good Gnards dead just to show that this home for the insane wasn't a threat!"

"And ten Terrans slain," Di remarked. "At least we haven't completely disgraced ourselves."

"Ten civilians," Kair said. "I'm not impressed."

"I'll be glad to be out of here—" Hadrak began as he pushed open another door and stepped through. Then he stopped in mid-sentence, frowning.

They had first reached the seaward side of the house at the great hall, which was clearly not what they were after. They had then turned and worked their way through half a dozen smaller rooms, all with spectacular ocean views, toward the back of the house, assuming that somewhere along the way they would find the promised garage.

However, Hadrak had just entered the study at the back corner of the house, a room that projected out of the south wall with windows on three sides. There was nothing beyond this on the seaward side of the house; they could see that clearly. They had crossed the entire side of the house without seeing any vehicles.

"I don't understand," Kair said. "She couldn't have been lying, could she?"

"Of course she could have," Di growled. "You can't trust these Terrans, even under torture. They're all crazy!"

Hadrak had crossed the room to the windows and was looking out at the moonlit sea, contemplating. A huge white thing fluttered by, but he ignored it.

"She said 'downstairs,' " he said. "And look there." He pointed at the view of the south wall of the house.

Di and Kair joined him and looked where he indicated.

"Another level," Di said, staring at the basement windows.

"And there's a light on," Kair said. "Not a very bright one, or perhaps it's deep inside, but definitely a light."

"This 'garage' could be right under our feet," Di said.

"I didn't see any stairs going down," Kair said.

"They must be hidden," Hadrak said. "Remember that room Bindar found."

"Then how can we get down there?" Kair asked.

"We could blast through the floor," Di said, lifting a KA-77—each Martian now carried two of the weapons, his own and one salvaged from a dead companion.

"No," Hadrak said. "We might damage the vehicles."

"Then what should we do?"

"We will search," Hadrak said. "We'll find a stairway somewhere."

"Your will," Kair said doubtfully.

Hadrak glowered at him. "There's no need to be subtle about it," he said. He lifted a KA-77, pointed it at an interior wall, flipped the selector, and fired.

The wall disintegrated into splinters and plaster dust, leaving a hole into the next room.

"No stairway there," Hadrak said.

Di blasted away at the wall on the other side of the doorway, and reported, "None there, either."

"Next room," Hadrak ordered, waving the squad northward.

In the front hallway Mark and Brenda heard the boom of the Martian weapons.

"That way," Mark said, hobbling on.

In the garage Bud looked up at the sound, then down at the Caddy.

He had refilled the radiator using plain old tap water; he thought that would be good enough to hold it for thirty or forty miles, and a search had failed to turn up any antifreeze. He'd found a case of oil on one of the shelves in the back room and filled the crankcase. The battery was being charged—the recharger had been right next to the oil. The tires *looked* okay, and he decided to trust them, since he had no real choice.

He had just been checking the transmission fluid when he heard the weapons. Something was going on up there—probably the Martians killing off more innocent tourists.

"Damn," he said. He still had maybe half an hour's work to go before he'd be satisfied that the Caddy was fit to drive, but he couldn't just stand by while people were dying. At the very least, he had to go see if José was okay, maybe try again to talk him into coming along.

He put down the rag he was holding and headed for the passage that led back to the swimming pool.

35

RENDEZVOUS
WITH TERROR

Bud leaned in through the door and called, "José? You still here, man?"

José waved. "Right here," he said. "Got a friend, too."

It took Bud a few seconds to recognize the man standing beside José; Stan was considerably more rumpled than when Bud had seen him last.

"Hey, Stan," he called. "Where's Susan? And Sid?"

"I don't know," Stan said. "Wasn't Sid with you?"

"Oh, we split up hours ago, when we saw one of the Martians coming," Bud said. "He was with those college kids, I think. Didn't he come back to the secret room?"

Stan shook his head.

"Oh, man, I'm sorry," Bud said. "What about Susan?"

"I don't know," Stan said. "We were both in the kitchen, and we heard the Martians coming, and I fell down the dumbwaiter and couldn't find my way back up."

"That sucks," Bud said.

"What're you doing down here?" Stan asked. "Hiding, like José and me?"

Bud shook his head. "No, I'm trying to get us a ride out of here. Been working on one of the cars in the garage."

"The cars?" Stan's expression made it obvious that he had completely forgotten about the cars.

"Yeah, old lady Gelman's pink Caddy," Bud said.

"The *Caddy*?" Stan stared at him. "Are you *nuts*? What about the *Bugatti*, for God's sake? What about the Duesenberg?"

"I thought the Caddy was, you know, more practical," Bud said, a little defensively.

"But the *Bugatti*, man—my God, that's a Type 46! It's *handmade*!"

"Yeah, well, I'd rather drive the Caddy." He hesitated, and looked down the passageway past the storerooms. "Listen, you said you left Susan in the kitchen?"

"That's right."

"I'm gonna go take a look, see what's happened to her," Bud said. "Wanna come along?"

Stan thought that over for a moment; he looked at José, then at Bud. José shrugged.

"It's not safe up there," Stan said. "There were Martians out in the corridor."

"They move around," Bud said. "Probably gone by now."

"Well, still . . . I think I'll go to the garage, okay? See if I can help with anything."

Bud shrugged. "Suit yourself. She's your wife, and all. I've already filled the radiator and crankcase on the Caddy, so don't mess with that, okay?"

"Sure," Stan said.

Bud waved, then walked on, leaving the door open.

Stan climbed up out of the pool, waved a hesitant good-bye to José, then headed for the garage.

As he walked down the corridor he found himself muttering in disbelief, "The *Bugatti*. What about the Bugatti?"

That damn greasy biker didn't understand, Stan decided. That was all there was to it. He didn't understand that that was a *Bugatti*, a masterpiece, one of the greatest cars ever built—and worth a bloody *fortune*. If they were going to steal a car, why on Earth take a measly

'59 Cadillac, when they could have a million-dollar machine like a '32 Bugatti Royale?

He stepped into the garage and looked down the row of cars—the sleek blue Duesenberg, the streamlined Auburn, the gleaming Cord, that gaudy tart of a Cadillac, and dominating them all, the very image of power and wealth, the blue and yellow Bugatti.

He stared at it.

There was no guide here now to stop him, he had no worries about propriety or police; he walked over and put his hands on the Bugatti, opened the door, leaned inside . . .

It was too much to bear.

He had no more family, his old life was ruined—Stan felt as if he ought to come out of this with *something*. And the Bugatti would serve. A million-dollar car . . . he couldn't bear to see it left here, abandoned to those murdering Martian monsters.

"If he won't take it, *I* will," Stan muttered. He straightened up, took two steps sideways, and opened the hood.

Betsy opened the door of the snack bar and leaned through, peering into the brightly lit passage beyond. She sucked in her breath at the sight of Nancy's corpse, sprawled beside the kitchen door.

"What is it?" Katie asked, leaning over to look past her mother. She had a candy bar clutched in one hand. "Ewww," she said. "Who was it?"

"Nancy," Betsy said. "I think."

"Oh, yuck. I liked her."

"So did I." She sighed, and looked her daughter in the eye. "So, honey," she said, "now what? Do we go on and check the kitchen?"

"I don't hear any Martians," Katie said. "Go for it."

Moving on tiptoe, the two of them crept out of the snack bar and down the corridor to the kitchen door. They peered in.

"Well, there's a Martian," Katie said, "but I don't think he's a problem."

"I'd have to agree with that," Betsy said. It was obvious that Dundat wasn't a threat.

"Mom, look," Katie said, pointing at the floor.

Betsy looked, and saw a 9mm automatic lying there, a few inches from Nancy's outstretched hand.

"Didn't do her much good," Betsy said. Then she looked at the dead Martian, hoping that perhaps it, too, had dropped a weapon. She frowned.

There was no Martian weapon to be seen—but it was also obvious that it hadn't been the pistol that had killed the Martian.

"I wonder what happened here?" she said.

"They shot each other," Katie suggested.

Betsy shook her head. "No, they didn't. The Martian wasn't killed by a bullet. And he didn't fall neatly as that, I'll bet, with his legs and arms straight. And where's his ray gun, or whatever those things are?"

"So there were other Martians," Katie said.

"But who shot this one?"

"One of the others?"

"You think they're fighting amongst themselves?"

"Maybe it was an accident. 'Friendly fire'—you know."

"Could be."

"Mom, does it really matter?"

"I guess not." Betsy looked around the kitchen, noting the open door of the walk-in refrigerator, the smashed window over the counter next to the sink . . . and the buzzing she could hear through that broken window.

"Bugs," she said. "I hear bugs out there."

"Me, too," Katie agreed. "Maybe we should get out of here."

"Let's see if we can find those cellar stairs, first," Betsy said. "You try that door, I'll start on this side."

Together, they entered the kitchen—then Betsy paused and took a step back to scoop up the pistol from the floor.

"Just in case," she said. She checked the safety, pulled the magazine, counted the five remaining rounds, then slid the clip back in.

Bud started up the stairs, then paused, listening. He could hear footsteps in the kitchen above him.

He couldn't see anything; the door at the top of the stairs was closed. He had left the stairway light turned off, to avoid alerting any Martians to his presence here. The light in the passage at the bottom of the stairs was on, however, so he wasn't in total darkness, just shadowy gloom.

He stood there in the dark, straining his ears, listening to those footsteps moving around. They didn't sound like the heavy tread of the armored Martians. That was good; they were probably human survivors, the people he was looking for. He took another few steps up . . .

And the door ahead of him swung open. He froze, startled.

In the kitchen, Betsy swung open the door, looked in, saw the stairs and started to smile, and then saw something standing there in the dark, something big, looking up at her. Startled, she aimed the pistol at the middle of that pale, faintly visible face.

Bud couldn't make out who the dark figure silhouetted at the top of the stairs was, but he recognized the outline as human, rather than Martian. He started to relax—and then he saw the gun pointing at him.

"Hey!" he said.

Betsy squeezed the trigger—but she had forgotten to release the safety she had so carefully set a moment before, and by the time she flipped it off, she realized that it wasn't a Martian on the stairs.

"It's me, Bud!" Bud called.

Betsy relaxed and lowered the pistol—and just then a tremendous smash sounded behind her. She whirled, gun raised, as a moth battered against the windows, shattering glass and scattering bits of white-painted mullion across the counters and floor. Katie screamed once, then dove for cover behind a table.

The moth fluttered wildly, each beat of its wings spraying shards of glass and splinters of window frame inward, but it was too large to fit through the hole it was creating.

"Katie!" Betsy called. "This way! I found the stairs!"

"Shoot it!" Katie shouted back.

Betsy hesitated, then shook her head. "It's too big," she said. "I'm not going to waste a bullet! Come on!"

Katie came, running across the kitchen with her arms wrapped around her head to ward off flying glass. Betsy helped her down the first few steps, then paused to close the door while Katie continued down.

The door jammed on a piece of window that had wedged underneath; Betsy tugged at it once, saw the sharp-edged bit of debris holding it, then said, "Screw it." She left the door ajar and followed her daughter down.

If any Martians came along, she told herself, they might see the open door, but they would have no way of knowing whether anyone had actually used it, or where in the basement they might have gone.

Bud met Katie halfway and led her the rest of the way down into the basement, where the two of them waited for Betsy to join them. "Is there anyone else up there?" he asked as he brushed bits of glass out of Katie's hair.

Betsy shook her head. "Not that we saw," she said. "Not alive, anyway. Nancy's dead."

"And Tiffany," Katie added. "Back in the big room."

"Did you see Susan?"

"No."

"Stan said she was in the kitchen."

"She wasn't," Betsy said. "There was a smashed-out window, though, even before that moth came. Maybe she went out that way."

"Have you seen *anyone* else alive up there?"

"Not lately," Betsy said.

"We thought *you* were probably dead," Katie said. "I'm glad you're not."

"So'm I," Bud agreed.

"Now what?" Katie asked, looking around at the basement corridor.

"I'm getting one of the cars ready to go," Bud explained. "Stan's down here, and José. Come on, I'll show you."

Together, the three of them headed down the passage.

36

FATAL PLUNGE

"**P**erhaps," Tenzif Kair said as he smashed open a window with one of his weapons, "rather than searching for the stairs, we should find a way to lower ourselves down to the windows of this 'garage.' " He leaned out, looking down the wall below.

Hadrak glanced at Kair, but did not bother to say anything.

The three Martians were in the so-called great hall, a soaring pseudo-Gothic extravagance a hundred feet long and two stories high, with immense stone fireplaces at either end, bear and tiger skins on the floor, and displays of medieval weaponry adorning the walls. Hadrak had hesitated to shoot up the walls in here for fear that any such destruction would damage the structure sufficiently to bring the ceiling down on them; instead he was poking small holes here and there, looking for stairs.

This had not seemed to be something that called for all three of them, so Kair had taken a break and gone to inspect the windows, whereupon an idea had struck him.

Now he was looking down a sheer drop of sixty feet or more onto black, wave-splashed rocks. Off to the side, however, he spotted the driveway.

The light was not sufficient for him to make out much detail, but he nonetheless guessed that this was just what they were looking for.

"Sir," he said, "I believe I have spotted the exit the stored vehicles use."

Hadrak and Di turned.

"Where?" Hadrak asked.

Kair pointed out the window. "Down there," he said.

Hadrak and Di crossed the room to join Kair at the windows.

And at that moment Mark saw his opportunity, and took it.

A few minutes earlier, as the Martians finished shooting up the billiard room immediately to the south of the great hall, Mark and Brenda had hobbled into the great hall.

Mark spotted the weapons immediately; his eyes lit up at the sight of them, and he grabbed a crossbow, only to find that the string had been removed years before, rendering it useless. He dropped it on a sofa.

He had then snatched at a flintlock and found it unloaded, whereupon he flung it aside. A sword was more promising, and he had held that in one hand while snagging a mace with the other.

He had some of his strength back, and adrenaline helped; he was actually able to swing the mace with some authority.

"Yes," he said. "This'll cave in those stupid helmets—the sword would probably just bounce off." He dropped the sword and hefted the mace.

"Mark!" Brenda called from the doorway. "Get the hell out of there! Are you crazy? They'll be in here any minute!"

"Let 'em come!" Mark wasn't quite up to a triumphant laugh, but he did manage a sickly smile.

Brenda stared at him. He was *definitely* recovering from the mosquito attack, but the damned fool didn't realize it yet, she thought, and he seemed to be caught up in his revenge fantasies. God save her from testosterone!

"Listen," she called, "if you just stand there, they'll blow you away before you get close enough to use that thing! Come on back here, and maybe you can jump 'em and get them by surprise!"

"You're right," he said. He joined her in the doorway, and together they retreated a few steps up the passageway, past the head of the cellar stairs—and just then the Martians entered the great hall.

Mark and Brenda could hear them conferring in their weird, harsh language—Brenda thought it sounded like cats spitting and growling. Mark crept closer to the doorway, and Brenda didn't dare hold him back, for fear of being heard; she cowered in the passage, trying to figure out what to do.

Mark used a glass-fronted bookcase in the great hall as a mirror, and saw the Martians split up; two of them were moving along the inside wall, but the third went over to the big Gothic windows.

Without warning, the Martian smashed out a dozen leaded panes with the butt of his gun and leaned out, peering down the cliff.

He looked so vulnerable there! Mark lifted the mace—then remembered the other two, with their nasty ray guns or whatever they were. He'd never get all three of them before they shot him.

But then the Martian at the window said something, and the others responded, and a moment later all three of them were crowding around the windows, their backs to him.

Mark saw his opportunity.

"Die, lousy alien bastards!" he screamed as he charged across the room, mace waving over his head.

The Martians turned, startled—just as Mark's foot landed on the outstretched paw of a tigerskin that slid beneath him. He stumbled, flailed about, and rammed into the Martians totally out of control. The mace smashed into the window over his head and tangled in the leading, while Mark himself tangled with the Martians. He had knocked down the one with the white-stained helmet, and caught one of the others around the neck.

"If I'm gonna die," he shrieked, "I'm taking you with me!" With that, he heaved the Martian whose neck he held upward, and dove out the window, taking the Martian with him.

"Mark!" Brenda shrieked as she saw her injured friend leap to his doom.

Slithree Di had received no warning of the mad Terran's attack; he was caught from behind, completely off guard. He had been looking over Kair's shoulder at the driveway when an arm suddenly slammed into his back and he found himself yanked bodily off the floor.

Now he was plummeting out the window and down the cliff with the Terran still clinging to him. He had a KA-77 in each hand, which left him with no way to fend off the lunatic; he flung one weapon aside, then used that hand to force the Terran away.

Then he opened fire with the remaining KA-77, punching hole after hole through Mark in the few remaining seconds before they both slammed head first onto the rocks.

The impact shattered Di's helmet and smashed open his armor; Hadrak, still standing at the window, could see as much. Whether Di had died from the impact, from Earth's atmosphere, or by drowning, Hadrak didn't know, but there could be no doubt that he was dead.

On the other hand, it was very obvious how Mark had died; by the time he reached the rocks, Di's weapon had blasted him to pieces.

Hadrak stared down at his dead trooper—and at the KA-77 that had landed on the driveway a few feet to one side.

What a shame, he thought, that it was the weapon, rather than Di, that had landed there! Armored as he was, Di might have survived a twelve-foot drop.

Sixty feet, though, had clearly been fatal.

"Sir," Kair said, getting to his feet, "there's another one!"

"What?" Hadrak spun around, raising his weapon.

"I heard it!" Kair said. "There's another Terran. It shouted 'target,' or 'set,' or something when the other went through the window."

Hadrak didn't wait for further details, he opened fire, spraying the far wall, and to hell with any worries about structural damage.

Brenda saw the Martian get up off the floor and point at her; she saw the other one turn and raise its weapon. She didn't wait for it to pull the trigger; she turned and ran.

She had no time for niceties like dodging; she just ran in the straightest course she could manage through the mansion's maze.

Hadrak and Kair, glimpsing movement, charged after her, Hadrak in the lead.

"Sir!" Kair shouted, stopping suddenly. "The stairs!" He pointed at the stairs leading down, stairs that Hadrak had charged blindly past.

"Later!" Hadrak shouted. "I'm going to get that Terran! I've had enough of this!"

Kair looked at the stairs, then sighed and followed his squad leader.

37

THE MOTH AT
THE WINDOW

Brenda dashed into the front hall and hesitated for a fraction of a second before choosing her path—there were so many doors!

But two of them led back in the wrong direction—the Martians might have split up, and she might run smack into one. Turning and running the full length of the hall to get to the stairs, or to one of the two back doors, might give the Martians a clear shot at her. Even the third door on the far side had that problem.

That narrowed it to two, and she simply headed for the closer one.

As she ran she could hear fluttering wings somewhere; she glimpsed some of the materials from the barricade scattered across the floor, and even had to jump over a fallen marble bust. She glanced up and saw that half a stained-glass window was gone, revealing black night beyond.

In the reception room she ignored the stairs and most of the doors and ran straight across into the parlor. The door on the far side of the parlor was propped open, so she continued through that, to save herself the time involved in pushing anything aside.

That put her in a little entry hall; she flung aside a velvet rope and ran on into the guides' lounge.

That was a dead end; the only other door led to a small bathroom. She doubled back.

When she burst into the entry hall, she could see the Martians in the parlor, heading her way. One of them raised its weapon and fired.

Brenda dodged sideways and the blast missed her, instead striking a life-size alabaster statue of a nymph and reducing the upper half to gravel.

Brenda dove through the nearest door, and found herself in a snack bar; the pilot lights of various appliances and a lighted Coca-Cola sign provided some illumination. Brenda could see used paper plates and bits of hot dog bun scattered about, and the blackened remains of a few hot dogs were still turning on the cooker.

She had no time to spare contemplating this, even though it was the first food she had seen all day. There was one other door, and she barreled through.

The corridor beyond was brightly lit; except for the front hall, she had been running through semidarkness. Here she could clearly see the blast marks on the walls, the cracks in the ancient plaster, the corpse on the floor . . .

She gulped air and glanced through the kitchen door.

A gigantic moth was beating its wings against the ruined frames that had once held a row of windows; broken glass covered everything in sight, including a dead Martian.

That did not look inviting; she turned and sped down a side passage.

A moment later Hadrak and Kair charged out of the snack bar into the passage and skidded to a stop.

"Which way?" Kair asked.

Hadrak hesitated, then heard the sound of movement in the kitchen. "That way!" he said.

The two dashed into the kitchen, where Hadrak saw that he had only been hearing the moth. He raised his weapon, aimed, and fired.

The bolt ripped a hole through the moth's abdomen, but the insect merely fluttered more wildly. A second bolt almost sliced off a wing; a third, striking the thorax, finally killed the immense creature.

Kair looked around at the ruined windows, the scattered glass, and Dundat's remains.

"You know, sir," he said, "those things are breaking in windows all over the structure. In the morning, when the wasps and other species return, this place will be uninhabitable."

"You're right," Hadrak said. He lowered his weapon.

The Terran had gotten away. He hated to admit it, but it seemed clear that the creature had lost them somewhere, probably by taking another route from the lit corridor.

On the other hand, he could see what appeared to be a staircase leading down behind a half-open door at the far end of the room, and Kair was quite right that the building would be full of deadly giant insects in a few hours. They had to escape. The only means to do so was the Terran vehicles stored in the garage, and the stairs behind that door presumably led down to the garage. Perhaps it was just as well they had turned in here, even if it did mean losing the quarry.

"The stairs," he said, pointing. "Come on."

"Ah," Kair said. "Excellent."

A blast from a KA-77 removed the jammed door; Hadrak fired another blast down the stairs to discourage any attempt at ambush. Then the two of them moved slowly down the stairs, weapons ready.

Brenda, meanwhile, had dodged and run and dodged. She passed a secret panel standing open, glanced inside long enough to see that there were dead bodies in there, and then ran on.

She considered calling for help, but she wasn't sure there was anyone left alive to help her, or that even if there were, that they would hear her, or that if they were alive and heard her, that they would be able or willing to do anything for her.

And the Martians might hear a cry for help. She wondered why they didn't seem to hear her as she ran. To her, her ragged breath, her footsteps, and her pounding heartbeat seemed deafening.

Finally, when she had zigzagged through a dozen rooms and run back through the front hall, into the courtyard, up to a balcony, and down a passageway, she couldn't run anymore; she collapsed onto a sofa in a huge, tapestried drawing room.

She lay there, catching her breath, for what seemed like hours; then she lay there and listened.

She couldn't hear the Martians. She couldn't hear any footsteps or voices.

She could hear the beating of giant wings, though, and the whine of a giant mosquito in the distance. If she listened very intently, sometimes she could hear glass breaking.

"You idiot, Mark," she muttered.

There had been three Martians in that big Gothic room, she remembered. One of them had gone out the window with Mark, and was presumably dead. That left the two who had pursued her.

Were they all that were left? Or were there dozens more lurking in this ridiculous maze of a place?

And what about the other humans? What had happened to Jennifer, and that Bud, and the rest? She had seen the corpse in the kitchen door, and there had been at least two or three bodies in the secret room—along with a dead Martian, which was the good news. That dead blonde was still hanging from the railing in the front hall, and of course the kid was still on the stairs.

Was she the only survivor?

Who knew? A place like this might have whole armies hidden away somewhere.

If there *were* other survivors, where would they be? She couldn't just roam around at random, she told herself; she had to approach this logically.

She remembered when she and Mark and Jennifer had first met the others in that smoking room. They'd given their names, and then the car outside had blown up, and the blonde, Marcie—was she the one hanging in the hall?—had said that was the last car anywhere, and Bud had said no, there were more in the basement garage . . .

That was it. The basement garage. That was where everybody was.

Maybe.

She remembered the stairs she had seen leading down, halfway between the room where Mark had gone out the window and the front hall where the dead blonde and the barricade were. If she could find those again . . .

The hard part, she thought, would be getting there without running into those two Martians.

And of course she couldn't be sure anyone else had actually reached the basement garage. But going there was better than sitting here doing nothing, waiting until the Martians found her, or the bugs smashed their way in and got her, or she starved to death.

She stood up and crept out of the drawing room and down the passageway.

38

BUGATTI ROYALE

"You're sure you won't come?" Betsy asked.

José shook his head. "I'm okay here," he insisted. " 'Cept . . . one thing, man."

"What?" Bud asked.

José looked embarrassed. He held up a chain saw. "Look, I got this from where they keep the gardening tools. I figure a Martian comes in here, it's better than nothin', you know? But I don't have much gas—couldn't find any there, an' the tank's almost dry. You think you could maybe get me some gas from the pump in the garage?"

"You got a can?"

José shook his head.

"Well, look," Bud said. "You got two chain saws, right? You bring 'em to the garage, we'll fill 'em up, and you're all set. I don't need that whole ten gallons—the Caddy's mileage can't be *that* bad."

"Sure," Betsy said. She glanced at Bud. The two of them were both thinking the same thing—if they got José out of his little fort in the swimming pool and over to the garage, maybe they could talk him into coming along.

They had stopped in at the pool, rather than continuing on through the basement lounge to the garage, in hopes of convincing José to accompany them, but without immediate success.

223

José thought it over, looked around at his redoubt, then shrugged. "Okay," he said. He handed a chain saw to Bud, then picked up the other. Together, they climbed up out of the pool, then up to the balcony and out through the door with the broken lock.

They were in the lounge, just at the foot of the stairs that led up to the corridor outside the great hall, when they heard an engine start up.

"What the hell . . . ?" Bud said, breaking into a run.

The four of them—Bud, Betsy, Katie, and José—burst into the garage just as the Bugatti started rolling. Stan waved to them from the driver's seat and rolled down his window.

"See you in Brownsburg!" he called.

Then he floored the accelerator and the Bugatti leapt forward through the big garage door Stan had opened, motor roaring like an angry beast.

They all heard the crunch, the squeal of tires, and the rending metal as the big car hit the wall beside the driveway. The roar of the motor ceased abruptly.

Katie and Betsy and José hung back, but Bud ran across the garage and out into the night.

On the driveway outside he stopped dead.

The Bugatti had smashed up across the low wall and was teetering on the edge of the cliff, both front wheels hanging out over empty space and one rear wheel spinning freely a few inches above the asphalt; only the other rear tire and part of the undercarriage were still touching anything but air, the undercarriage balanced precariously on the scarred top of the wall.

Stan was still sitting in the driver's seat, bleeding from his nose and a cut on his forehead where he had hit the steering wheel. He turned to look at Bud.

"Whoa," he said. "Lot of power there. Took off faster than I expected. And the steering's a bit rough."

"Did you check the steering?" Bud asked. "I mean, it hasn't been lubed since the Second World War . . ."

"No, I didn't think of that," Stan said. He laughed nervously, and looked up—a fifty-foot moth was fluttering overhead. "Guess you were right about taking the Caddy. All I did was put in water and oil and gas, and hot-wire it; I thought that would do it. And hey, I left you half the gas . . . Good thing, I guess, since I'll be coming with you after all." He swung the door open and started to climb out.

The shifting weight was too much; the Bugatti's tail suddenly swung upward, and the car plunged over the cliff, taking Stan with it. The last Bud saw of him was an expression of utter astonishment on his face.

Bud winced at each crash as the heavy car bounced down the cliff; then finally, the fall ended in an immense splash.

Bud waited, half expecting a Hollywood-style fireball, but there was no explosion.

He glanced up at the sky; no wasps or mosquitoes were in sight, and the moth seemed more interested in smashing itself against a lighted window somewhere than in bothering anyone. Bud crossed the driveway carefully and peered over the edge.

The Bugatti lay upside down on the rocks at the foot of the cliff, waves breaking on the running boards and headlights.

Theoretically, Bud supposed that Stan might still be alive, but he wasn't about to go down there to check.

He'd want to check the Caddy's steering carefully, Bud told himself, and pull out of the garage nice and slow.

He glanced around before going back inside, and the gleam of something lying on the edge of the driveway caught his eye. At first he thought it was a piece of wreckage from the Bugatti, but then he realized it was in an unlikely place for that. He took a closer look.

It was one of the Martian weapons.

He approached it carefully, half expecting some sort of booby trap or ambush, but nothing untoward happened as he reached down and picked it up, or as he stood there holding it, looking around.

He looked up at the wall of the mansion and saw that one of the big Gothic windows had been smashed out. The weapon must have been flung out through the window for some reason, he decided.

"Well, hell," he said, hefting the thing. "If this sucker still works, then we've got some bug repellent."

It was lighter than it ought to be, he thought, which might mean it was out of ammunition, or charge, or fuel, or whatever it used—or maybe the Martians just built weapons light. He pointed it out to sea and pulled the trigger.

It worked.

"Cool," he said.

Then he looked at the broken stretch of wall where Stan had sent the Bugatti to a watery grave. He hadn't expected Stan to do anything like that. He had thought he could trust the other humans here, but maybe that had been naive.

Stan had taken the Bugatti, instead of the Caddy, so at least he and the others still had a fair chance, Bud thought, but he decided he didn't want to overdo the trust from now on. He took off his denim jacket and wrapped it around the Martian gun.

Then he stepped back into the garage.

"What happened?" Betsy called.

"He went over the cliff," Bud said. "He's gone."

"What've you got there?" Katie asked, looking at the bundle Bud held.

"Some tools he dropped." He crossed to the Caddy and dumped the bundle in the backseat. Then he looked over at the space where the Bugatti had been.

He froze, and a cold anger grew in his gut. If he'd seen that before, he thought, he might have pushed the Bugatti over the cliff himself.

Stan had pulled the Caddy's half-charged battery and used it to jump-start the Bugatti; the battery and jumper cables were still lying on the floor. Now he would have to start the recharge all over again, and it might be another hour or two before they could get out of here.

Meanwhile, though . . .

"So, José," he said as he closed the garage door to keep the bugs out. "You still thinking of staying, or do you want to come with us?"

"Staying," José replied. "Let's get that gas."

39

MEN, MARTIANS, AND CHAIN SAWS

Betsy and Katie waited in the garage; Betsy was pumping the remaining gas into the Caddy's tank, and Katie was looking over the other cars, when Bud and José headed back through the lounge toward the swimming pool.

They were in the middle of the lounge when Bud froze. "Listen!" he hissed.

José stopped and listened, and heard footsteps. "Martians!" he hissed, holding down the chain saw's trigger and reaching for the pull cord.

But then Bud relaxed. "No," he said. "It's not. Look." He pointed.

José looked, and saw a tall, thin black woman—little more than a girl, really—wearing only a red bikini, coming down the stairs.

"Who the hell is *that*?" he asked.

The girl started at the sound of his voice. "Hello?" she called. She squinted, peering into the dark lounge.

"Hey," Bud called. "Brenda, right? It's me, Bud."

Brenda continued hesitantly down the stairs. "Bud?"

"Yeah, it's me, and José," Bud said. "Glad to see you! Is anyone else alive up there?"

"I don't think so," Brenda said. "The moths broke in all the windows in the front hall, and I think I heard mosquitoes. A lot of broken windows up there. And dead bodies." She shuddered. "The Martians shot the kid, and Mark went out the window over the cliffs and took a Martian with him."

"Did you see Marcie or Nancy?"

Brenda shook her head. "There was a dead blonde in the front hall," she said. "Maybe that was Marcie, I didn't look close. I don't know Nancy. Was she an overweight brunette in a leather jacket?"

"That's her," Bud said.

"In the corridor by the kitchen," Brenda said. "The Martians got her."

"Damn!"

"Are the Martians still there?" José asked.

"There were two of them left, last I saw," Brenda said. "I saw a couple of dead ones."

Bud and José exchanged glances. "Still want to stay?" he asked.

"Yeah," José said. "I feel safer here. You sure you guys want to leave?"

"Damn right," Bud said. "You heard what she said about the bugs breaking in. Sooner or later there'll be termites or carpenter ants or something, and this whole place'll be history."

"Naah," José said. "I don' buy it. I'm stayin'."

Bud shrugged. "Your funeral," he said.

Brenda shuddered at Bud's choice of words.

"How about you?" Bud asked. "We've got a car almost ready to go, and there's room for a couple more."

"Definitely," she said. "Get me *out* of here!"

"Just go through there to the garage," Bud said, pointing. "I'll be back in a few minutes and we'll get going."

Brenda nodded and headed in the direction indicated. Bud and José watched her go, then headed on across the lounge. They were almost to the door when it suddenly opened and a Martian stepped in.

"Martians!" José shouted, backing away and yanking the pull cord on his chain saw. The motor roared to life.

Bud fired up his own saw, suddenly wishing he hadn't been so quick to stash that ray gun.

José swung his saw straight at the Martian's armored belly, and a horrible scraping of metal on metal tore the air; Bud winced at the sound.

He couldn't cover his ears, though, because he was holding a running chain saw. Instead he swung the saw's whirring blade at the Martian's arm.

The teeth snagged on a flange in the Martian's armor, and the saw bucked and vibrated in Bud's hands; he struggled to pull it loose.

The Martian was struggling, as well—Bud could see its skull-like face and bloated head, despite the thick patch of gooey-looking white stuff that was plastered across the top front of the thing's transparent helmet. Its red eyes were wide and staring, and it was trying to pull its arm free of the jerking chain that held it. It had dropped one of its weapons—it had been carrying two, one in each hand—and was trying to fend off the chain saws with an armored fist.

That white stuff on the helmet—what *was* that? Bud remembered the dead Martian in the room with Steve's corpse, lying there with its helmet cracked, dead of exposure to Earth's air . . .

"José!" he shouted. "Aim for the helmet!"

"You got it, man," José shouted back. He brought his saw up in a long, sweeping arc.

The blade spun across the clear plastic, scraping at it without biting into anything—and then hit the white gunk.

Teeth ripped through the patch, scattering little curls of white wound sealant in all directions. Tenzif Kair screamed in horror, and without bothering to aim, he fired the one KA-77 he still held.

The blast tore across the lounge and demolished a beveled-glass mirror.

Bud's chain saw came loose—and so did José's, as he hauled back for another swing. Kair seized his opportunity, and as Bud swung his saw at Kair's helmet, Kair fired again, this time aiming his weapon at the approaching blade.

Bud's saw disintegrated—and so did his left hand, which had been holding the top handle. He screamed, dropped what was left of the saw and fell backward, away from the Martian.

He landed sitting on the floor, his left arm raised; he stared at the blackened stump where his hand had been. There was no bleeding; the blast had cauterized the wound.

It hadn't stopped the pain, though; Bud saw the stump, and the entire world, through a red fog of burning agony.

Meanwhile, José connected again, and this time the chain saw's teeth ripped into the plastic of the Martian's helmet, biting into the existing cracks, widening and elongating them.

Kair swung his weapon around, trying to bring it to bear on José, but the Terran dodged wildly, swinging and twisting the chain saw as he did, trying to maintain contact with the Martian's helmet.

And then a chunk of Kair's helmet snapped off.

Kair knew then that he was dead; there was no way to prevent his death from atmospheric poisoning. He was determined to at least take the Terran responsible with him; he took his KA-77 in both hands and turned it toward José . . .

Just as José brought the whirring chain saw down on that soft, bulbous Martian skull that was now exposed and unprotected.

Dark Martian blood sprayed, and Kair's fingers tightened convulsively on the firing stud.

The blast punched a hole a good six inches in diameter through José's belly and spine.

Both combatants toppled to the floor.

Bud stared past his missing hand at them. José was still moving, he realized—and so was the Martian, though the Martian's movements were just spasmodic twitches.

He had to finish the Martian off, Bud decided through the haze of agony, and then see if José should be put out of his misery. He still had one good hand; he could pick up one of the Martian's weapons and use it. He struggled to his knees and reached for one of the ray guns.

That's when the other Martian charged in through the door, weapon ready.

40

UNWILLING PARTNERS

Quisaz Hadrak had turned aside for a moment to check on what lay behind a door with a broken lock; he had not argued when Kair went on ahead without him. After all, there were hardly any Terrans left, they probably weren't anywhere near this part of the building, and it was only a matter of a few paces. Hadrak knew he would catch up in a few seconds.

Then he heard the alien buzzing of some sort of Terran machinery. He heard Kair scream. He heard Kair's weapon fire, once, twice, a third time.

Hadrak forgot about the odd accumulation of containers down in the hollowed-out section of floor; he slammed out through the broken door and charged down the passageway.

He was too late to save Kair, though; the med-rep's helmet was broken open and his brain sliced messily open. Kair lay beside a dying Terran, a hole through its gut.

And another Terran was kneeling a few feet away, its left arm ending in a scorched stump.

"Stop!" Hadrak shouted in the Terran language, aiming his KA-77 at the kneeling Terran.

He almost went ahead and fired, but he had been too hasty in killing Terrans before, and this one was crippled and unarmed. It might be useful in operating the Terran vehicles; the instructions provided by the female with the yellow head filaments might not be complete.

The Terran froze and stared at him.

Hadrak stared back for a second, then down at the others. He shuddered.

There was nothing else to be done for Kair. Regretfully, Hadrak pointed the KA-77 at his subordinate's exposed head and pressed the firing stud.

Then, with a glance at the crippled Terran, he did the same for the Terran who lay dead or dying.

That left just the two of them.

Taking the Terran captive would be difficult. Now that he was alone, Hadrak knew he would have to remain constantly on guard. He could not risk putting down his weapon. Perhaps, though, the Terran might be convinced to help anyway.

"I am Quisaz Hadrak," Hadrak said. "What is your name?"

"Bud Garcia," the Terran said. Its voice seemed weak and uncertain—doubtlessly due to pain from its injury. Hadrak was no med-rep, but he knew a few basics; he knelt, keeping the KA-77 trained on the Terran as he did, and fumbled with Kair's pack.

A moment later he had a nerve-deadener in hand; he set it on maximum and applied it to the Terran's shortened arm.

Bud had watched as the Martian—the *last* Martian, perhaps?—put José and its own companion out of their suffering. He had been astonished when it had introduced itself.

None of it had seemed really important, though; the pain was what mattered. Everything else was secondary. That was why he had not resisted when the Martian pulled out that gadget and pointed it at the stump; nothing could possibly make the injury worse, and the Martian acted as if it were trying to help.

Then the gadget touched the stump and a soothing numbness spread up through his arm. The red haze of agony lifted, just blew away and vanished.

He looked at the stump in amazement. "Wow," he said.

"How? Is that what you said?" the Martian asked.

"No, I said 'Wow,' " Bud replied. "You speak English?"

"Yes," the Martian replied.

"What did you say your name is?"

"Quisaz Hadrak."

"Quicksand Hatrack. Okay, why not?" Bud grimaced.

Hadrak did not bother correcting the Terran's pronunciation; "Quicksand Hatrack" was close enough for now.

"We must work together to escape this place," he said.

Bud stared at the Martian. "Escape?" he asked.

"Yes," Hadrak replied. "You have vehicles?"

"Why do you want to escape?" Bud asked.

Hadrak waved at the ceiling. "The insects will make this place . . . uninhabitable? Is that the word?"

"It'll do," Bud acknowledged.

"We must go before they do this," Hadrak said, choosing his words carefully in the unfamiliar language.

"You can't control them? Or call in your friends to pick you up?"

"No," Hadrak said. "We have had equipment failures."

Bud snorted. "I'll bet," he said. "Nice to know that happens everywhere, and not just to us Earthpeople."

"You have lost a hand," Hadrak said. "Your vehicles require two hands, do they not?"

"Well, sorta," Bud admitted. He realized that the Martian didn't know there were any other humans left; apparently, it didn't have any sort of heat sensors or high-tech tracking devices.

"I have two hands," Hadrak said, "but I have little knowledge of your machines or your roads."

"So you want to make a deal?" Bud asked. "Go partners?"

"Yes."

"Your people killed about a dozen of mine here, not to mention what you've been doing all over the planet," Bud said. "Why should I help you? Why should I trust you?"

"Because you cannot drive yourself," Hadrak said.

"And if that's not a good enough reason?" Bud demanded.

"Because I have the weapons," Hadrak said, hefting the KA-77. "I would prefer to do this as free partners, but I will use the weapon if you leave me no choice."

Bud thought that over. He looked at the various weapons scattered on the floor—one chain saw and two of those Martian things. He couldn't reach any of them, and he couldn't operate a chain saw with one hand.

"Okay," he said at last. "I'm convinced."

"Good," Hadrak replied. "Lead me to the garage."

Bud shrugged and led. Hadrak took a few seconds to snatch up Kair's dropped weapons; he now had a total of four KA-77s, which was awkward, at best. But until he had a satisfactory accounting of all of the humans, he couldn't afford to leave any weapons behind. He kept one ready in his hand and bundled the rest under his other arm.

When Bud entered the garage, the three people there all turned toward him, smiling, relieved to see him alive after having heard the sounds of combat from the lounge. Betsy tucked something away quickly.

"Is José—" Brenda began.

Then Hadrak stepped into sight, weapon trained on Bud's back, and the three females froze.

"This is Quicksand Hatrack," Bud explained. "He wants to come with us."

"Let him find his own ride!" Brenda shouted.

"What about the other Martians?" Katie asked.

"That's a good question," Bud said. "What *about* the other Martians, Hatrack? You running out on your buddies?"

"I am the last survivor of my squad," Hadrak replied. "You and your friends have killed the others, as I and my troopers disposed of many Terrans."

"And why should we believe you aren't going to just kill us, too?" Brenda demanded.

"Because I need Terran assistance to operate one of these vehicles."

"So you need *one* of us," Brenda said.

"Hey," Bud interrupted, before Brenda could continue or Hadrak could reply, "it's all or nothing here, and I think Mr. Martian Hatrack understands that—if he hurts any of us, that's it, no more cooperation. Right, everyone?"

"Right," Katie said at once.

Brenda glanced at the others and then said, less enthusiastically, "Right."

"*Damn* right," Betsy said. "You touch my daughter, you Martian son of a bitch, and I'll rip your stupid red eyes out if it's the last thing I do."

"I have already observed the ferocity of Terran females acting in defense of their young," Hadrak said. "You need not fear for your offspring."

"Good," Betsy said.

"So how's the car?" Bud asked.

"All gassed up," Betsy reported.

"Battery's mostly charged," Katie said. "Should be enough to get us to Brownsburg."

"Good!" Bud said. "Now let's check the steering—you saw what happened to Stan."

Hadrak heard that remark with interest. He noticed the gap in the line of vehicles, remembered odd sounds he had heard, and put these facts together.

"Stan" had presumably operated a vehicle that had been insufficiently prepared, and had died as a result—that made his own decision to rely on a Terran driver that much wiser in retrospect. These machines were plainly not as easy to control as the female prisoner had implied.

And if Stan had died, and there were four live Terrans here, then who was that lying dead beside Tenzif Kair? Who went out the window into the sea with Slithree Di? The prisoner's count had made it clear that no more than five Terrans, at the very most, were still alive and free at that time, yet here were four, and three others had perished.

Clearly, the female had lied, despite Kair's emphatic questioning techniques. There had been more than fifteen Terrans in this place.

Terrans could not be trusted.

Right now, though, if he wished to get out of this deathtrap of a building, Hadrak had little choice but to rely on these Terrans. The vehicles were dangerous to operate.

Once they were safely clear of the insect hordes, however . . .

Hadrak smiled to himself and fondled his KA-77 as he watched the Terrans making their final inspection of the selected vehicle.

41

DEATH DRIVE

Bud slammed the hood and looked around.

"I don't suppose any of you ever hot-wired an ignition?"

The three women—or two women and a girl, really—shook their heads. The Martian simply stood there, clearly not understanding the question. Bud sighed.

"I guess I'll give it a try," he said.

"Are you sure the keys aren't around somewhere?" Brenda asked.

"They're probably in old lady Gelman's purse," Bud said. "I looked through everything on the key ring, and all through the garage area for a Peg-Board or something—"

"Did you look in the glove box?"

"Oh, come on, who keeps car keys in the glove box?" Katie asked.

"It won't hurt to look," Brenda insisted. She opened the passenger door and leaned in, emerging a moment later with a key fob dangling triumphantly in her hand.

"Well, I'll be damned," Bud said. "Give 'em here!"

"What, you think *you're* driving?" Brenda asked.

"But you only have one hand!" Betsy said.

Bud looked down at his left forearm. "God, you're right," he said. "Then who drives?"

"Not me," Brenda said. "I'm a city girl—I never learned."

"I'm too young," Katie said.

Bud and Betsy glanced at the Martian; then Betsy said, "I guess that leaves me."

"Good enough," Bud said. Then he looked around the garage. "Is there anything we want to take with us? If we've got the keys, we can use the trunk."

"I'll open it," Brenda said. "*That* I can do."

She suited her actions to her words, and Bud loaded in a few useful tools and supplies from the garage shelves.

Then the Martian stepped over.

"This storage compartment cannot be accessed from the interior of the vehicle," Hadrak said.

"That's right," Bud said.

"Excellent." Hadrak dumped three of his four KA-77s into the trunk, and a small pack of other supplies and equipment, then slammed the lid before anyone else could react.

"Wait a minute," Bud said. "I want to put my jacket in there." He opened the rear door on the near side of the car and reached in for the bundle.

This was the moment. He hadn't had a chance before, but now was the time. He could pull the Martian ray gun out of the bundle and drop old Quicksand Hatrack . . .

He looked up, through the back windshield of the Caddy, and saw the Martian watching him.

He also saw the Martian's ray gun pointed directly at Brenda's head.

He sighed. Okay, he thought, so maybe this *wasn't* the moment.

He looked about the interior of the car. Maybe he could slide the ray gun under the front seat, and snatch it out at some point . . .

And maybe he couldn't. The Martian was cautious, constantly on the alert. If he spotted the weapon, he would probably take it very badly.

With a sigh, Bud picked up the bundle and brought it around to the back. Brenda reopened the trunk, and Bud dropped the jacket and ray gun in on the heap.

Then the trunk slammed shut.

Bud stared at the curving, pink-painted metal for a moment, thinking of all that firepower tucked away in there. If they *did* ever make it to Brownsburg, that arsenal ought to be worth something to whoever was in charge—and it ought to help a little in the war against the Martian invaders.

Bud just hoped it wouldn't all wind up back in the hands of Hatrack's friends.

"Okay," he said at last. "All aboard!"

"Brenda, give me the keys," Betsy called. Brenda tossed them over.

Katie clambered into the backseat.

"Give me a hand with the door," Bud said to Hadrak.

The Martian replied, "No. I will take my seat now." It opened the front door on the passenger side and slid into the shotgun seat, its helmet brushing against the fabric-lined ceiling. Bud could see Betsy flinching at the Martian's presence so close at hand.

"Brenda," Bud called.

Together, the two of them opened the garage door and looked out at the night.

Stars shone brightly overhead; the sea sparkled far below. And in between moths were fluttering about, banging against windows and walls. Broken glass tinkled somewhere.

"Come on," Bud said. "Let's get aboard."

He slid in behind Betsy, and Brenda behind Hadrak.

"Here's hoping it starts," Betsy said as she turned the key.

The starter whined. The engine coughed, sputtered—then roared to life.

"Take it nice and easy," Bud said. "Remember Stan."

Betsy nodded, put the car in gear, and inched forward. She flicked on the headlights as the Caddy rolled out of the garage onto the driveway.

They took the first turn at a crawl; Betsy had no intention of following the Bugatti over the cliff. She eased past the line of garage doors and onto the ramp; the headlight beams swung upward.

And a fluttering monstrosity descended from the heavens. The car jolted to a stop as the wings of a gigantic moth battered against the hood.

"It's drawn by the light!" Brenda yelped.

"Turn off the headlights!" Bud shouted.

"But I can't see without them!"

"Turn 'em off!" Bud repeated.

Betsy obeyed—but the moth didn't retreat.

Hadrak looked at the chrome-plated controls on the inside of the door. "Which of these operates the window?" he asked.

Brenda leaned over the seat and pointed, and Hadrak began cranking the window down.

When he had it almost fully open, he leaned out and blasted at the moth.

The insect fluttered away, wounded.

"Looks like you're *really* going to ride shotgun," Bud said.

Hadrak looked at him, but said nothing. The Martian turned to Betsy and said, "Drive."

"I need the lights—"

"Use what you need," Hadrak ordered.

Betsy turned on the lights and inched the Caddy up the ramp. She made the turn into the parking lot and wound her way past the blackened wreckage of her old Chevy, past the burned-out hulks of the other three cars . . .

Everyone felt the bump when she drove over the dead Martian; everyone heard the sickening crunch. Bud wondered whether she had done it deliberately, or whether it had been the only way out of the lot.

Then they were on the entry road—and the moths were coming at them again, three of them. Hadrak fired half a dozen times before two of them fled and the other fell fluttering into the leafless, broken trees at the roadside.

"Is it possible for this vehicle to move faster?" Hadrak asked.

"Are we clear of all the wreckage?" Betsy asked. "You're the only one who knows, Mr. Martian."

"I am not aware of any further obstacles," Hadrak replied.

"Good," Betsy said.

She jammed her foot to the floor.

The Cadillac roared magnificently and took off down the entry road, while Bud and Brenda held on for dear life.

"Go for it, Mom!" Katie yelled from the back.

Hadrak took a second or two to adjust to the increased velocity, then began firing at approaching insects.

At first there were only moths, but as they tore down the road, tires squealing at every curve, Bud was sure he saw other species—june bugs, perhaps, or damselflies, or gnats—he couldn't be sure, as they were either blasted out of the sky by Hadrak's weapon or passed and left behind by Betsy's driving.

And then she slammed on the brakes, and the Caddy fishtailed, spraying gravel, as it skidded off the entry road and onto the highway.

The burned-out wreckage of a dozen cars and trucks was strewn along the asphalt; once they had made the turn Betsy paid no attention to any of it. She slammed down on the accelerator and headed north at eighty-five, dodging wreckage like a skier running a slalom. Wherever the full width of the highway was blocked, she swerved onto the shoulder without slowing.

The insects kept coming at them for almost a dozen miles, and Hadrak blasted them out of the sky, one after another, before they could come close enough to be dangerous.

Then the intervals between blasts began to lengthen, the sound of the KA-77 dropping from a steady drumbeat to a slowing, sporadic cadence. The trees beside the road began to have more leaves.

"We're outdistancing them," Bud said as he scanned the sky from his window and saw nothing but stars.

"About time," Brenda said.

"Stop the vehicle," Hadrak said.

Betsy reacted instantly, shifting her foot from accelerator to brake; the car screamed to a stop, leaving wide trails of smoking rubber on the asphalt.

"What is it?" she demanded.

"My weapon is low on charge," Hadrak said. "I must replace it with one from the storage compartment. Give me the key." He held out his hand.

Betsy stared at him. "How low?" she said.

"That is not your concern," Hadrak replied. "Give me the key."

"In a minute," Betsy said. "First, I want to get straight just where we're heading. Brownsburg, right?"

"We will rejoin my unit."

Betsy shook her head. "I don't think so," she said. "I think we're going to Brownsburg, where we'll join up with the defenders there. You'll be a prisoner, but you'll be alive."

"I do not think so," Hadrak said, pointing his weapon at her head. "Give me the key."

"I knew it." Betsy pulled the keys from the ignition—then tossed them to Bud, who made a quick one-handed grab, catching them in midair.

"You open the trunk for him, Bud," she said.

Hadrak hesitated, then spun and grabbed the door handle.

He couldn't shoot the driver; none of the others could operate the vehicle, and he was still a long way from his pickup point. He couldn't let the other Terran open the trunk unless he was there, either—if the Terran got hold of a KA-77, their little interplanetary alliance would be over. He got out of the car, watching the Terran called "Bud" closely.

This was the one the prisoner had said was a fighter. Even with one hand missing, it might be dangerous.

Hadrak was so focused on Bud that he never saw the gun Betsy pulled from her pants. His first inkling of its presence was the report as she fired, at point-blank range, at his helmet.

The first round shattered plastic; the second punched through Hadrak's skull. He tumbled out of the car and lay on the pavement, dazed but still alive and conscious.

Bud shouted, "Nice work, Betsy!" He hurried to the trunk, popped the lid, and hauled out the Martian ray guns, one by one, with his one good hand.

He passed them out to the people in the car—everybody got

one—then he slammed the trunk and tossed Betsy the keys. That done, he took his own captured weapon in hand and walked around to look down at the dying Martian. Hadrak lay there semiconscious, coughing as Earth's air poisoned him.

Bud thought about what he could say at this point. He thought about the stirring speeches he could make, about how no damn Martians would ever take Earth away from its native inhabitants, about how a technological advantage and a surprise attack weren't going to be enough, about how Earthpeople would fight on no matter what the odds, about how they would never surrender.

He thought about pointing out that it was ordinary people, not soldiers, who had wiped out Hadrak's squad, despite being disorganized and virtually unarmed. He thought about saying that Earth *itself* was resisting the Martians, with its toxic air and its uncontrollable insects. He thought about claiming vengeance for his blasted buddies, for Marcie and Nancy and Lenny and Blitz and even Screwy Joe, and all those poor tourists, and Steve and José. He thought about loudly avenging the loss of his own left hand. He thought about saying this was in return for Toppwood, the beginning of the end for the Martian invaders.

Then he decided not to waste his breath. He pointed his KA-77 at Hadrak's face and made his speech, the final sound that the Martian squad leader would ever hear.

"Asshole," Bud said as he pressed the firing stud.

Then he climbed back into the car and slammed the door, and the wheels spat gravel as Betsy put the Caddy in gear. The car roared on through the night, heading toward Brownsburg at eighty miles an hour.

ABOUT THE AUTHOR

Nathan Archer was born and raised in New York City, and discovered science fiction as a boy. His mother threw out his original Mars Attacks cards, but she let him keep the comic books and paperbacks and continue watching *Star Trek*.

After working for the government since college budget cuts left him unemployed in 1992, he decided to try his hand at writing.

So far he's been lucky. He's the author of *Star Trek: Deep Space Nine #10: Valhalla*, *Star Trek: Voyager #3: Ragnarok*, *Predator: Concrete Jungle*, and *Predator: Cold War*, as well as *Mars Attacks: Martian Deathtrap*. He hopes to someday soon sell a novel that doesn't have a colon in the title.

Archer lives in Chicago and has no children or pets. His eyes are green, and now that he no longer needs to please employers, he wears his hair in a ponytail. Other details are still classified.

.